OF MUNICIPAL
BONDAGE

OF MUNICIPAL

BONDAGE

Dan Gillcrist

To order additional copies of this book, contact:
Xlibris Corporation
1-888-7-XLIBRIS
www.Xlibris.com
Orders@Xlibris.com

CONTENTS

ACKNOWLEDGMENTS

Over the past two years I slowly compiled a list of people, mostly from the muni bond business, who made some contribution to this project either knowingly or unknowingly; directly or indirectly; wittingly or unwittingly; consciously or un consciously; inadvertently or directly; tangentially or perpendiculary. The list had over 40 names at least. When I showed it to several friends they pointed out that I had left some people out. So as not to offend anyone, I chose to eliminate the list and simply say that everyone in the bond business who I know had some influence on this project. The help was mainly in the mainly in that most, but not all, of them simply managed to be themselves, and maintain a body temperature of 98.6 degrees.

Particular acknowledgment, goes to my son Dan who has one of the finest ears for humor I've ever been around, and who's stories and hilarious personal experiences have entertained the Gillcrist family ever since he was about three. I hearby offer him, publicy for all to read, my heartfelt apologies for my flagrant, wonton and shameless theft of many of his funny stories and observations. I have assured him that if he wants to write a book, he should fell free to use the stories I stole since nobody will read my book anyway.

My friend Marc Greer was of great help in several areas including remembering stories and people out of the past. He read the manuscript and contributed both suggestions and a review. Bob "Junior" Jones with whom I worked for many years was a great help as well. I always marveled at how he remembered every trade he ever did, but it turned out that he remembered every zany muni bond anecdote as well.

Finally, this is a work of fiction and any similarity between the characters in this novel and actual people is purely coincidental. It will be tempting, and may be fun, for muni people to try and figure out who Johnny Cannon or Jack Armstrong are, but the fact is they, like all my other characters, are fictitous.

PROLOGUE

The phone rang in the bond department of Searl, Patrick and McNulty and Elvira, the leading secretary picked it up saying, "Bon Apartment". Leon Walla, the firm's muni trader who had finally gotten a chance to read the *Journal*, peered over the top of the paper to look with some disgust at Elvira as she talked over a trade fail with someone from another firm. It always irritated him when she answered the phone that way. He felt like shouting, "D's, D's, goddammit, there are D's in there!" Bon Apartment sounded like something French for heaven's sake, and Leon hated everything French . . . and English for that matter. Every time a certain lady at his buddy Johnny Cannon's firm answered the phone, she said, "Vestments" instead of "Investments." Each time she answered he was tempted to ask, "Have you any habits?" But he knew with the certainty of death and taxes, that the woman wouldn't have a clue—women didn't ever get his jokes.

While Leon was from Pasadena, Texas and had a pretty heavy Texas accent, at least he pronounced his words properly and entirely. Sloppy speech drove him crazy. Texans often pronounced words with the accent on the wrong syllable, or they'd drop one entirely. This was another little pet peeve of Leon's. Actually he found it a bit embarrassing. He had to be a little careful though since he didn't know the rules of English either. Leon had won one of life's lotteries wherein he was born to parents who spoke English properly. An accent was fine so long as the person pronounced every word properly. Texans too often said INsurance instead of inSURance and ceMENT became CEment. Leon made a big distinction between sloppy talk and colloquial or colorful speech like "fixin ta," "y'all" and "winda." That was one reason he liked country music so much. He could understand every word of a country song—they spoke English—although he would be the first to admit that they dealt far too much with trains, trucks, the highway and easy women. But you could at least understand! With rock and roll, you had to read the album cover to understand the lyrics they were yelling into the microphone. In addition to the French and English, Leon hated rock and roll—particularly its performers. He would only attend a rock concert at gunpoint.

He would not admit it but he was feeling real low since his friend and desk-mate, Jack left the business a few days earlier. Jack was a salesman and a constant source of fun and humor at the desk and Leon realized that things had changed for the worse, and he feared, forever. Sitting there moping, pretending to read the *Wall Street Journal*, the first smile crossed his face since Jack left.

Leon was recalling the time that Dowling called Jack with a bond offering. This guy Dowling worked for their buddy Johnny Cannon who ran the bond department of a competing firm. Cannon held the unpleasant distinction of having the world's stupidest bond salesman working for him.

Everyone knew that "original issue discounts" (OIDs) were unique, particularly in their treatment by the IRS. The bondholder got the coupon interest over the life of the bond as well as the accretion from, say, a discount of 92 up to 100 at their maturity. The IRS's policy concerning this treatment is known as the "de minimis" rule, an arcane concept that almost no one understands, including IRS auditors.

Leon looked at Jack and said, "Jack, it's Dowling on the direct line for you."

"What does that dopey bastard want now Leon?"

"Jesus, just pick it up Jack, what do I know?"

"Armstrong." Jack answered—an old Marine Corps habit of his.

"Jack, I think you ought to look at these bonds, they're cheap. My client wants to sell them and I wanted you to have the first shot." Jack thought, 'Dowling wouldn't know 'cheap' if it bit him on the ass.'

"Thanks Dowling, what are they?"

"OK, I've got 500M Valdosta, Georgia—Electric Revenue bonds. They are 5.50% due out in 2010 at a price of 92." Jack thought immediately of the IRS rule since this one sounded like it might apply.

"That's pretty close to de minimis isn't it Dowling?"

"Now Jack, I'll admit that I don't know exactly where in Georgia Valdosta is, but I do know it's a damn good bond."

Leon recalled that Jack had to hit his mute button so he could laugh and not offend this dolt. Finally Jack got back on,

"Sorry Dowling, it's a client. Gotta go." Jack hung up and said to Leon who was now laughing like crazy, "hey, call over to Cannon and tell him to just pull the life support system on Dowling because he's fucking brain dead!"

He thought Jack was one funny guy to have around. He had been hilarious at his own going away party a week earlier. Leon half expected rim shots after each one liner. Jack said a few remarks after the Houston bond guys sort of roasted him, and gave him a few silly gifts. He had grabbed the mike from Sammy David Stein, the perennial master of ceremonies, and acted like some Lake Tahoe lounge act.

"Sammy, talk to me after this gig, I want to buy the movie rights to your bullshit . . . it's my retirement plan." (bah dum pum!).

"Looking out at you guys reminds me a lot of the bar scene in *Star Wars*." (bah dum pum)

"With the exception of my wife Mary here, known to you all as Radar, I don't think there is a completely functioning liver in the room. In fact, my neighbor is a surgeon at St. Luke's and he told me Houston was a net consumer in the National Liver Transplant Program. I think I know why." (bah dum pum!) Leon remembered Jack pausing here when nobody laughed. So he went on,

"Net consumer, net consumer . . . in the liver program. What's wrong with you people?" That was when Marc Rapoport yelled; "We got the fucking joke already. We aren't laughing because the joke stinks!" Then everyone started laughing and throwing stirrers at Jack.

Just then Leon's little daydream was interrupted—he heard the phone ring and Elvira picked it up, "Bon Apartment–oh, hi Jack! Leon, it's for you—it's Jack!" Leon thought, 'the guy's gone for two days and she screams when he calls—typical woman.'

"I'm sorry sir, we've already filled that position with a real bond salesman. I can recommend a bucket shop here in Houston though. Where *are* you anyway?"

"We saw the moving truck off about 9AM and I'm not two miles north of Huntsville and the girls had to take a leak already. God, this trip's going to be awful. Leon, do me a favor and phone ahead to Washington and line up a divorce lawyer—we'll probably need one by the time we get there."

"Does that mean you'll be back selling bondos?"

"Shhheeeetttt no! Are you nuts? I'm on my way to our Nation's Capitol, Leon. The august and steaming hot, crime ridden Washington D, by God, C to make a difference."

"Yeah, right Jack, you'll be there maybe a month before you'll be selling influence and indulgences like the rest of them. You'll make the Catholic Church and the thirteenth century look like amateur night."

"Now *there* are two things you know nothing at all about Leon. Hell, you have never even been in a Catholic church, and I know that the only damn thing you ever learned about the thirteenth century was that it closely followed the twelfth." Leon overheard Elvira answering a call in the background. They were all of a sudden getting busy.

"Bon Apartment . . . Leon, its' Danny McKay."

"Hey, Jack, Wide Load is on the other line. I'm gonna put you on hold."

"HOLD? HOLD? Wait! I'm out here in the field, in a phone booth that's as hot as 11 Mexicans burning mesquite stumps—outside some fucking Stuckey's—and by the way, it *smells* like all 11 of them took a leak in here—and your gonna talk to that fat ass? What am I, chopped liver? I'm out of the business for what?—maybe 48 hours?—and you're already treating me like shit, Leon—like retail for Christ's sake." Leon put him on hold anyway and was laughing when he picked up McKay.

"What is it Wide Load? Hurry up. I got Jack on the other line and he's about to die of heat frustration."

"It's prostration."

"What?"

"It's prostration Leon, prostration, not frustration. Frustration is what you get from talking to muni traders. And what's so funny anyway?"

"It's just Jack being Jack. You know, it's a full time job. What did you want anyway?"

"Who are you guys going to get to replace him?"

"That's what you interrupted us for? The body is not even cold for Christ's sake Wide Load! I'll call you later."

"I'm back Jack, sorry." There was no answer, but Leon could still hear the trucks go by on the Interstate in the background and figured Jack was either away from the booth or was just messing with him.

"Tell you what Leon, I wish I could put your little ass on hold, but even if this phone had a hold button I'd be afraid to touch it. This is nasty in here man. The phonebook looks like it's 8 inches thick and I know Huntsville doesn't have but 20,000 people and a quarter of them are in the slammer here and don't even have numbers." Jack saw his error and added, "Well, at least they don't have phone numbers. How do you suppose it's that thick Leon? Anyway, I'm getting a can of Lysol for the rest of the trip."

They were both laughing as they screwed around on the phone like they always did. Leon felt awful now. He was laughing and felt lousy at the same time knowing that a great time was over. He could hear the trucks in the background as Jack signed off.

"The girls are back Leon, I've got to go now. Shit, Mary bought them Cokes! We won't get 10 miles before they have to go again. At this

rate we might make it to DC in time for the next election. 'Bye."
Leon was feeling sorry for himself when the direct line from his pal
Marc Rapoport, the brokers broker lit up.

"You missing Jack yet Leon?"

"Naaahhh, I'm fine. We'll just get another salesman, that's all."

Leon and Rapoport both knew that was a bunch of bullshit—like
whistling in the graveyard. They'd never have another friend quite like
Jack Armstrong.

CHAPTER 1

Danny McKay was one of those guys from the Deep South with a heavy drawl and no idea that he was Irish. Somehow those guys never got the word, Danny's name could have come out of "Deliverance" for all it mattered to him—he was a Texan. It is probably just as well that the assimilation of all the riffraff from Ireland 150 years ago was quicker in the South than it was North of the Mason-Dixon line. A freckle-faced guy with a south Boston accent named McKay was one thing—a complete picture. But the same type guy with a Port Arthur, Texas accent, made you think he was adopted or something.

McKay had a bit of an eating disorder. It wasn't that "over achiever girl" kind though, his disorder was that he never stopped eating, and he only threw up when he got really shitfaced and started mixing up what he drank. Which would indicate he also had a "choice of what he drank" disorder.

He was in the municipal bond business and they had a financial procedure called a partial refunding, part one way and part another, which sometimes reminded him of his own body type. When you checked him out from the head downward he looked pretty good until your eyes got to about his chest where he began to tear drop into an enormous ass.

No telling where he would even begin getting his suits. His little, skinny assed buddy Leon Walla nicknamed him "Wide Load."

"Wide load! Over here" Leon shouted out of the darkness of the bar.

McKay heard Leon but couldn't see a thing and nearly impaled himself on the corner of the little half wall near the entrance.

"Aagghh!!, Jesus Christ Leon why the fuck do we come to this place? It's as dark as your large intestines in here, goddam place is dangerous. I think I broke a rib or something." Walking out of the Summer Houston sun into a basement bar was like having a flash bulb go off in your face. Leon was grinning when Wide Load finally felt his way to the table and sat down.

"What is so funny, you skinny little son-of-a-bitch?" he said, rubbing his ribs.

"You. You ought to get your cones and rods checked out boy!"

Danny said, "I'll bet that is the only thing you remembered from that chickenshit, little no-account, boondocks, high school you went to. Did you actually graduate by the way?"

"Don't be a wise ass, Danny. You know damn well I finished. How else would I have gotten into UT?" Leon said with a bit of irritation.

"Name dropper" Wide Load was wiggling around in his captain's chair to get comfortable.

"You want to move to a booth or something? Seriously Danny, how do you get that huge ass of yours into these captain's chairs anyway?"

"Getting back to your education Leon, how long were you at UT before they had your number anyway?" Danny continued, paying no attention to Leon's wisecrack. Leon looked at Danny through the darkness,

"Hey, who bought Conroe ISD (Independent School District) this morning? Answer is, I did, that's who. Where was that brain dead underwriter you guys had on this deal? Probably tucked in there with those fifth to tenth guidos out of New York. Shit, I beat 'um like a runaway slave!"

Conroe, a little town just north of Houston, had sold a new issue of schoolhouse bonds earlier through competitive bidding and Leon's little group won. He was happy as hell about it. He'd made his firm some serious money with today's Conroe ISD deal. Most bidding syndicates have a half dozen members, spreading the risks, but also diluting the profit potential. Leon had only one partner on the Conroe bid. He was some smart hombre and loved that about himself—probably about the only thing he liked. He was not good looking and was not at all imposing in any physical sense, but he was smarter than the other traders in town—he knew it—and loved being one up on them.

Conroe was a home run. It was a $44 million issue and the takedown, or gross profit, was a point and a half, split two ways. Searl, Patrick and McNulty, Leon's firm, would probably net well over $300,000.00. What made it even sweeter was the fact that they had put the bonds away within the two-hour order period. He knew the other dealers were dying to find out where he had sold all those bonds so fast.

"Danny, your facing Lung, try and get his attention, I need another Stoli-rocks. Shit, there's nobody in this place and you can't get this assholes attention. HEY LUNG!"

The big Chinese bartender ambled over to the table. By this time Danny's eyes had adjusted to the dark and one look a Lung's face told him he was having problems, probably at home. Danny thought that Lung's wife JuJu might be on to the fact that he probably had a 'squeeze' stashed somewhere.

"Jesus Lung, you look like shit. What's the matter? You're as yellow as a ghost," Danny said, and started to laugh at his little joke. Everyone thought Danny's attempts at humor were a little weak. He was the only one who usually laughed at his jokes.

"Very funny Danny. You're a riot you know that? What are you gentleman having?" Lung said this with a smirk.

"Stoli-rocks," said Leon as he polished off the little bit of cube-melt left in the glass.

Danny thought a second and said, "I don't know. Is happy hour on yet Lung?"

"Not 'till 5:30 as you well know. How come you two are here so early anyway?"

Leon looked sideways at his friend, Wide Load, "What do you give a shit if it's happy hour all of a sudden?"

Danny ignored the question and looked up at Lung, "Now Leon here, 'MISTER' Leon to you Lung, made him a shitpot full of money this morning and talked me into leaving the office early to celebrate."

Leon's eyes widened, "talked you into it?! You can't be serious Wide Load, I hardly got the sentence out of my mouth and you were half way to the "Sewer". Talked you into it my ass."

Once again Danny paid no attention, "Tell you what Lung, a Heini, I'm all dried out from that block and a half walk over here."

The basement bar was actually "The Padded Sewer" to the Houston bond crowd. It was yet another example of Houston's attempt to be something other that it actually was. The city was so hot, so flat, so humid and so uninteresting that every conceivable attempt was made by its millions of inhabitants to make believe the city was someplace else. The Sewer was a perfect example of an attempt to copy one of those New York bars out of those 50's B-movies. It was full of padded booths covered in red, with what Danny called "Genuine Unborn Naugahide."

By this time Lung was back with the drinks, setting them down and wondering where the hell Rose, the cocktail waitress, was. It was four o'clock and she still wasn't suited up in her low cut, maroon polyester outfit with the stains.

Lung's name of course wasn't "Lung" at all, but one of those unpronounceable Chinese names. He had a pretty bad smoker's cough from the tons of cigarettes Chinese men seem to smoke. The nickname the muni guys gave him started out "Shy One Lung," because of his coughing, and over time, it evolved simply into Lung. He was not the least bit offended. In fact, he really liked these bond guys who religiously stopped off at the bar each day. They were his kind of people. They smoked, drank, gambled, liked ladies, were funny and had balls—plus, they were not like most Anglo Saxons. Normal Anglos were interested in him because of his Chineeseness, asking questions like, "so, how do you like thousand year old eggs?" or, "so, do you think we ought to unleash Chiang Kai-shek to invade the mainland and kick ass on those Commie bastards?" The muni bond guys never asked such questions. They didn't give a shit about Chiang Kai-shek, and they never even heard of a thousand year old egg.

Leon was facing the wall when Danny noticed Sammy David Stein enter the bar blinking, trying to get his night vision going. At least Dave was smart enough to have taken off his shades when he entered the building, unlike Danny, who still had them on when he rammed into the half wall earlier. Remembering the wall, Danny rubbed his ribs and thought of how the bruise he would surely have would look and knowing it was highly unlikely any pretty woman would ever see it. All the guys liked Danny, but he figured, correctly, that a guy with a pair of National Geographic globes in the back of his trousers had a pretty shitty chance at getting anywhere close to one of those racehorses who stopped by the Sewer during happy hour.

"Stein, over here!" Leon and Danny got up to move another table next to theirs. They knew the routine. More of the boys would soon show up and they always sat together.

Samuel David Stein was not Jewish in spite of the name. He was a pretty big guy, a former Marine captain, brought up in the Bronx. He was a hilarious man with the most infectious laugh. Whenever he got to the table the fun started! He grew up on the Grand Concourse in the Bronx where the population had to have been 95% Jewish. He pronounced it "The Grrreann Koncus in the BRONx". He had a repertoire of Jewish jokes and told them in a perfect dialect, which would have shamed Jackie Mason. He'd hold court at the tables telling these jokes, never seeming to repeat himself, while everyone held their sides, including Marc Rapoport, the broker's broker and one of the few Jews in the business, at least in Houston.

After he got his drink Stein said, "Know what the trouble with this place is Leon? Food. If they had decent food we'd all stay longer, drink more and the owner here would make more money. How hard is that? Is this guy stupid, or what?" Leon listened and turned his head toward the "free food/happy hour table" to his right to see if it was still there. Sammy noticed and said,

"Leon, don't even think of mentioning that prefab, plastic, make believe excuse for food in that steam table thing. God . . . fried chicken wings, tater tots and chips and salsa. I'll bet they don't spend ten dollars on all that crap. Plus, it's loaded with salt on the misguided notion that we'll drink more . . . dopey bastards. That's the trouble with American businessmen, they've all got their head up their asses."

Leon said, "Jesus Stein, who the fuck wound you up? Lighten it up . . . relax, have a drink for Christ's sake!"

"Hey Sammy, I think you should exempt Mr. Leon Walla here from your 'head up the ass list,' since he beat *your* ass as well as the rest of us today on the Conroe bid." Danny nodded toward Leon when he said this.

"Oh yeah Leon, nice bid. I can't believe you, Jack and Freddie put that loan away in just two hours!," Stein said hoping he'd get lucky and pick up a few tidbits about the accounts which had just bought $40 million bonds from Leon's firm. Leon, however, hadn't fallen off the back of the Dilley, Texas melon truck that morning, and he just smiled at Stein. Just then Stein noticed Rapoport entering, squinting his eyes and Dave waved him over to the tables.

"Shalom my fellow tribesman!" Dave said expansively in his great Yiddish dialect.

"Up yours Stein. Where is that shiksa waitress with the tits? Oh, there she is. HEY, ROSE!, wine and fresh horses for my men here!"

Lung looked up over the bar, through the smoke and thought the boy's rowdiness was exactly on Q, in about 17 seconds happy hour began at the Sewer.

CHAPTER 2

It didn't matter what time he got to bed, Leon Walla got up at 5AM, even on weekends, drank a pot of coffee and read the *Houston Chronicle*. He knew it was sort of a shitty paper but it was the only "AM" in the city and he was addicted to the morning paper. The paper's editor was a rich guy named Lobby who had inherited it, and was the poster child for the concept of *primogeniture*. Leon thought the guy should have been delivering the paper, not editing it.

He was very predictable with all of his routines, and even though he felt pretty lousy from the prior evening's excesses with the boys at the Sewer, he showered, dressed and drove downtown to his office.

The government bond traders were almost always there before anybody else. New York, the center of the known world, was one hour ahead and if you wanted to look good to management up there and be a player, you had to be in early and make yourself known over the "squawk box" the government bond guys communicated on all day. Glen Williams picked it up and called the government bond trader who traded the longer maturities,

"Billy Berniscone, New York, where are you on the 30 year?"

"Morning Glen, I'm 99 and 3/32 offered for up to 5 million bonds. What have you got to do?"

"USAA wanted to get a post on the long bond as soon as I got in this morning. I'll get back to you in a few minutes. To be honest, I don't know whether he's a buyer or seller."

"Let me know Glen," Berniscone said as he hung up. Berniscone thought most institutional salesmen were a bunch of greedy, covetous prima donnas. He wished there was a way, maybe with the computers some day, to link the traders directly with the institutions and eliminate these assholes. When he positioned half the government bonds in the Western Hemisphere, these guys couldn't sell them…"too high," they'd say. On the other hand, if he had nothing on the shelf, they bitched about not having any reason to call the accounts. Yesterday he put a bid on $25 million of the 5-year Treasury bond for one of the salesman on his own desk and when they found out that he missed by 1/32, a lousy 32 cents on a thousand dollar bond, the guy gave him a dirty look! 'I'm not falling on my sword for these jerks,' he thought.

Twenty minutes had passed and Berniscone had a little lull in the action and picked up the squawk box and said, "Glen, have you got hold of USAA yet? What do they want to do? Oh, and the market's changed. I'm no longer good on the market I gave you awhile ago, so check me again." Glen picked up his squawk and said, "Billy, I'm trying." Berniscone thought, 'Glen, you are *very* trying.'

Leon walked into the trading room and weaved toward his desk on the other side of the room from Glen and the government bond people. The star muni salesman, for some odd reason, was already at his desk. Leon thought that the guy's dog must have gotten loose again. Sarge, a huge, goofy black lab, was always getting loose from Freddy Brister's yard and he spent a lot of time driving up and down his neighborhood shouting, "Sarge, Sarge" out the car window.

As Leon slumped into his chair he asked, "little early for a big hitter like you, isn't it Freddy? You in the dog house or something?"

"Naaah, I've been looking for Sarge since 4AM and I'm exhausted. I bet I drove 17 miles."

"Tell me something Freddy," Leon asked, "How the hell does that goofy bastard keep getting out of your yard? I've seen your back yard and it reminds me of San Quentin for God's sake."

"I think the maid left the gate to the alley unlocked when she took out the trash." Leon thought, "Jesus, this guy makes four times what I do and he is a dip shit. Spends his off hours yelling 'Sarge, Sarge' . . . God I feel lousy."

Jack Armstrong, the only salesman Leon really cared for, walked into the room and took his place next to Leon at the trading desk and said,

"You look like shit Leon, you know that? Did you hit the Sewer with the boys again? You really need to start taking better care of yourself amigo."

"God, I feel awful", said Leon under his breath, "I even stopped by Ben Taub Hospital on my way in, just to get an estimate." Leon slid open his pencil drawer and took out two bottles—Bayer Aspirin and Maalox and, in an attempt to lighten up the mood of the desk said, "I believe I'll have a bowl of aspirins and milk for breakfast this morning." This was not the first time Jack and the others had heard this little joke out of Leon, but it was funny nevertheless. Leon headed for the coffee pot, poured himself another mug full and added a quarter cup of sugar.

From about age eight Jack Armstrong had been a little mad at his parents for naming him Jack. 'What a cross to bear' he thought, 'people giving me grief all my life and thinking it was cute.' The odd thing was that Jack was just like the fictional character—big, blond, handsome and smart. He was a decorated Huey pilot, a Captain with the Marines in Viet Nam, and he married a girl who looked a lot like the girl in that new Bond movie, "Goldfinger." He was in some ways the antithesis of Leon, and yet they were friends. Neither one of them thought much about the paradox. They would go to lunch to their favorite chili place, looking like Mutt and Jeff on the down escalator.

The phone rang and before Leon could answer, Elvira, the head secretary of the bond department, picked it up, "Bon Apartment."

It always irritated Leon that Elvira slurred her words and talked through her nose. He felt like shouting, 'Bond Department, for God's sake, Bond Department!,' but decided against it. She would end up screwing him over somehow if he ever said anything. He knew she'd figure a way. He once overheard Elvira counseling a young female margin clerk, who had somehow been offended by a sales-man, "don't worry Mary, his ass will swing my way one of these days." The call was for her anyway.

At 10:30AM Archie, the black shoeshine guy, came into the bond department and started to work his way around the room. Most of the guys got a shine every time Archie came up there because he did a great job and he was entertaining. It was almost symbolic, an act of prosperity, real or imagined. A shine could be a little reward for just having done a trade.

Freddy often wondered how much Archie made shining shoes. 'All cash' was Freddy's kind of business. He also wondered how the hell Archie got past the lobby rent-cops. Going through the 53-story Shell Building at four dollars a shine seemed like a very nice business. Freddy won-dered whether shinning shoes might just be a better business than 'jam-ming' bonds into his client's portfolios, and considered taking Archie to lunch some day to pick his brains. Freddy, the pillar of the community, had somehow avoided military service and was thinking, 'I wonder how you shine shoes? I could learn . . . hell, I learned about munis.'

When Archie finished, Freddy handed him a "pound" and waved away the change. The next customer was Leon who was on the phone; he just swung a foot up onto Archie's shine box. He hung up and said, "how are you doing, Archie?" He always gave the same answer, which he apparently thought was funny,

"If I felt any better it would be a frame-up."

"I mean what's new with you?" Leon asked.

"Oh, I'm just ridin' around, you know. What you got on your agenda Mr. Walla? What's the chairman o' the board doin' these days?" Archie said looking over the top of his pulpit half-glasses with a big, white toothed grin.

"I'm going on a cruise to St. Thomas in two weeks, Archie. I'm pretty excited actually."

"I been there," Archie matter-of-factly said tapping Leon's already shined shoe to start on the next one. Leon thought, 'shit!, I've got to get a raise for Christ's sake. Even the fucking shoeshine guy has already been to St. Thomas. This is a bunch of bullshit!' He reached into his pencil drawer again for more aspirins and lit another cigarette. It was 11AM and he was feeling a little better.

At 11:08 the direct line from the broker's broker, Marc Rapoport, lit up and Leon answered,

"Yeah?"

"I can't even see you and I know you look like hell," said Rapoport.

"What's this, Sons of David day or something? What do you want?" Leon said with feigned annoyance. He liked Marc Rapoport, they were good friends.

"Bid wanted by 1PM our time on 750M LCRA 71/8s of 7-15-90 . . . do you care?"

"Yeah, I'll be back to you." Leon hung up the 'direct' line and raised his voice to the salesmen,

"Does anybody care on size LCRA's of '90? Billy, what about that guy in the Valley?" Leon turned to his desk partner and continued, in a lower tone,

"Jack, what about Henry Bell, these LCRAs seem like his kind of stuff?"

"What level are you thinking?" asked Jack.

"I don't know . . . a 5.40% yield less some spread? Where do you think you can get an order?" Jack responded, "a 5.40 probably works. Let's get outta' here, I'm starving. Want to go to Cyclone's?" Leon did some quick figuring and turned in his bid, and they headed for the elevators.

There were three ways to eat lunch; 1) at the desk, if they were either too busy or too lazy to leave the building, 2) there were at least 20 places within an easy walk of the building, or 3) they could drive somewhere. The bond guys didn't go to the trouble of driving too often, so when they did decide to drive somewhere, it was always sort of festive and took a lot more time.

Jack started the Nova and reached for the paper ticket to initial, as they drove toward the exit of the City Parking Garage which he used month-to-month. Leon grabbed the ticket first and said, generously, "I'll get this," and then signed Jack's initials on the ticket with a flourish. Leon did this every time they left the garage in the

Nova and each time they'd both laugh. The fact was that Jack was billed monthly and Leon generously initialing the ticket as though he were picking up some big tab in New York City, and it didn't mean shit. Leon was a cheap, tightwad and he was not at all bothered by it. Jack ribbed him about it all the time but it honestly never bothered him either; it was just how Leon was.

Cyclone Anaya's restaurant was their favorite Mexican place. It wasn't necessarily great, but they just liked being there. Cyclone had been a professional wrestler and there were black and white pictures of this guy as a much younger man in wrestling poses all over the walls. Two of the indicators that it wasn't a particularly great place to eat were the shuffleboard table and the duck shooting game in the corner. Jack didn't think too many people used the shuffleboard table from the looks of the aging can of that sawdust shit they had to "lubricate" the table so the puck went faster. He had never seen anyone shoot ducks.

"Are you ready to order?" asked what was probably one of Cyclone's heavyset daughters. Jack went first because Leon was trying to decide between the carne adovada and the special described on the blackboard on the wall over the duck shooting game. "I'll have a Dos Equis and the Mexican dinner plate." Leon decided on his standby, carne adovada and of course, a Dos Equis also.

"Leon, why do you even consider the rest of the menu when we both know what you'll order? You are the most predictable son-of-a-bitch I ever met. Have you *ever* ordered anything but carne adovada? I'm serious, your a masochist, you'll have heart burn the rest of the afternoon. Maybe even a heart attack"

"Give me a break Jack, all right? It's my stomach and I pay for the Rolaids, so it's no skin off your ass. You're like a den mother. The thing you don't get is that I don't give a shit about a heart attack. When my number is up, it's up, and that's it—I'm toast. Then you'll have to find another trader and another friend who'll put up with all your nagging."

"Hey, all I'm trying to do is make you a bit healthier, get you to shape up. It would change your whole life Leon, being in shape, feeling good, probably improve your sex life too."

"What sex life? I'm already the recording secretary for the local chapter of 'Sex Without Partners.' Another thing about you Jack is that in spite of the fact that you run five miles, or whatever every day, it doesn't mean shit. Hell, it's probably bad for you. How do you know?"

"Leon, that's got to be stupidest thing I ever heard you say!"

"Look at you Jack, your body is confused, don't you see? You don't feed it enough; you ask it to run five miles and then to sit at a desk all day. There is probably a meeting of your organs being held under your liver right now, a protest meeting. I can just see those guys saying, 'what does this asshole want from us anyway? Why didn't we just walk the five miles? What's with this running shit anyway?' And another organ says, 'Yeah, and what is it with all this water, I'm about to drown down here for Christ's sake!' You see Jack, I think they are going to get pissed off at you one of these days, and they'll *give* you a heart attack. Some bum looking for aluminum cans will find you along Buffalo Bayou some morning. Now my organs don't even have meetings because they are perfectly content. Shit, they have plenty of rest, all the booze they want, lots of fats, so that they slide around with no friction. I don't ask my guys to do anything except keep everything working and to squeeze when I take a crap."

As Jack drove back to the office, he realized they had pretty much blown the afternoon as far as bonds were concerned. Leon's logic was appalling . . . meetings of body parts . . . shit. The aluminum can guy was a whole lot more apt to find *Leon's* body with its distended belly behind some dumpster, than to find a physical specimen like Jack along the Bayou. Jack knew Leon was just messing with him anyway, he was always doing that.

When they got back to the office from lunch, Freddy Brister was over across the trading room reading the long piece of paper, which had rolled off of the Munifax machine over the past several hours. The machine was in every bond department throughout the country and it printed stuff all day long. It was about half news related to the business and half "bid wanteds" on blocks of munis dealers needed to sell. It always irritated Freddy that no one seemed to pitch in and at least tear off the paper and attach the pieces to a clipboard hanging on the wall for just that purpose. Freddy was a bit of a martyr, always righteous, and felt that he was always contributing more than his share, no matter what it was. His marriage was even that way.

The reason Freddy was not on the phone was that the banks he called on had closed for the day. Leon and Jack were still at the trading desk reading—Jack, the *Wall Street Journal* and Leon, a well-worn *Playboy*. Leon dropped the magazine into his bottom drawer and said, "get out the board" to Jack.

They had a pretty consistent ritual every afternoon when things slowed down—playing backgammon at the desk. They would open the upper file drawer between them and lay out "the board" which they kept under Leon's desk. Jack had introduced Leon to backgammon and realized, almost immediately, that he had created a monster. Leon was a serious gambler and took to backgammon right away. He even read books on the game. Their playing always bothered Freddy who had no interest in playing himself. He thought gambling was inappropriate in a brokerage house. It never occurred to him that a brokerage house *was* a gambling establishment for God's sake! Jack and Leon, as usual, paid no attention to Freddy, set out the men, put the doubling cube on two, agreed to a dollar a point and rolled for who went first.

CHAPTER 3

Glen Wilson was at his desk across the room with the other institutional salesmen who sold government bonds to pension funds and insurance companies. Leon was watching him look out the 49th floor window he sat next to. 'He was real good at that,' Leon thought, 'he's probably still trying to figure out what all that yellow/greenish haze is.' Leon knew exactly what it was, and where it came from as well. He grew up in Pasadena, just on the Southeastern edge of Houston. It was near the Houston Ship Channel and was virtually covered with oil refineries—huge ones. In high school, they used to poke fun at their town and say, "come to Pasadena, where the air is greena."

Leon saw Glen pick up his phone. He knew Glen had this really big bond swap up with one of his larger accounts, and had been nervously waiting for a response. It was probably why he had been staring out at the green air for the last half-hour. Just then Glen's face started to turn red and he slammed the phone onto the receiver from a good three feet up in the air! Leon thought he saw little pieces of black plastic bouncing off of the desk, but he was certain he saw that little microphone from inside, land on the secretary's desk next to Glen's.

"GODDAMN ASSHOLES! SON-OF-A-BITCH! F—KING BUREAUCRATIC PISSANTS! JESUS H. CHRIST!"

Leon loved it when Glen blew up over a trade, because it gave him an opening he enjoyed and always took advantage of. He yelled across the room, "Hey Glen, quit holding back like that and tell us what you really think, you can't keep bottling up all those feelings." The rest of the salesmen chimed in with similar comments. Glen was the classic 'little guy,' he had the entire syndrome down pat.

Jack watched the whole thing sitting next to Leon and shook his head. He thought that sort of display was pretty pathetic. Glen needed the trade pretty badly, Jack knew that, but this shit was ridiculous. You don't act like that. They'd have to get another phone; it looked like Glen totaled his this time. Jack turned and said, "Hey, Leon, Radar is out of town seeing her mother in Oregon, lets bag a few drinks after work. How about it?"

Mary didn't know it, but her nickname among the bond guys was 'Radar.' She watched Jack like a hawk and somehow had the ability to track him down anywhere within the city. Of course there were only a couple of bars she knew Jack would go to with the boys, and she knew the numbers by heart so it wasn't much of a trick really. They all loved the name though. It was really funny when Lung would cover the phone with his palm and shout over to the table, "Yo, 'Jack-san', it's Radar for you."

Lung always called him 'Jack-san' because they both spent time in Japan and shared the same feelings about the Japanese. Neither one was particularly fond of them for reasons the rest of the guys were not familiar with. At any rate, Mary left town Thursday and Jack would have the weekend free since she took the two kids as well. Leon said, "Sure, I've got nothing going on, unlike you and all the other poor married slobs, I stand before you, unattached and free to do anything and anybody."

Jack knew that was baloney, Leon was basically a lonely man and he and Mary always included him in their holiday celebrations and those sorts of things. "Lets go early though, this goddamn office depresses me sometimes," Leon said looking at his watch. "As a matter of fact, unless you've got something cooking, lets just go now." They put on their suit coats, headed across the trading room and as they passed by the secretaries desk they both said, "going to a meeting," which Elvira Moore knew meant the 'meeting' was at the Sewer. Leon noticed as he passed Glen's desk that he was still trying to get that little microphone back into his phone. Just then he heard someone yell, "Leon, it's the direct line for you."

"Christ, wait a second Jack, get an elevator, I'll just be a second." Leon ran to get the phone, "What is it? I'm on my way out"

Johnny Cannon was on the 'direct' (line) from G.K. Hill & Co. Leon liked him; everyone liked him for that matter. He was a really nice guy, but you had to catch him before he went to lunch to do any business because he had a bad drinking problem. If he had been an asshole, like some traders, he would be fair game even after lunch when Leon's *caveat emptor* rule kicked in. Johnny was too nice to 'pick off' when he was drunk, but Leon had, more than once, sold high priced bonds to competitors he did not care for, who were stupid enough to get loaded at lunch and come back to the trading desk. Leon's rule for himself was to take the rest of the day off if he planned to drink at lunch.

Johnny Cannon was about to say his usual, "hey pal" introduction when Leon interrupted him, "Johnny, I am running out with Armstrong and I can't talk. We'll be at the Sewer if you want to join us." Leon hung up and ran out of the trading room into the hall in time to see Jack Armstrong holding the elevator door open for him.

"That was Cannon. I told him we were stopping by the Sewer, he may join us."

"'May join us' my ass," Jack said to Leon. "When has Cannon ever turned down having a drink? When they finally take him to Ben Taub Hospital and inject him with dye and look at the X-rays of his liver, it's gonna' look like he swallowed first base. He's put a lot of mileage on that liver of his."

Leon knew Jack was right about Cannon. He remembered some time ago having a conversation with Johnny about living wills and the nobility of donating organs and that sort of thing. Leon hoped that Johnny had not included livers on the back of his Texas driver's license, and thought, 'if anybody ought to get his liver, it ought be the Smithsonian, and not one of his unsuspecting fellow Texans.'

They were a half block from the Ten Ten Garage building where the Sewer was located in the basement when Jack stopped and turned to Leon, "God I hate going to this place, its a friggin' dump, Leon. I don't know how you guys stand it. The one night I get to go out on the tiles with some friends, I go to the Sewer."

"What a fucking weenie this guy is," Leon turned away, as if speaking to someone else, "the guy gets medals in Vietnam, and he's afraid of a bar. I don't want to hear it all night, so let's just go to the Cellar Door." They turned and headed in the opposite direction.

"Hey, I'm not afraid of the bar so much as I'm afraid of what I might contract in that place. The last time I had those shitty *hors d'oeuvres* they have, the plate I picked up looked like a petri dish for Christ's sake."

"Jack, how is Cannon going to know where we went in case he wants to join us?"

"Shit, he'll figure that out in a heartbeat—the guy has supernatural powers when it comes to that stuff. Don't worry about it Leon, we're probably doing him a favor." As it turned out, Cannon was not five minutes behind them when he walked into the Cellar Door. He also had a bit of a head start on Jack and Leon from his lunch with the 'Dipper.'

Kitty McDonald was real tall, and someone started a rumor that he had seen her actually dunk the ball one time, which of course was bullshit. She had been asked to move from her very blue blood roots in New York to Dallas when Solly opened their office there. She told Jack once that she could not stand the arrogant, pompous assholes Saloman Brothers seemed to hire. There was one she briefly dated who's goal seemed to be to date every female at the firm. She referred to him as a serial monogamist. So she quit, moved in with her lawyer boy friend in Houston and finally ended up as a trader with Danny McKay's firm.

Kitty thought Jack was handsome and liked him a lot, but only in the platonic sense. When they talked on the phone during the day she always called him "Pork Chop," once explaining the joke about the girl who was so ugly that the family had to tie a pork chop around her neck, just to get the dog to play with her. The guys never used the nickname 'Dipper' around her, but she knew about it and didn't care. She seemed to posses that confidence that really good looking, blue blood women seemed to have. Being tall and the nickname didn't bother her in the least.

Everyone thought that Kitty was beyond 'good looking'. Once during a conversation with Jack she referred to her days back in New York, after work,

"My room mate Francie and I would go out Friday nights after work, you know to those cool bars over on the East Side? Francie looked a lot like Michele Pfeiffer—she was just drop dead good looking. Anyway, the bars were full of mostly young traders and lawyers. It was lots of fun for us—easy picking's—like clubbing baby seals."

When Johnny Cannon had a few drinks in him, he was actually delightful to be with. You sort of had a window between drink #3 and drink #9—maybe two hours or so, when he would regale the boys with stories. Beyond drink #9 things went down hill. He wasn't belligerent or a pain in the ass, he just became an invalid everyone had to take care of.

"Jack, have I ever told you about my cousins the steeplejacks in Ireland?" It was Cannon starting to hold court.

"You've told us about all those cops and firemen up in New York. I want to party with those guys. How about you Leon?" Leon began to answer when Johnny Cannon talked right over him,

"No, no. Not those guys, I'm talking about the steeplejacks back in Ireland. One of them had this terrible fall, working in England and was killed. They decided to take him back to their village in Ireland where they all came from. When they got off the ferry with the casket, a borrowed car from the village met them. It was one of those old British jobs with the rounded top. The only way they could deal with the casket was to tie it on the top of the car, with the ropes running through the open windows, which of course meant they couldn't open the car's doors, you know, to get in and out. Well, naturally, being Cannons, they couldn't pass by a pub and so they hit every one on the way home. Each time they climbed in and out of the windows laughing like crazy. Then when they were all out of the car, and ready to go into the pub, they'd all say, 'We'll not be a minute or two Dan, so don't go anywhere!' Then, roaring laughing, they'd go in for another pint. The entire affair took nearly all day, and it was the most fun they ever had. It was really a fucking mobile wake, if you get the picture. Yeah, they are still talking about Dan's wake over there.

"Anyway, the roads were pretty shitty, being Ireland and all, and every time they'd hit a pot hole the casket would shift and it sounded like the thing was about to fly off the top. So, all the cousins would lean out of the window and shout, 'ARE YOU THERE DAN!?' Jesus, those guys have fun."

"Do me a favor Johnny." Jack said with a big grin, "When any of these guys come to New York, you've got to promise me that we all go up there. I want to party with the Cannons by God!" Jack knew it wouldn't ever happen but it would sure be some fun.

CHAPTER 4

At least once a year, usually in the summer, Searl, Patrick and McNulty summoned Leon and the two salesmen, Jack Armstrong and Freddy Brister, along with traders and salesmen from the other 'regions', up to New York for a municipal bond conference. Leon always thought that while it had some value, it was mostly a bullshit thing, which had little real value to his particular desk and ended up costing too much money. The thing that annoyed him the most, was that the expenses he incurred going up there, came out of his profit center. It was *their* goddamn conference, *they* wrote the rules and the agenda, and Leon and the other regional traders paid for it. He thought it was a crock. The good side was that every time he went up there he had a good time. Not of course during the boring meetings, but afterward. He also liked to scope out the new ladies who worked on the New York desk with whom he talked all the time, but had not yet met. It was always fun to finally put a face, or in Leon's case, a chest on the voice, and often they were damn nice faces and chests to be sure. Jack knew that Leon got pretty clubby with several of the girls on the New York desk and suspected that he knew them also in some biblical sense.

These conferences were always over a weekend and invariably at some fancy country club up in Westchester County somewhere. It was the usual, meetings/golf/tennis /dinners and cocktail parties. Jack always liked these things because he paid for nothing and he happened to be very, very good at golf/tennis/eating and cocktail parties. Searl often did a half assed job at important things like hiring the muni department head or some big shot public finance guy, but never with their muni conferences—they were always top of the line affairs.

Every guy at the first night's cocktail party, with the exception of the out of towners, had on something made of madras. Either their slacks were madras and the cotton jackets were lime green, or the color of some other fruit, or it was the other way around! Leon thought they looked a lot like the members of that black fraternal order of something or other back in Pasadena, Texas when he was a kid. Leon and Jack wore the Houston equivalent, which were a blue blazer, khakis and a white knit golf shirt. Leon disapproved of all that madras and Gatorade colors, and, being stubborn, would not concede, even in his own mind, that the Houston uniform was just as conforming as all that madras.

"Jack, this looks like a picnic for black life insurance salesmen for Christ's sake. Look at these blue blood, up-east people, even the women look the same." Jack turned to Leon and looked at the same blazer he had on, only four sizes smaller and smiled at Leon.

"Leon, lighten up for Christ's sake, and lets have a good time; and try to act civil; and watch your drinking. And another thing Leon, don't let that eagle brain of yours overload that humming bird ass. The last time you picked a fight, you looked at me as though you expected me to be your stand-in. Just be nice tonight."

"Anything else Mom? You're a fucking nagger, you know that Jack? You're worse that my ex-wife. The difference is, I could get rid of her."

Just then Freddy Brister walked over to Leon and Jack in his own blue blazer and khakis. Freddy was a lot of fun as long as you got him away from the office. When it came to business, he was a pain in the ass, but when it came to a party he was fun to be with. Freddy was a runner and he had just gone for a jog around the golf course before the party and he was feeling nice and mellow. Leon only enjoyed Freddy's company when his endorphins were up—Freddy's endorphins that is—Leon's were permanently in hiding. Freddy had already gotten his first Heineken and was replacing body fluids the way he liked and said,

"Look at all these assholes in those Jamaican outfits, they look like a shelf full of Gatorade bottles". Jack turned toward Freddy,

"That is exactly what Leon just said and I want to warn you two not to start anything tonight 'cause I'm not bailing your asses out this time. Besides they'd probably fire you if you make a scene."

The next morning there was a compulsory meeting in one of the club's big meeting rooms. The New York planners had left the afternoon open for a golf tournament, and the morning meeting turned into one of those free-form discussion and bitching sessions. There really was an agenda, which they would eventually get through, but the session bordered on the mutinous, with everyone a little hungover, making comments, butting in and talking right over the top of one another. The main topic was prompted by all the many mergers, which had been taking place among the Wall Street brokerage firms. This consolidation had made many sales positions redundant or, at least produced the problem of double coverage of big institutions. A salesman would be doing pretty well with State Farm for instance, when his firm was merged with another whose salesman did five times as much business with that account. It didn't take a brain surgeon to figure out who ended up with "The Farm". This bothered Freddy a lot because he covered bigger institutions where Jack mainly called on the country banks in Texas, which were definitely not considered institutions by anyone's definition. Freddy was following the discussion carefully. The senior muni manager was making suggestions that these impacted salesmen ought to be broadening their types of business away from institutions into, say, rich individuals, trust departments and corporate treasuries. Freddy raised his hand and told this big shot with the ideas,

"Scott, what you have to realize is that this is not so easy to do. You know I've been institutionalized for ten years now." Freddy sat down; satisfied that he had made a point, while everyone who knew him was moved by his confession.

Leon and Jack always moved down to New York City after these conferences to kiss the ring at the main offices while Freddy invariably flew right home. Jack and Leon debated whether he missed his business or his wife. They would check into the Westbury, on Madison Avenue, and on Monday, cab it downtown to Searl's headquarters and spend the day hanging out on the trading desk. Someone on the desk was usually either sick, just fired, or on vacation, so there was room for them to make a few calls and sometimes do some business. Both Leon and Jack liked the faster pace of the muni desk in New York, but neither would ever consider a transfer up there—a couple days in the Big Apple was fun, but enough.

Leon, as usual, had been up since 5 A.M. and was ready to head downtown when, at 7:30, he called Jack's room, only to discover he had just gotten out of the shower. "Come on Jack, move your ass, I want to get to the office in the next two hundred years, sleep when you get back to Houston. I'll be in the lobby in a half hour."

Jack stepped off the elevator exactly on time with his hair still bit damp. He kept that fairly short hair cut from his Marine days, even though the trend was to look like the kid on the "Dutch Boy" paint cans. Every time he saw one of those trendy, dopey looking hairdos he felt like smacking the shit out of the guy. He knew that was ridiculous though, since half the "men" wore their hair like that.

After a few minutes they managed to hail a cab. Through inexperience, some cunning and devious natives aced them out of the first two cabs. One guy went half a block uptown and shortstopped the first cab and with the second one, they simply got muscled out by an elderly woman.

"New Yorkers are assholes", Jack said after they finally got into a cab. He realized what he had said and quickly looked at the drivers name on the hack license mounted on the dash, hoping it was unpronounceable—it, of course, was.

"I can see your side of that." Leon said, "How about the one at La Guardia on Thursday night, the guy who told you to wait your turn? I thought you were going to hit him with your attaché case!"

"Right Leon, all I needed was to get into a fight with some Guido who's brother was either a cop or a wiseguy with the Mob. Shit, Searl would really enjoy the additional PR from us while we were up here. I'd end up so deep in the Tombs they have to feed me with a slingshot."

"Jack, what the fuck do you know about the Tombs? As soon as we get up here each year you start to talk like these people. We're here maybe twenty minutes and it's 'dees and does' and places like the 'Tombs'. Why not just move up here and get it over with? You'd fit right in."

"Let me tell you something Leon, 'When in Rome', OK? As soon as these people suspect you are from out of town, they try to take your head off. This driver, from Addis Ababa or wherever, probably thinks he can get us downtown by way of Queens just because he heard that twangy Texas accent of yours."

"That is so typical of that paranoid and twisted mind of yours Jack, I swear to God. Anybody from a place like Addis Ababa isn't going to be able to tell the difference between an accent from Texas or Thailand."

"Why do you do that Leon? You know you turn me on when you get mad", Jack said as he reached across the back seat to try to kiss Leon.

"GET THE FUCK AWAY FROM ME JACK, YOU GODDAMN HOMO! You act like you're thirteen, you know that? Jesus, now the driver thinks we are a couple of queers. I hate it when you do shit like that!"

Jack always pulled things like that with Leon. He knew Leon was homophobic and tried to embarrass him. Leon noticed the driver's eyes in the rearview mirror and said in a lower voice,

"The guy's looking at me Jack, why do you do shit like that? They probably castrate you in Addis Ababa if you're queer. I think you have some queer in you Jack, you know that?" Leon moved his attaché case off his lap and stood the thing up on the seat between he and Jack. Jack was laughing so hard that he got his handkerchief out to wipe his eyes.

Jack remembered the Thailand remark and started to laugh some more. He'd been there several times when he was in Vietnam and he thought the country was the world's biggest whorehouse. It was pretty sick he thought. He was as red blooded as the next guy, but he thought Thailand was pretty evil when it came to their women and girls. He and his pilot buddies always pronounced it "Thigh Land".

Searl's offices were in a building right on Hanover Square near

Wall Street. The bond department was on the twentieth floor with a view of the East River from where the government bond people were, and a view of Harry's Bar from the muni side of the floor. When Jack first noticed this a few years earlier, he thought, 'How appropriate?', the bond trader's watering hole. That was no doubt where Louie Napolitano would take them for lunch. Louie was the head muni trader in New York, and a good friend of Leon's. He traded the longer maturities of the local names like Triborough Bridge and Tunnel—everyone called them 'Tribes'. Most munis had short names for obvious reasons. Who would want to go through the formal names all day long? So, it was 'Tribes', 'Ports', 'Dorms' and 'Cities' instead of Triborough Bridge and Tunnel Authority, Port of New York and New Jersey, New York State Dormitory Authority and The City Of New York.

Jack and Leon had not had any breakfast, so they went over to a little snack bar, just off the trading floor, for a buttered roll and a cup of coffee. The New York muni desks preferred that the traders not leave the floor for lunch. There was just too much going on, so they always made lunch easy, and most everyone ate at their desks, unless they had out of town firemen like Leon and Jack. In that case, they'd go to Harry's. Louie would take them across the street for lunch later on. Some firms actually catered lunch right there on the muni desk so no one would leave.

They sat near Louie and each time he would start to say, "So, Jack how did you like the conference?", someone would yell across the consoles, "LOUIE—MERRILL" and he'd pick up his phone. So, they never got much of a chance to talk to anyone up there.

The sales people in New York always left Jack with the impression that he was from the boonies somewhere. They made him uncomfortable somehow. He realized however, that it could just be his imagination. It reminded him of that *New Yorker* magazine cover with the cartoon map of the United States, where there was only New York City on one side and Los Angeles on the other side and a bunch of grass and a few little cows in the middle. Jack figured that these people thought that if you were from west of the Hudson River, you couldn't possibly know shit about the business. The truth was that he did feel a bit lost with everybody shouting about Tribes and Ports. It always took him a morning up on that desk to realize that he did not give two shits about Tribes and Ports anyway! The last thing Jack's clients in Texas wanted to hear about were New York bonds. He knew that they wouldn't care if that paper were yielding 25%. The place was poorly managed, and was going to belly up any day, and they hoped that Gerald Ford would not acquiesce to a bailout. All Jack's Texas clients felt the same, "Fuck New York City"!

"Louie, I just remembered that a client wanted me to check out the possibility of really short paper and I forgot to do it before I left Houston. I guess floaters would work except we don't do them here. Any ideas?" Jack felt like a dope for forgetting.

"First Chicken has all that shit Jack. They must have five traders doing nothing but Treasury bills and muni notes—you know, TAN's, RAN's. First Chicago has always been big in short paper. Give them a call. In fact just pick up line 44 over there, it's direct."

It rang a couple seconds before they answered,

"Bill Trader."

"I need the muni note trader please."

"Bill Trader."

Jack thought, 'Is this guy stupid, not listening, or just from Chicago?'

"Look, I don't want bills OK?, I want some muni notes. Are you listening?"

"Yeah, I am listening wise guy. My name is BILL TRADER, it's short for WILLIAM TRADER, which I'd prefer not to use if it's all right with you. So, what do you want?" Jack felt like a complete fool and country bumpkin, reaffirming his suspicion that they all thought Texans were a bit slow. He'd have hung up except it was the direct line and there was no place to hide. He sheepishly wrote down what he was told and said he'd call Trader back in a few days. He also knew he wouldn't make that mistake again.

Louie put down his phone and said, "Where do you guys want to go to lunch, Harry's or Harry's?"

As usual, Harry's bar was three deep with traders and salesmen.

The muni guys thought of the place as their own, but in fact there were plenty of stock people there as well. Louie got the *maitre d's* attention and they were seated to the left of the bar at a table near the high windows. They all ordered Stoli martinis and before Jack and Leon picked up the menus, Louie said, "The Wellington. Get the Beef Wellington. It's the best thing they have here, and they only have it once a week."

Jack took a sip and asked, "Louie, I heard someone on the desk awhile ago call you Boom Boom. I never heard that before. Where did that come from?"

"It's an Italian thing…nicknames." said Louie.

"You guys discovered America, developed the meatball and the radio, now you're claiming nicknames? Millions of people have nicknames Louie, it's not just Italian."

"Jack, I am not talking about variations of the name your parents gave you, I'm talking about the names your associates give you. There is a difference. When you think about it there are only two groups that do this. Fighter pilots and Italians."

"Wait a second Louie, I've got to think about this. It sounds like bullshit though." Jack paused and took a sip.

"Then do Italian fighter pilots have two nicknames? I can see it, 'My I introduce Tennente Vito The Stick—Strafer Provalone'."

"Jack, just look in the goddamn papers. Every Italian has a nickname and the press *always* uses it. Mario "Two Fingers" Columbo, or Vinny "The Guinney" Polozzi, you know, shit like that. Wasps like you don't have names like that. Can you imagine, Nathanial "The Hammer" Williamson, or Buffy "The Mattress" Huffington? Don't exactly roll of the tongue do they?"

"Come to think of it, we had a biology teacher in college we called "Fat Fingers". We heard he taught because he couldn't get into dental school because he couldn't get his hands in anybody's mouth."

"He was Italian, right Jack?" asked Louie.

"Ciaravino, Professor Sal Ciaravino. God he was fat."

Jack always thought of himself as pretty worldly. He'd been all over the place in the Marine Corps, but surprisingly, he was not that familiar with ethnic groups. He had a white, Anglo-Saxon experience for the most part. He ate plenty of Italian food, but had no idea about their culture and language. Maybe a stereotype or two. The same for Chinese, Greeks, and all the rest. He had once seen a movie, which he thought was hilarious, called *A Fish Called Wanda*. There was this character who spoke in what sounded like Italian, but actually was just a bunch of nonsense. This character was really an American who wanted to jump the bones of the movie's good-looking girl. He'd string Italian sounding syllables together with all the proper inflection, and the result got the girl in bed every time, because she was enamored of the sounds of Italian. Once Jack passed a construction site in New York, on one of his yearly visits, and heard the guy delivering the cinder blocks yell and wave his arms at some other guy in a sleeveless t-shirt, "*Ba fongule!*", and Jack loved the sound of it, and repeated it over and over as he walked,...*ba fongule, ba fongule, ba fongule*. The other word he loved was *pasta fagule*. He didn't know what that meant any more than *ba fongule*. He'd repeat it in his head sometimes. This was his way of dealing with that distinctly American inferiority—the complete lack of any foreign language skills. It always bothered him that the average German knew several languages and he, and everyone else he knew, didn't know 'come here from sic'um", when it came to other languages.

The waiter was typical New York, condescending, rude and a little surly. The plates hit the table a bit too hard for Leon—the Southerner. The waiter's attitude went right by Louie, who ate all his meals in the City and was accustomed to shitty service. Neither Jack nor Leon commented. They had been in New York for four days and had already begun to acquiesce, as did most visitors, to abuse. They all began to eat when Jack said, "Oh my God, this stuff is great!"

Leon just nodded and kept on eating and then added, "This is the best Wellington I've ever eaten."

Jack looked sideways at Leon and said, "Probably the *only* Wellington you ever had."

"Jack, just because we eat at Cyclone's or James' Coney Island every day doesn't mean I am some kind of a philistine. You don't know where I eat at night while you're out in suburbia making franks and beans for the kids on your smoker. Jack, see this crusty stuff around the meat? It's called brioche . . . brioche Jack. Did you know that? I didn't think so."

Louie tried to change the subject and said, "Why don't you guys stay a couple more days? Come to the office and work out of there and we'll go out at night. See a show and I'll take you to my favorite restaurant over in Greenpoint . . . Bamonte's. The food is great and you get to see all the wiseguys with lumps in their coats. It's the place they had the victory lap after they shot Joe Bananas or one of those Mob guys out in Coney Island."

While Leon and Jack looked at each other as if deciding, Louie went to the full court press and said, "Come on guys, stay over and we'll go see *Hair*." Jack's eyes widened and he asked, "No shit Louie, can you really get us into that show? I thought it was the hottest thing in town. Mary wouldn't talk to me again if I got to see that without her."

Louie shrugged and said, "I've got a buddy who is a scalper, a paisan . . . we went to high school together until he decided to drop out and run errands for some of the boys . . . if you get my drift. He's in the Guiness book for hearing his Miranda Rights the most times. He can get you tickets to the Last Supper!" Leon and Jack burst out laughing just as the asshole waiter handed Louie the check.

Louie pulled up in front of Bamonte's the next night in his brand new Mercedes and decided to park in the little fenced in lot next to the restaurant. He had talked Leon and Jack into extending two more days. They were early and there was one space left. As he passed the owner at the door Louie said, "Paulie, I've had this car all of six days, do you think its safe out there? I'd hate to get it stolen or something." Paulie looked shocked and said, "Louie, are you *serious*? A guy would have to be fuckin' crazy to steal a car from this place!" Louie immediately realized how dumb the question was. An expensive new car parked at *this* restaurant was certainly owned by a mobster, and everybody knew that if you fucked with it you *would* sleep with the fishes.

CHAPTER 5

Jack left through the kitchen door, walked over to the garage door and started to raise it. He wondered how the hell little old ladies did this. He worked out a few times a week, was six feet three and the door was not too easy to raise even for him. He also worried about throwing out his back since he was never warmed up enough at 5:30 in the morning or 'the middle of the night' as he referred to it. Maybe it needed an adjustment or something, maybe some grease, who knows. He thought, 'I'll ask Bob Welton on Saturday, that son-of-a-bitch knows everything.'

Everything in Welton's house ran and worked perfectly. He was Jack's next-door neighbor. Jack thought the guy was a little anal about his house and particularly his yard. He got Yard of the Month a couple times this year. Jack remembered both times on Saturdays when the committee stuck the sign, *YARD OF THE MONTH,* into Bob's lawn. Jack was pretty intimidated being this guy's next-door neighbor, when his own lawn looked like the Third Armored Division had done a recon on it.

As he drove downtown to the 'YMCA' he tried to figure the odds of getting Yard of the Month twice. The radio in the old Nova was lousy; Jack never turned the thing on, so that didn't interfere with the mental math. He thought, 'Lets see, there are about nine or ten streets, each a long block with maybe fifteen houses on each side. So there are about 300 homes and surely they don't give out the goddamn award in the winter months.' Jack thought the odds were like winning the Lotto. If it weren't for being able to pick Welton's brain, and borrow his tools, Jack would rather not live next to the guy, it was just too much pressure. He didn't want to live next to a slob exactly, but he'd prefer something in the middle. In other words, a guy who could help him but whose yard looked a little bit shitty also.

Jack's trip downtown was pretty easy since he left so early . . . speed limit the entire way. His commute was so awful when he left at a conventional hour, that he developed the habit of working out at the Downtown YMCA before going to the office. He carried a shirt, tie, suit, and he slipped on his dress shoes and put socks in his pocket. He had a Dopp kit in his locker and the 'Y' supplied the towels and workout stuff. Jack would occasionally forget his socks and was not the least bit embarrassed to walk around downtown Houston in a suit and no socks. Since it was December 10, he would play racquetball rather than running along the bayou in shorts and a t-shirt, with socks on his hands, turning beet red in the process. A good workout, an apple juice, banana and strawberry smoothie, and he was good to go.

There were several fitness guys among the Houston bond community apart from Jack, but for the most part the traders were physical wrecks. They smoked, drank and ate too much, and the only identifiable exercise they ever got was waving their arms to get the waitress' attention at the Sewer. Jack always thought that having the Texas Heart Institute near downtown was one of the hidden perks of their jobs. He was still thinking about this as he sat down at his desk next to Leon,

"Hey Leon, remember that guy at Woodhouse who worked with Sammy Stein—the guy who dropped dead right in front of me in their lobby?"

"Yeah, he was a stock jockey, I only know the bond people there. Didn't you work on him . . . give him CPR or something? I never asked but did you put your mouth on his?" Leon shuddered visibly and made a face, "Jesus I couldn't do that, no way hombre."

"Hell Leon, if the guy is dying and you can save his life you'd do it, believe me."

"No way Jose, not me. I don't put my mouth on blue people with saliva coming out of their mouth. And certainly not some cigar smoking MAN, sheeiiittt no!" Leon made another face. Jack just looked at him for a second,

"You know what that's all about don't you? It's your homophobia again, you're a mental case about that shit Leon, I swear. By God, if that had been that racehorse receptionist they have up in their bond department, you know the one with that Boone & Crocket body? If she had a fucking heart attack you'd be through the crowd around her like Sam Huff looking for the pocket! You wouldn't think twice about saliva and all that other shit. Hell, you're just jacking me around on this anyway."

Leon remembered that Boone & Crocket was that big game hunters record book, the one with the guys who shot the biggest trophy deer or whatever it was, and he began to laugh at Jack's little joke,

"Actually Jack, that was pretty funny . . . Boone & Crocket body, that's good. Well, you sure have her pegged; she's as strong as train smoke! I remember at their Christmas party last year she was at the door in some stretch, short, skintight kind of thing. God. it was almost pornographic. When she stuck one of those "Hello, I'm____" paper name tags on me, I nearly swallowed my tongue."

Leon was thinking about whether the racehorse would be at this year's Christmas party over at Stein's office, it wasn't too far off he thought. Just then Archie walked into the trading room making the rounds, shinning shoes. Leon and Jack always got a shine from Archie, but this morning they would have to wait a few minutes since everyone seemed to want one all of a sudden.

Each Christmas the bank in the lobby of the building had musical groups put on little shows. Every day they had a different organization, always around lunchtime. One day it would be those ladies with those bells with different tones, the next day it would be a bunch of old ladies singing carols. They all made Leon uncomfortable, it was too staged and phony with store bought cookies and lobby temperature punch.

Archie put down the shine box in front of Jack and started to work, "Jack, family man like yourself should go down to the lobby and get into the Christmas spirit, they putting' on a good show today. Bunch a kids down there."

"Is that right? Well Leon and I are going to grab some lunch and we'll hear them on the way out." Turning in his seat he asked, "Leon how about James' Coney Island? I'd kill for some chili today, as cold as it is out."

Archie kept talking about the music in the lobby, "They got a orchestra down there today, none of those old ladies with those bells 'n shit, they got a bunch a kids today. Tell you what Jack, it warms my heart seein' all them kids; black kids, white kids, Mexican kids. All playin' in a real orchestra together, you know, playin' Mozart, Rembrandt and all that shit, it's a beautiful thing really." Jack looked over to Leon and thought he was probably trying to recall just what music Rembrandt had composed. Leon was a big country music man, the classical stuff made him want to run screaming into the night.

Billy Bob Joiner was the building maintenance man for the top third of their building. He opened the hallway door to the department, and then went back out for his big long stepladder. Jack never saw one as big as the building used and thought his neighbor, Welton probably had one too. Leon thought Billy Bob showed up a lot around Christmas, 'Probably trolling for a big tip from the company. The rest of the year you needed Interpol to find the lazy bastard to come and change the fluorescent light tubes. Today he's up here changing stuff that doesn't need changing.' Leon thought the guy was a real asshole who had that whole Pillsbury doughboy thing going. He noticed Billy Bob's beer gut was getting a little bigger, his membership in the globally feared Texas National Guard, notwithstanding. Since he was a teenager, Leon called this condition 'Dunlap', after the old tire company. One time Archie, who had an entirely different slant on almost everything, defined the 'condition' by saying, "It's when a man's belly done laps over his belt." Billy Bob's jeans rode down on what used to be his hips, and his polyester uniform shirt rode up the opposite way showing the top of the crack of his ass. Jack once said, referring to Billy Bob, "The son-of-a-bitch never met Wil Rogers." Just then Jack piped up,

"Where you been Billy Bob? I haven't seen that coon ass of yours since that infestation of crickets in the parking garage. You been good?" Jack knew what was coming next. This guy would start whining about how hard he worked. He didn't get a chance because Leon joined in,

"Last time I saw you was just before you went off with the National Guard this fall. How did that work out, what all do you guys do in that two weeks anyway?"

Billy Bob started up the ladder with another tube, "They were having problems showin' Ortega n' them that we mean business and decided to send the Texas Guard down to kinda show the flag, 'least that's what I heard the sergeant say anyway. Went to Guatemala for our maneuvers."

Jack was interested in just who all these people down there were. In school they told you about the English and the French and the Germans, but nothing about Central and South America, he wondered how that was,

"Billy Bob, what are those folks down there like, I mean, they must have a lot of Indian blood in them. Did they brief the outfit on demographics?" Jack knew that Billy Bob probably knew all about *pornographics* but wouldn't know about *demographics* if it hit him upside the head. Billy Bob just shook his head; he was at the bottom of the ladder to get another unnecessary fluorescent tube. "What kind of people are they down in Guatemala anyway, Billy Bob?" Jack asked sincerely.

Billy Bob started back up the ladder and said, "Awwhh, there just a bunch a Mexicans." Leon had to act like he was looking for something under his desk, he was laughing so hard. He didn't want to offend Billy Bob even though he didn't give a rat's ass about him really.

Jack said, "Lets go to James', I'm behind on my fats. Leon, tell me something, how the hell do you stay so skinny? We eat together all the time so I know what you eat and how much, but I've gotta' run five miles a day to keep even and I know damn well you don't do shit except sit around with McKay at the Sewer and smoke?" Leon said one word, "Metabolism" and changed the subject.

There was no one on the elevator on their way out to lunch when Leon started up on Billy Bob to Jack, "Can you believe how fucking stupid that guy is? Jack, how can the National Guard have people that stupid? I can't imagine any sane, responsible person giving that son-of-a-bitch anything loaded. By the way, where do you want to go for lunch? Still James'?"

The first of the James' Coney Island chain of chili and hotdog joints was the only one Leon and Jack patronized. It was on the seedier side of Main Street and Leon was convinced it had the original grease on the walls. The place was loud and frenetic—all the noise coming from *behind* the counter. The customers just ordered, ate and left. The only noise they made was the spoons in the chili bowls and maybe a burp on the way out. James was a Greek immigrant and they had every single cousin in the clan, behind the counter yelling at the same time.

Leon and Jack each got down their trays from the big stack; silverware and an inch high pile of cheap paper napkins and started down the line,

· "Bowl of red with beans and two all the way . . . Hey!, a Doctor Pepper and a bag of Fritos too." Leon *never* altered his order. The Greek cousin yelled to his left, "CHILLA BINS and a DOCTA." Jack wasn't much better, "Bowl of red no beans, two all the way, a Big Red and a bag of Fritos."

This particular James catered to the polyester uniform people, the guys with embroidered patches with stuff like Otis Elevator, or some cleaning service on them. Guys in suits were tolerated but held suspect. The seats were those lecture chairs you had in college with the right arm that formed a big teardrop covered up with initials.

Leon was salivating as he poured the Fritos on top of his 'chilla bins', "Chilla bins, chilla bins. Goddamn I love their chili". Jack always started with the hot dogs first and made short work of them. James' hot dogs were 'all time' as far as Jack was concerned. They didn't cut the bun the whole length so that it would hold all that shit they put on the top like chili, onions, cheese out of a gun and mustard to top it all off. Jack said,

"I'd never take my kids here until they were older. You really need an adult sized mouth to handle these hot dogs when they are 'all the way'. I can't imagine a little kid trying to eat one of these, it would not be pretty, I'll guarantee you". The first things Leon would have when they got back to the office would be Rolaids, a cup of coffee and a cigarette. He thought, 'Life is good.'

As soon as he sat down at the desk after lunch, Leon pushed the direct line to his pal the broker's broker, Marc Rapoport, to see if he had been successful on any of the bids he turned in earlier on the 'bid-wanted' list Marc had out. While Leon's primary job was underwriting, he also doubled as the firm's trader for the secondary munis issued within the Texas region.

Marc said, "I'll bet you are dying to find out if you bought anything. If you'd eat at your desk like a real trader, you would already know."

"Spare me the bullshit Rapoport, and just tell me what I bought. It's Christmas time for Christ's sake" Leon thought that sounded pretty clever . . . Christmas for Christ's sake, "Goys like me lighten up a little; take time to get into the spirit; have long lunches with their friends; you get the picture. Although, the friends part probably confuses you." Leon knew Rapaport was grinning on the other end of the line as he got his bid list in front of him and marked down the items he was buying as Marc read them off. He thought he had done better than expected as he hung up. Jack had been listening and asked, "What did we buy?" Leon held up his hand to Jack as a sign to wait until he put reoffering prices on the new bonds.

Just then, Antonio Manuel Miguel Jesus Jimenez y Homosillo glided into the trading room. Antonio evidentially came from pre-Castro Havana's upper crust and rumor had it that, while he was one of the cashiers in the back office, he was rich and really didn't have to work. Both Jack and Leon always thought that was probably bullshit, since neither of them could conceive of working if you didn't have to, particularly as a cashier in a brokerage office! They

usually tried to stay, as Jack put it, about a hand grenade away from
Antonio at all times, because they were convinced that he was
homosexual. Jack would always refer to him as just 'Homo' for
short, but never to his face. Once he told Leon, with a straight face,
that "Homo" was the diminutive of the Spanish surname
"Homosillo". Leon was so homophobic that Antonio drove him
crazy whenever he came back to the bond department. Jack, on the
other hand, considered Antonio' visits entertainment because they
made Leon so uncomfortable. But both considered Antonio about
one enchilada short of a combination plate.

Antonio was the self-appointed, resident director of all that shit
secretaries did at any other firm. He was always in on the baby showers;
he took up the collections when a secretary left for another job; he was
the United Way representative; he organized the decoration of the office for Christmas and stuff like that. This particular visit was on behalf
of this year's office Christmas party.

"Yak, I hope that dis year ju are coming to the party. Lass year ju
dint show up and we had so much fun Yak. All those cute girls in the
backoffice ass me, 'Where was that big handsome Yak'?" This guy wore
tons of cologne, combed the hair from his temple clear over the top of
his head and walked from the knees—three strikes as far as Leon was
concerned.

Leon saw his opening and said, "Yeah Yak, where the fuck were you
last year anyway? Antonio is right you should go to stuff like this; show
your humanity; be a little more social; mix with the philistines from the
cage; dance with the secretaries, you know there all hot to trot for you.
Shit, I saw one of them smell one of your tickets last week—swear to
God, Yak" Jack just stared at Leon trying to make his eyes say, 'Screw you
Leon!' Leon's eyes stared right back at Jack and they said, 'I'm having
some fun with this one big guy!'

At this point Leon was just looking at Jack with a grin on his face
and Antonio was still there chattering and waving his arms as usual.
Antonio didn't use facial expressions like most Latinos, Jack thought,
rather he used his body movements to punctuate what he was saying.

Leon put his feet up on his desk and said, "You dint answer my question handsome. How come you let the girls in the cage down last year?"

"Don't worry Yak, dis year we are goin to have good music to dance to, because the manayur said I can rent a yukabox dis time." Antonio said excitedly. Leon's feet came off the desk as he said, "Hold on, hold on Antonio. Am I missing something here, what the fuck is a yukabox?"

Antonio looked at Leon as if he were stupid and said in a raised voice, "A yukabox, a yukabox, with records which ju push the buttons! Dint ju have those? We had, in Habana, big ones." Leon thought to himself, 'Yeah Antonio, ju got big ones all right. Como se dice *asshole* en espanol?'

Leon stood up and said, "Jack, I need a ride home, have you got the good car or does Radar have it as usual?"

"You know damn well I've got the Nova. Hell, you ride in it three or four times a week Leon. Besides she can't carpool the kids in the Nova, it's not big enough. Lets go." Under his breath, he said to Leon, "That cologne Antonio has on is about to make me sick. He smells like a Honolulu whorehouse." Leon stopped at the elevator and said,

"Wait Jack, it just came to me."

"What came to you?"

"The name of that cologne. I remember that smell. It's *eau de* petroleum jelly."

Across the street from their building was city hall and its little reflection pool surrounded by 50 live oak trees all chuck full of grackles making an enormous racket.

"They really ought to do something about those nasty birds Leon. I mean there has to be 10,000 of the goddamn things—just listen to that!"

"I'll tell you what, the noise bothers me a lot less than the fact that they are all crapping on the sidewalks. They must save it up all day. It smells awful and you know it's a health hazard. Why doesn't the city do something about this Jack?" Leon said this as he tiptoed through the bird droppings.

"Leon, you know the answer to that. They don't want to offend

those tree hugger, animal rights people. That really bothers me.
They are so damn inconsistent. I mean they will pack a city counsel
meeting about some plan to deal with the pigeon problem or these
nasty grackles, but they'd never think about complaining about killing
rats. Hell, pigeons are just flying rats anyway. It kills me to see them
demonstrating with signs that say "don't kill the animals", and they
are standing there in their fucking Gucci loafers! They must think
that the cows supplying the leather died of old age or something."

By this time they were nearly to the parking garage, and Jack was
thinking about how Leon constantly bummed rides home and how dis-
paraging he was about the Nova. It really was a piece of shit though,
with its throwup green color and that awful shag carpet the previous
owner installed. The guy actually put some leftover carpet in the rear
window area where the Houston sun had buckled and ruined that original cardboard shit that came with the car. Jack had meant to take the
stuff out when he bought the car, but never got around to it. He thought
it was like an advertisement to the car behind, which said, *"Don't even
think of running into this guy, because anybody with shag carpet in the rear
window deck, had to be uninsured."*

"You know," Jack started up as they left the parking garage, "Has it
ever occurred to a cheap son-of-a-bitch like you to contribute to the gas
bill of the car that takes you home three times a week? I mean you dump
all over this car, then ask for another ride."

Leon answered, "Look Jack, offering money would only encourage
you into keeping this piece of shit, when you really should call that guy
at that 'midnight auto sales' place we pass on the way to my house, and
ask him to just take it off your hands."

Each Christmas the entire Houston bond community looked forward to seeing Sammy David Stein and Leon Walla dress up as Santa
and his elf. Stein was one of those career Santas with his own costume. It
wouldn't matter where or what he did for a living, he'd be Santa; he even
did it when he was in the Marines. Nobody could figure out why Leon
would humiliate himself dressed as a little elf. But they did it every year.
All the bond departments were downtown within walking distance of

each other and on a particular day, usually the last working day before Christmas, Stein and Leon would dress up and visit each firm.

Nobody got any work done on this day of the season, because it was an office party at all the firms. Not the official one. Not the one at night where all the men get loaded and make passes at all the women, but the one in the office where everyone brings in food which is bad for you.

Stein and Leon went to *every* firm in downtown Houston and they stopped into both watering holes—The Sewer and Cellar Door-both of which were worth at least three drinks on the house. When they were at Stein's firm, Woodhouse, Leon took the opportunity of talking to that gorgeous racehorse of a receptionist they had.

"Hiya, I'm Leon. You know, I keep seeing you at these bond functions and I never seem to get a chance to talk to you. We are going to be finished with this Santa stuff in a couple hours. How about meeting for a drink after?"

Miss Racehorse was looking at Leon in his green elf costume with the red shoes turned up at the toe into a big loop, and burst out laughing. Pretty soon she had tears running down her face and she was bent at the waist, nearly hyperventilating, slapping her gorgeous thighs. Leon felt like a fool and went over to the trading desk to get another drink

CHAPTER 6

Elvira Moore was the most senior secretary, not only in the bond department, but also in the entire office. In fact, she was senior, in time at the firm, to all the folks in management as well. In a wolf pack, she would be the 'alpha female'. Mess with her and she'd kick your ass *with* the approval of the pack. *Nobody* gave Elvira grief in spite of what she might have thought. Grief was, after all, relative. Leaving the top up on the Xerox machine was not, in any metaphysical sense, grief, but it pissed Elvira off. She was paid on a formula just like every other secretary or clerk in the firm, but Elvira was the undisputed 'alpha female'.

She actually liked Jack and Leon and loved it when they made jokes and screwed around with each other at the trading desk just across from hers. The three had sort of a *rapprochement*, they paid her the appropriate homage and respect due the 'alpha female' and she treated them civilly most of the time, and nicely some of the time. In spite of a sour, outward appearance and demeanor, Elvira had a very good sense of humor.

This "alpha female" syndrome came with the territory. If you were there long enough, and you started to look a little beat up, put on a few pounds and your lips got thinner, you'd get snappy with people.

Then the 20-year-old secretaries would begin to show respect and deference.

Jack was particularly nice to her, being charming and bringing in pictures of the kids and generally including her in what was going on in the Armstrong household. Elvira loved being included like that. Jack would often think, 'Ole Jack's mama didn't raise no dumb son-of-a-bitch.' Elvira loved it when Jack's kids took the bus downtown to come by the office and have lunch with their dad. They were really sharp, squared away youngsters. Elvira's kids, on the other hand, were grown up and regrettably, fucked up as well. Her life was constantly dealing with her "kid's" problems. It seemed they were always getting either fired or divorced. The Cleavers they were not.

Jack thought Elvira looked like a cross between the farmer's wife in the painting *"American Gothic"* and that little cop in *Car 54 Where Are You?* He would refer to her as Vampira whenever she was in one of her lousy, irritable moods (not to her face naturally). Jack attributed her appearance to the hard life she had. Leon, on the other hand, didn't think too deeply about Elvira. He loved beautiful women, but had little regard for plain looking ladies and once told Jack that Elvira looked like somebody had staked her out face up in a hailstorm.

Jack was sitting at his desk thinking about how much Elvira reminded him of Cecil Holmes, a Gunnery Sergeant in his Marine helicopter squadron in Vietnam and the irony of having two totally different kinds of humans actually appear to be very much alike. Elvira was 'top kick' in the bond department. She processed all of his expense reports and medical claims and the like, and as a consequence had power. She could make things easier or harder for you. Same thing with this sergeant. Jack was an officer and theoretically had power over this guy but the sergeant could do the same kinds of things Elvira could do and, he could also find excuses to avoid doing things for you.

Jack found out early on that showing Gunny Holmes some respect and being nice to him produced wonders. He could get Jack a new engine for the worn out piece of shit Huey he flew and he was always *finding* great stuff for the squadron.

Jack thought a lot about Vietnam. He once told Leon that he

often got nauseous when he heard a helicopter fly over downtown Houston. The 'bar back' kid who helped Lung at the Sewer reminded him of his door gunner, Manning. They were both a bit wacked out, Jack thought. Once he heard this Manning open up with his M60 and shouted, "Manning, what the hell are you firing at?" The answer came back, with a smile and a little slurred, "Captain Jack, you know, door gunners and whores don't give a fuck for nothin'" Jack thought, 'Jesus, they get the worst mental case in the entire Marine Corps, and they give him an M60 machinegun on *my* helicopter! I can't wait to get out of this asylum.'

Elvira brought him out of his daydream, "Bon Apartment . . . line four is for you Jack." Jack acknowledged with his eyebrows and picked it up.

"Armstrong."

"Jack? Henry, are you still long any of those Trinity River Authority bonds you showed me earlier?" Jack was, all of a sudden, completely out of Viet Nam and back in the bond 'world', because he knew that Henry Martin never bought less than million bond blocks for his big bank in Corpus Christi. Jack never covered the mouthpiece of the phone because he wanted to appear totally open when his clients called and he had to talk to his trader Leon.

"Leon, this is Mr. Martin calling back on the TRAs, where do you stand?" Leon answered,

'Two and a half million left Jack, same way as before."

Jack began, "Mr. Martin?" when Henry interrupted, "I heard him Jack, I'll take the bonds" Jack always wanted to sound real cool when he got a big order, "Thanks Mr. Martin, you're confirmed the two and a half million bonds, settlement is regular way for Thursday. I'll send you the Texas Municipal Report on the authority" They both hung up.

"Nice trade Jack, you're big you know that? I mean, who's bigger than you?" Leon said this with a mixture of sincerity and mockery designed to keep Jack from getting a big head. "I just read an ad here in the paper, says Norton Claymore is having a sale today and tomorrow on men's suits. I thought a man of newly acquired wealth, such as yourself, would want to know, particularly since lately, you've started to look like you slept on some bus on the way to work. Want to check it out at lunch?" Leon knew, of course, that Jack had just put $15,000 commissions in his pocket!

"Tell me something Leon. Do you trade any better in a nice suit? Do you really think that some trader in Baltimore you happen to call gives a shit what you are wearing? Do you think, Wide Load and McKay or Lung care whether your suits are a bit worn?" Jack had a serious face on.

"Jesus Christ Jack, lighten up! What is this Perry Mason? It's only a suit for God's sake, not a cure for cancer. Besides you need to wake up to the fact that we work in a tall building, downtown in a big city with thousands of asshole bankers and lawyers and stock brokers and we can't go around looking like we live on Buffalo Bayou somewhere. What about the dignity of the bond department?"

"Look Leon, all my clients are out of town. They never visit Houston unless it is absolutely necessary, so, I don't need to look like one of those peacocks out in the Board Room." Jack was a little cheap and felt uncomfortable with his defense.

"You are missing one important point Jack. When you go on the road and visit all those little hick-ass country banker clients of yours, in Dime Box or wherever, you need to look superior, like you actually know something about bonds. When the dipshit banker comes out into the lobby to see you in his plaid, polyester sports coat with the two inch white belt holding up his bell bottoms, by God, you'll be standing there in your new, stunning, summer weight, wool suit from Norton Claymore, looking like the goddamn Chairman of the Fed! Hell, he'll probably pee his polyester pants at the very sight of you." Leon actually stood up for this last part. "By the way Jack, I do trade better in a nice suit. Do you want to go to Norton's before we eat or afterwards?" Leon tried not to ask open-ended questions of Jack. It was never, "What do you want." but, "Do you want the red one or the blue one." He learned that at the only self-improvement seminar he ever attended.

Norton Claymore was on the street level of the old Nellie Esperson building. The building was well built and quite elegant and exactly the kind Houstonians love to demolish and replace with those ugly glass boxes they seem to be so fond of. The store was well organized with the section for businesswomen on the left and the men's stuff on the right. The women's section sold those business outfits designed to convert pretty women into men. Leon frequented the store and could never figure out why some nice looking woman banker working at Texas Commerce Bank down the street, would pay for dark suits with shoulder pads so she could look powerful. Oddly, for a conservative guy, Leon was all for women's rights in the business world. If they could do a good job, they should be permitted to do virtually anything in business and be paid the same as everyone else. To Leon, the idea that they had to dress like men seemed ridiculous.

"Ah, Mister Agajanian, *inch besses*?" Leon said, attempting the only Armenian he knew, shaking the hand of his pal the sales guy for the young men's section of the store. "This is Jack Armstrong, as you can see by his appearance, he is in need of professional help."

Aram Agajanian looked at Jack, shook his hand and said, "Nice to meet you Jack. How come you're out with this character, are you guys on a Twelve Step treasure hunt from the noon AA meeting? Let me guess, they told you to find a lava lamp. I suggest you try Leon's apartment." It was obvious that Aram and Leon were friends and had done plenty of business. Leon was a pretty natty dresser who correctly figured that since he could do nothing about his looks and stature, he could at least dress smartly to call attention away from himself. Jack was just the opposite.

Aram asked, "You a 44-long Jack?" Jack began to smile broadly, thinking about that old joke about the guy with migraine headaches, who was advised to have himself castrated to get relief, only to be told by his haberdasher, too late of course, that the cause was wearing tight Jockey shorts. He chose not to relay the joke. Jack went through the 44-long section with Leon watching and shaking his head. It appeared to him that all Jack cared about was the price tag on the right sleeve. "Jack, quit looking at the damn prices and think about how the thing will look on you. Knowing you, you'll have the thing for ten years anyway, so if you amortize a $300 suit it's only $30 a year. Just a small hill for a high-stepper like you."

Jack had found one he really liked and was starring at the price. He looked at Leon and Aram with resignation and shaking his head, said, "I used to get a week's R and R in Bangkok out of the price of this suit. Shit!" Leon smiled, "He'll take it Aram. Let's get going before he backs away from the trade." Jack stood in front of the mirror while the tailor made his chalk marks for the alterations. He noticed Leon turning away when the tailor measured his inseam. That was the only bad part for Leon about buying a suit—when the guy measured his crotch.

Leon was starring across the trading room and feeling very uncomfortable. For one of the few times in his career, he was at a loss for what to do. He'd never heard any of his acquaintances in the trader community ever mention counterfeit bonds. Do I tell my manager in New York? Do I call the cops? He was sure that someone had gotten into his nickers and the only thing he could think to do was call the FBI. Leon thought, "How the hell do you get in touch with those guys . . . the yellow pages? Feeling like a fool, he called information and in a low voice while facing away from the trading desk asked, "Do you have a listing for the FBI?" "Yes, wait for the number please." Leon dialed the number, Special Agent Kelly answered and Leon explained that he had what he thought to be some sort of scam involving counterfeit bonds and he'd like a little guidance. "Mr. Walla, for the sake of privacy, why don't you come over here to our office. Can you do that?" Leon told him that would be fine, got the address down town, put on his coat and told Elvira he had something to do the rest of the afternoon and he was unlikely to be back.

He passed Jack coming back from the men's room, "Another half day Leon? You traders have it by the balls, you know that?" Leon thought, 'Yeah, right. Spent a half million dollars of the firm's money this morning on what I think are counterfeit bonds, I've got to talk to a bunch of G-men and I don't know what the fuck I'm doing. Life just doesn't get any better than this.'

"Mr. Walla? Agent Kelly, nice of you to come by. How can I help?" Leon looked around and decided that the FBI wasn't wasting his tax dollars on fancy office space. The offices looked like they backed up the truck to the GSA warehouse and took their pick of the used stuff. He found a chair by Kelly's metal desk, sat and let out a long breath. Kelly started with, "You are probably going to have to tell your story a few times before we get you to the right people, so lets get started."

"I'm in the municipal bond business—a trader actually—with Searl, Patrick and McNulty. My job is to buy bonds out for the bid in the secondary market. I bid on stuff all day long. Most of the time I am asked to bid through the brokers networks which cover the country, and sometimes I'll bid on client bonds directly, you know, bonds owned by the firm's customers who want to liquidate for all sorts of reasons. When we bid through the broker systems we are of course blind to the seller, that is, there is a firm between the seller and me. All we 'see' is the selling firm who is responsible to deliver bonds, as we say, in good form. When we buy bonds from a customer, they have to deliver in good form as well, but they usually don't know what they are doing and rely on firms like ours for the process. Anyway, about six months ago I was asked by one of our offices in Texas to bid on a particular block of 500M LA DWAPS."

"Hold on Leon, do you mind if I call you Leon? And Frank is fine for me. What are LA DWAPS?"

Leon realized that he was sliding into 'shop talk' and said, "Los Angeles Department of Water and Power. Lots of bonds have nicknames, sorry. So I bid the bonds, the office took them in, the customer got his half million dollars and we all went down the road. As I said, I do this all day. Well, today the same office called in for a bid from the same customer on exactly matching bonds. I figured that the guy had quite a few and was selling maybe the remainder of his position of the name. Every time I bid a bond, I check it out in the big blue Moody's book to be sure the guy had the description right. You know, if we get sloppy and sell a badly described bond it becomes a nightmare making good delivery—you know, "in good form"-so we are very careful. We're short one thing and long the wrong thing and, you don't need to know all that anyway. The point is, that when I looked in Moody's, I found out that there were *only* 500M of these bonds in that maturity to begin with, and I'd already bought them six months ago. There *can't* be any more of this particular description. Frank, I don't know what is going on but these bonds have to be counterfeit.

It was pretty clear to Agent Kelly that Leon was upset. He wasn't scared, he was just very uncomfortable because he was involved in something he couldn't control and knew nothing about.

"Next step Leon, is for me to present the situation to my boss and get back to you. When will this settlement or payoff be by the way?" Leon said it would be in five business days, next Thursday. "OK, I'm getting started on this as soon as you leave. Go have a drink or run five miles, but relax Leon and I'll get hold of you tomorrow."

As he waited for the elevator Leon thought, 'Let me see, run five miles or stop by the Sewer for a drink, what will it be?'. He was laughing when the doors opened up. 'Agent what's his face in there obviously doesn't know who he's dealing with yet. I'd probably get all of 150 yards of the five miles before my coronary.' Leon looked at his watch, 'Wonder who will be at the Sewer at 4:45?'

CHAPTER 7

Houston is not at all like New York when it comes to transportation. You just don't hail a cab in Houston; they are all at the hotels waiting in line to take out of town conventioneers to topless bars and Mexican restaurants. You really have to be lucky to find cabs roaming about, and even if you found one cruising you practically had to throw yourself under the damn thing to get it to stop and pick you up. Leon had a bit of a walk on his hands since the Sewer was at least seven blocks from the FBI office. He naturally didn't have an overcoat on, he didn't even own one—nobody in Houston wore the things, it was unsportsmanlike conduct for a guy. On the eleven cold days a year which occur in Houston, all the rich, rail thin, society ladies wore full length furs for the 60 foot walk from the valet parking stand to the door of Tony's. An early winter 'blue norther' had blown into town during Leon's little chat with the G-man and now he thought he'd better just fast-walk it to the Sewer and try not to think about the fact that he was freezing.

It was dark out by the time he got to the bar and there seemed to be no perceptible difference inside—the bar was just as dark as the street. Leon wondered if they ever turned the lights up, maybe to clean the place in the mornings. He hoped so. The possibility that they never cleaned the place and kept the lights low to disguise the dirt was disturbing–it was why Jack hated the place.

Johnny Cannon was the first to see Leon and waved him over to the table. The 'usual suspects' were not yet there—just Cannon and the Dipper so far.

Kitty said, "Hiya, Leon. You look like you're freezing, where's your overcoat?"

"I *am* freezing, it's as cold as a witches ti..sorry, and I don't own an overcoat Kitty, and after you're here for a year or two, you'll throw yours out I promise. All Yankees who move to Houston throw out their winter stuff within eighteen months. It's like a rule or something. You get your Texas drivers license, Texas plates, and then throw out your winter shit."

"Leon you don't have to watch your language around me. I know you're a gentleman but it *is* as cold as a witch's tit out. I just walked over here myself. Plus I have three brothers and I've been a trader for six years, so I don't think there are too many surprises out there."

Lung arrived at the table for drink orders, having been waved over by Cannon, "What do you want to drink Leon?" This coming from a 6'2" northern Chinaman. "Do you want to know what the ancient Chinese drank when they were freezing *their* asses off?"

Leon smiled and said, "What ever it was Lung, bring me one, I'm a candidate. Tell me what it is though, I might be allergic. Hey Lung, how tall are you anyway? You've got to be the tallest Chinaman in America"

"Six two, and there's not a chance you're allergic to it Leon, you've already field tested the stuff a hundred times . . . they drank Jamesons...neat" Lung turned and returned to the bar. Leon tried to remember that old saying about the Chinese being . . . was it "inscrutable"? He thought that it would have been helpful if he ever bothered to look up the damn word. He didn't have a clue and once again swore to look it up this time.

Lung returned to the table with the Jameson's plus a plate of their lousy, dried up, free hors d'oeuvre and said,

"Leon, anytime you see a tall Chinaman it means that he is from Northern China. We ate wheat up there and the little spindly guys along the coast ate rice. It must be some dietary thing. As you can see we are handsome as well as tall. It must have been the Visigoths or the Huns or someone raping our ancestors." Lung then left for a table full of secretaries across the room. Leon quipped,

"If he is handsome, I'd hate to see the little ones on the coast." Then he tried to change the subject. Johnny had no idea why he brought up the subject to begin with and thought, 'I mean who gives a shit about that? Only Leon brings stuff like that up.'

"Johnny, what did the market do this afternoon? I was out at an appointment."

"Dead as Kelsey's nuts Leon—like a Jewish holiday for Christ's sake."

"Is that why you're here early?" Leon asked.

"I walked in just before you Leon. I got stuck in the office with trying to explain housing bonds to Dowling, remember him? One of my salesmen? He is so fucking stupid it's pathetic. I don't know how he ever got in the business. There is nobody home with this guy Leon, he's legally brain dead."

Leon was laughing by this time. Dowling *was* stupid. Leon meant to ask how he ever got hired to work with Cannon in the first place, "What exactly did he have a problem with? I mean it's pretty straight forward, not brain surgery."

"Extraordinary call provisions, you know the one from unexpended funds? About the fifth pass, I made it verrry simple. 'The city sells bonds and attempts to lend the funds it just raised with the bonds to first time home buyers at attractive rates through their area lenders—the ones who do home mortgages. If rates stay the same, no problem—all the funds are loaned. If rates go down than nobody is going to want to borrow the city's money, since they can go down the street and get a lower rate'. I think what he doesn't get is that the city can't, obviously, adjust to the market and lend lower than the rate on the bonds they sold."

Leon finally got to ask his question, "How did he get hired? I know you'd have black balled him."

"It was typical political bullshit Leon. Did you know his father was in the business? Must have been back when you could afford to be brain dead to sell to the country banks. I heard his father wasn't any code breaker himself. The only thing I can think of is that the old man either saved the life of, *or* had compromising pictures of, the firm's president."

Leon saw Sammy David Stein working his way toward their table, so he slid across the banco to make some room for him. "Dave, you look nice and healthy", said Kitty. "Yeah? The rosy cheeks say it all Kitty, I ooze vitality, sexuality and plus it's cold as a well diggers ass outside. Johnny, did I ever tell you about the two Jewish brothers in the garment district in New York? Where's Lung, I need a drink?"

"How long a joke is this one Stein, I retire in 14 years?" Cannon said, rolling his eyes, knowing Stein never told a one liner in his life.

Stein started in with his Yiddish accent, "Irv and Moshe owned a shirt factory on 6th Ave. Irv was the smart one, the business end and Moshe was one of only six stupid Jews in America, and he ran the floor where they made the shirts. Anyway, Irv hadn't had a vacation in ten years because he was always afraid to leave Moshe alone because he knew they would be out of business before he got back from the Borscht Belt. So, he says to Moshe, 'If I don get away soon I'm goin to jump in front of a bus Moshe, so when I leave, lock the door, don answer the phone for ten days 'till I get back from Grossingers. Can you do that for me Moshe?' His brother tells him no problem, yea, yea, yea and off Irv goes.

"Three days go by and there is a knock at the door and Moshe lets this good looking Irish guy in from Burlington Industries who, with maybe a four second sales pitch, sells Moshe 10 bolts of fuchsia silk. It's the ugliest shit they ever made and the Irish guy probably gets a bonus just for getting rid of this shit, OK? Anyway, Moshe puts all of his Ricans to work making all this shit into shirts, and by the time Irv gets back, there entire inventory consisted of 110 gross of fuchsia silk shirts, which he is very proud of.

Irv has one look in the back at all these really ugly shirts and grabs his heart, 'OI, OI, OI VAY!!! We are out of business, I'm ruined for God's sake.' Then he looked at Moshe with his face turning red and started chasing him all over the factory, 'You *mesuggah* you, I'm gonna kill you, I swear to God Moshe, you fuckin' *schlemiel* !' Meanwhile they are both sveting and running, and sveting and running through the machines with the Ricans leaving through the fire escape. Irv finally sits down panting, 'I told you *not* to answer the door, and you buy all this *dreck* and make these *shmatte* fucking shirts we won't sell in a hundred years! You ruined me Moshe. We'll have to burn the place down for God's sake! Papa is turning over in his grave.'

'Stop your fucking *kvetching*, we'll sell the shirts already, for God's sake.' says Moshe, keeping a healthy distance from his brother.

"Next morning, in walks the Goy buyer from JC PENNY and says, 'I've looked everywhere on 6th Ave. and I can't find what we need. This is my last stop. No one has anything we can use.'

'So vat are you looking for Mister J C Penny?' Irv asks the guy.

'There is a whole new trend for sort of wild colored shirts, good quality, you know, silk would be good.' Irv looks at Moshe with a 'DON'T EVEN OPEN YOUR FUCKING MOUTH ' look, and casually says to the Penny buyer,

'I don't know, let me look in the back.' Now he *knows* he's having a heart attack! He brings back a sample of Moshe's shirts and the Penny guy goes nuts. It's *exactly* what he wants and he places an order for all the shirts and says, as he is leaving, 'You guys know the JC PENNY rule, the home office has 24 hours to cancel otherwise the deal is done and they cut you a check.'

They lock the door, put on a pot of coffee and start smoking to sweat out the 24 hours. 23 hours go by and there's a knock at the door and Irv says, 'I can't stand it. I'm having a heart attack already, I swear to God! Moshe, you answer it.' So, he opens the door and there is the Western Union guy with a telegram. Irv says, 'OI, OI, I can't take it anymore. I'm jumping out the window.' Moshe opens the telegram smiling and says, 'Good news Irv, Momma died.'

Stein laughed for three whole minutes with the entire bar watching because he was always so loud, particularly laughing at his own jokes. Kitty had tears running down her face, Leon and Cannon just smiled. New Yorkers loved Steins jokes; the Texas boys didn't really get them.

Leon was a bit loaded when he finally left the Sewer and headed for the parking garage. He had taken Agent Kelly's advice to relax a little more seriously than Kelly had intended. As he was driving through Memorial Park on his way home he saw the flashing lights of the 'gumball machine' of one of Houston's finest and said, "SHIT." The only place he could pull over was into the only commercial area in the whole park, a little, grandfathered gas station.

Leon got out of his car, lit a cigarette and waited for the cop and all the bullshit he knew was coming his way. After showing his license, Leon decided to try the honesty bit and, squinting at the cop's nametag, said, "Look, officer Skipper, I'm sorry. I know I had too much to drink, but I had some bad news today and I'm working with Special Agent Kelly, with the FBI on it. I've got to see him again tomorrow so I'm hoping he doesn't have to interview me in the clink, if you get my drift. I'd really appreciate a little latitude on this and, again, I am sorry." Officer Skipper looked at Leon for some time, obviously thinking, and finally said, "Well, Mr. Walla, I'm going to overlook this but I can't let you drive tonight. You'll have to leave the car here 'till in the morning, Ok?"

Just as Leon was thinking about whether to wake Jack up to come get him, a hippie kid stopped to gas up his motorcycle. Leon thanked Officer Skipper and headed for this hippie kid with the bike.

"How you doing?" Leon asked. "My name is Leon and I just got busted by the man in blue over there, he thinks I've had too much to drink, can you imagine? and he won't let me drive home. How about I give you $25 to take me home?" The kid was thinking about it when Leon said in an irritated tone, "I mean, it's not Oklahoma, it's not but three or four miles from here . . . and I'll make it $30." The bike was a real piece of crap with Duct Tape covering the entire seat and Leon thought that he maybe over bid for the ride home, but it was too late . . . ever the trader he thought.

There was nobody on Memorial Drive at this time of night. The kid asked,

"Can't figure how you got off man." Leon's tie was flying over his shoulder, he couldn't hear for the wind and noise and he was absolutely freezing.

"WHAT?"

The hippie turned sideways and asked, "How come the fuzz back there let you off a DWI man? They'll throw my ass in jail for drinking fuckin' prune juice, and they cut a suit like you some slack. It ain't right man." Leon's teeth were chattering as he thought, 'Hey asshole, you don't work, you don't pay taxes, you do drugs, you look like a anarchist with a bomb in his pocket. Who the fuck's gonna cut you any slack?'

The cold was numbing Leon's wits because he missed the turn and had to tell the hippie to turn around. Then he told the kid to make a right instead of a left, which really pissed the hippie off. Leon said, defensively,

"Hell I never come this way. I'm a *right* off Memorial when you're coming from downtown."

"We ain't coming from downtown man," the hippie was saying as he slowed to do another U-turn, " I hope you ain't plannin' nothin' complex tonight man, 'cause you are pretty wasted, you know what I mean?" They finally spotted the apartments where Leon lived. He thanked the hippie, paid him the $30 and went in to take a hot shower to warm up.

CHAPTER 8

The phone rang just once. Jack wondered who the hell would be calling at 6:20 AM. and said,

"Armstrong."

"Jack, I need a ride, can you pick me up?"

"What happened to you, car break down or some bad vodka? I'm walking out the door, so tell me about your shallow life when I pick you up."

Jack decided to pass on going to the YMCA since he was now picking up Leon, and if he attempted to bring Leon into the 'Y' he would turn to a pillar of salt. He didn't have to honk because Leon was watching for him from just inside the front door of the apartment building and jogged out to the car.

Leon got into the Nova wheezing and said, "That was fast."

"OK, lets hear about it."

"I got pulled over last night and the cop made me leave my car at that little gas station on Memorial Drive. So, drop me there and I'll meet you for breakfast at the Pancake House. In fact I'll *buy* you breakfast. I got something to tell you.

"You won't mind if I bring in my Polaroid . . . I want to get a picture of you picking up the tab. I'll send it in to the *Bond Buyer*."

When they got to the restaurant, Leon told Jack all about the trade involving the counterfeit bonds and the FBI interview. It was pretty obvious that he was upset and the whole thing was getting to him. Jack tried to tell him to put the thing in perspective, to relax and all that seminar bullshit. It appeared that his efforts were in vein, however, since Leon couldn't eat and just ordered coffee. Jack was hungry and ordered off one of those plastic menus with actual pictures of the food. He thought, 'A dead giveaway. When they have a picture of the dish, it has to be shitty food. Good thing it's only breakfast.'

He scanned the restaurant to see what kind of people ate in these formula, chain places and figured the guys in suits were drummers and the others looked like deliverymen. The thought that he was just another 'drummer' also, depressed him a bit. He tried to rationalize by thinking that selling bonds was a higher calling than selling aluminum siding or perpetual care plots door-to-door, but knew he was on shaky ground.

"Hey Jack, your eyes are glazing over Bud. I need some help on this counterfeit bond shit. How about it? I'm seeing the FBI guys again today."

"Leon, the way I see it, is that you should not be worried at all. I think you are over analyzing the hell out of a simple thing. You committed for the bonds, but you don't settle and *pay* for them for a week. The "client" who happens to be a crook, has to make "good delivery" right? Leon, are counterfeit bonds good delivery? Shit no! So, you didn't loose any money for the firm, since you have not paid for them, and you're not going to pay for them. So you don't look foolish, hell, you'll probably get the good citizen award for helping to catch this scum-bag."

"That's what I like about you Jack! You're no Phi Beta Kappa, but you sure can cut through the fog and net it all out. You really gave me some relief on this thing. I feel better already"

"Phi Beta Kappa my ass. I don't see you applying for a job down at NASA."

"Jesus, lighten up Jack I didn't say you were stupid, what I meant to say was that you are very insightful . . . your strength is in your ability to identify a problem and put it into perspective like you just did."

Jack thought for a couple seconds and said, "Yeah, well, whatever. Lets get out of here and head for the office. I don't like this place, the food stinks and the waitress is way too happy. Who gives a shit about her new puppy anyway?"

"Yeeessshhh! Jack you're in a lousy mood today. Sounds like the old "excess sperm buildup syndrome" to me. Is Radar out of town or something?"

Jack and Leon walked into the office a little late and picked up their messages off Elvira's desk. Leon had one from Agent Kelly, which he returned first, "Agent Kelly speaking." Leon identified himself and Kelly told him what they had decided to do about the counterfeit bonds. "Leon, we really don't need you for the moment. Maybe at some later time as a witness if this goes to trial. Right now, we plan to have one of our agents go to Waco and pose as the cashier and nab this guy as he passes the phony bonds. Since there really isn't going to be a trade, I see no reason for your firm to do anything. I will need to have the name and number of the firm's general counsel. I think we ought to put him in the picture on this—sort of a courtesy. Can you get me the number?"

Leon said, "I have given this whole thing a lot of thought since our meeting Frank, and you guys ought to be aware of a potential problem, related to all this which dawned on me last night. A few years ago "zero coupon" bonds were introduced which pay no current interest but which sell at a deep discount. When they mature the investor gets his yield. They aren't a gimmick. They help in quite a few financing situations and there is an appetite among the public for them. Anyway, there are a number of issues, which had come to market prior to the industries' switch from "bearer bonds" to "registered bonds". If someone figures out that they can counterfeit bearer zeros, sell them into the market-place and not be found out for 15 years or so, you know, until they mature, there will be big trouble."

"I'm not following you Leon, run that by me once more."

"Look, a normal bond pays every six months. That means that some investor has his hand out looking to be paid interest every six months, right? So, if you counterfeit a regular bond, we will know about it around the next payment date because there won't be any interest for the new owner of the bogus bond. The issuer makes funds available for all their legitimate bonds and when these phony bonds go unpaid, it throws up a red flag. With a bearer, zero coupon bond, it sits in some old man's safety deposit box until maturity at which time he sends it in for payment only to find out, way too late, that he got major league screwed."

Kelly was pretty bright and saw where Leon was going with this. "What can we do about this Leon?" Leon said, "Well, not much. I am going to tell my salesmen to notify the affected clients to send their bonds into the trustee to be put in registered form—they can do that. This way they can be assured that they have real bonds and not make believe stuff." Kelly thanked Leon for another bond lesson and hung up.

Leon wrote up a memo on the problem and solution, asked Elvira to type it up and to make sure it got distributed throughout the firm right away. He felt almost giddy with relief. Jack had been right. He had let the fear of this episode get out of hand. He also felt like rewarding himself and getting out of the office.

He left the building and headed for the Cellar Door a half block away. He felt great. He realized that there were two things that began to approach good love making—making a bunch of money on a trade and solving a big problem with all its accompanying anxiety. He was not good at coping with fear and anxiety—they tore him up. So, with the monkey off his back, he was seriously thinking of getting a little loaded.

The place was pretty full for the middle of the week and he scanned around for a familiar face. At the bar sat Danny McKay. He walked up behind Wide Load, put his finger under his armpit and said, "Turn your head and cough."

Leon ordered a drink and asked, "Wide Load, what did you think of Stein's daughter's wedding last week? I want a second opinion. This was the first wedding of a friend's kid for me."

Sammy Stein was older than most of the boys in the Houston business. He was a Marine for four years and did something else prior to the business. Plus he got married right out of college, so, anyway, his daughter was the first kid of the bond club guys to get married.

She had gone one year to Texas then transferred to Berkley and immediately, to the eternal chagrin of her Marine father, became a Hippie. To make matters worse, she fell in love with another hippie who was a Jew. Not that falling in love with a Jew was bad to Stein, it was trying to stuff all those stupid Catholic rules down this poor guys throat that he found offensive.

Wide Load said, "First of all you got to understand his profound relief at having Lolita finally get married, you know she had an affair with the high school wrestling coach." Leon interrupted,

"No, no Wide Load, you've gotta be making this up! The wrestling coach? Not the guidance counselor?, the fucking wrestling coach? Jesus."

McKay took a long slug from his gin and tonic as if he were going to give a lecture, "When she was 13 or so Stein began to get visibly nervous because she had these Sophia Loren, va-va-voom boobs, and like a twelve inch waist and had this whole Lolita thing going. I mean it was unbelievable. Stein used to take her sailing with us all the time, I guess to keep an eye on her. Anyway, Stein turned into this protective pit bull of a father. I pitied her dates in high school. Can you imagine some goofy sophomore with zits and a skinny neck showing up at the house with Captain Sammy "Godzilla" Stein, USMCR, answering the door? Jesus, the kid's probably in the Radio Club or on the school paper and wouldn't even think to cop a feel, and Stein probably doing a body search on the poor kid looking for rubbers. I'm sure Stein laid awake at night considering why he didn't have some normal kid with freckles who got up every morning wondering when her tits were going to pop out. Instead he gets the playmate of the month." McKay took another long pull on his drink and Leon assumed there was more. He was right,

"Anyway, after four years of Stein hovering over her and scowling at her poor dates, and I'm sure embarrassing the hell out of her, off she goes to college, becomes a Hippie and gets into this sex and music thing people talk about."

"It's 'sex, drugs and rock and roll' Wide Load." Leon corrected,

"Yeah, well whatever. Anyway, she ended up at Berkley I'm sure walking around in a t-shirt and cutoffs causing fender benders all over town."

Wide Load said, "I had a long conversation with Stein during the preparations for the wedding and it was pretty funny stuff—almost operatic—you know, three opposing forces? First there is Leona, the mother who wants a big Houston statement wedding with all the right people, a white gown, correct music, rice and all that other shit. Then there is Stein the brainwashed Catholic school kid—taught by the Jesuits—who insists on the whole nine yards. High mass, big church, pointy hats on the priests and all the smoke and mirrors money can buy. Then comes Becky, the hippie, who wants the whole thing out in the fucking woods in Memorial Park. Peace signs all over the place, you know, flowers all over her, with some asshole playing *The Age of Aquarius* on a sitar or something. The whole idea was a fucking nightmare, not to mention this poor sap Jewish hippie from New York. When this guy got a load of the Stein family all screaming at each other, he was probably feeling his pocket for his bus ticket on The Hound back to the Big Apple."

By this time, Leon was laughing like hell and started coughing on his gin and tonic. Wide Load could be pretty funny Leon thought, and said, "Great way to begin a marriage—everybody is pissed off at everybody."

A soft voice came over the sound system, which, a minute ago, had the guitar player du jour, playing some Denver tunes, "Leon, your pizza is ready. Leon, your pizza is ready." They turned around to see Jack at the far end of the room sitting on the guitar player's stool, smiling with a drink in his hand. He got up and made his way through all the tables full of laughing secretaries and drummers.

"Jack, what the hell are you doing here? Married, father of two, ought to be home cooking his world famous franks n' beans instead of downtown with all us functioning alcoholics."

"Well, Leon, an unmarried man such as yourself, with prospects as shitty as yours, doesn't need to know this, but at Christmas time, *we* go out to buy presents for each other. It's an old custom you, obviously, are unfamiliar with."

"Is that where Radar is, shopping with the girls? Shit, I've got to shop one of these days too."

Wide Load piped-up and said, "Good, Leon, take your time, there's all of ten days to shop left and the selection gets better, the crowds thin out, the sales clerks get in a better mood and are more cooperative—it just keeps getting better!"

"What do *you* know Wide Load? Hell, *you're* not married either and your prospects have got to be worse than mine. You don't have but two friends, and you never buy them shit at Christmas anyway."

CHAPTER 9

The New York trading desk had the Federal Reserve Bank (Fed) Chairman Paul Volker's testimony to Congress patched into the hoot n' holler speaker on Leon's desk. It was known as the Humphrey Hawkins something-or-other for reasons Leon neither knew nor cared about. Jack was making a pretense of listening, but he also had a copy of *Field and Stream* open on his desk. They both found it almost painful to hear the profound ambiguity of "Fed-speak". Leon always thought that anyone who professed to understand the testimony was either a liar, or someone he did not care to be around. Volker was now talking about the modulation of M1 (money supply) being a little out of sync with that of M2 (also money supply but somehow different...go figure) and all that that implied, with respect to foreign currencies, in particular the Deutsche mark. Jack broke the ice,

"Leon, my head is starting to hurt with this guy. Have you any idea what he's talking about? Why doesn't he just simplify this shit? You know like, 'More people are working and earning, and they are not saving; instead they are spending it, and it is putting upward pressure on rates and causing inflation.' Instead, he gives us the *Deutsche mark* two-step." Jack lowered his voice and leaned toward his buddy, winking, and said, "Or should I say *Deutsche mark* goose step?" Jack thought that was funny as hell–Leon didn't get it.

"That's too easy Jack. People like this want everyone to believe that their job is hard, and that they are indispensable. The members of this committee are even worse—they're politicians—they are lawyers or they own the Budweiser distributorship in Bumfuck, Iowa. Wait till you hear some of their questions—they don't have a clue. If you and I don't know what he's talking about, how is that dopey broad on the committee, you know, the one from LA? Going to understand him. Her staff has got to be putting her questions together. God, she is so stupid, I mean there is nobody home Jack…the elevator doesn't go all the way to the top. Know what I'm sayin'? Plus, she's mean as a snake. Oh, and, by the way, what the hell is 'the wealth effect' anyway? That's the latest street buzzword. This guy must have a speech writer—some government geek who makes this shit up as he goes along."

"I'll tell you what Leon, whatever the hell it means, it has not had any influence on old Jack Armstrong's pocketbook. 'Wealth effect' . . . ssshhheeeiiittt." Jack looked at the 'hoot n' holler' speaker box, made an obscene gesture, and shouted, "Hey Volker, I got your wealth effect right here!"

Leon was getting a little depressed about the muni market over the last few months. Just as soon as he bought bonds for his position, rates would inch upward and he would end up selling them at a breakeven if he got lucky, or, more likely, at a loss. Year to date he was under water and any chance of a bonus at year-end was fading fast. The salesmen, on the other hand, were doing better than usual. Spreads, and therefore commissions, were widening and with rates of return up, many banks were buying more than they usually did. Since salesmen like Jack and Freddy worked purely on commission, they didn't care whether the firm made money. All the traders were in the same boat with interest rates rising. Leon and Johnny Cannon met for a drink at the Sewer nearly every afternoon to commiserate about their losses. The day before, Cannon had quipped, "A rising tide swamps all boats." To which Leon had responded, "I loose a little on every trade but I make it up in volume." The direct line to Cannon rang as Leon was mulling all this over,

"What do you want Johnny, a bid on all that shit you still own?

Are you listening to this guy Volker? More to the point, are you *understanding* this guy Volker?"

"I can't hear him from out on this window ledge Leon. The coil extension cord is not but 12 feet long, so when I jump the line will go dead as I pass the 14th floor. So don't be insulted, it's not like I'll be intentionally hanging up on you or anything. I would like to clear up any fails our firms might have working before I jump if you have a minute." Leon was getting the drift of Cannon's gallows humor and replied,

"Johnny, I got to go. I've got Dr. Kervorkian on the other line." He then hung up on him and began to laugh along with Jack who had heard the conversation.

"Jack I can see why you're in such a good mood—laughing and carrying on and all. You salesmen are making all the money while Cannon and I are getting our asses handed to us; the 'wealth effect' notwithstanding. Forget about bonuses this year. Hell, the firm is liable to send me a goddamn bill!"

"All right Leon, lighten up. I'm getting all misty-eyed here thinking of your plight. Tell you what, call Cannon and I'll take the pair of you out to lunch." Leon pushed the direct line to Cannon before Jack could change his mind.

"Johnny, come in off that ledge, Mister Big Shot Jack Armstrong here is buying lunch for us and stupidly failed to make any stipulations, so we can pick some upscale place like Tony's. He is over there rolling his eyes. Are you free?"

"Christ I'd kill just to get out of this office. James' Coney Island would do me but don't tell that to Jack. You already know this Leon, but I got to tell you, Dowling is the most annoying and dumbest son-of-a-bitch in this business, but I'll tell you about what happened at lunch. Tell Jack he probably just saved Dowling's life because I was about to kill him when you called."

Jack was sitting there wondering how he got trapped into lunch at Tony's when he heard Leon tell Cannon to meet them at the exit of the Ten Ten Garage.

Johnny "Table for One" Cannon was leaning against a *Houston Chronicle* vending box when Jack pulled up in the Nova with Leon riding shotgun. He squeezed into the back seat pushing all Jack's smelly gym stuff to the other side, and they headed for Tony's. Jack had already decided that no matter how hot and humid it was out, he was not going to pull up to such a tony place as Tony's in such a piece of shit of a car, and planned to park somewhere over near Oshman's and walk.

"Finish up about Dowling," Leon demanded.

"Every day, actually several times a day, this dope asks me what time it is. He wears a watch, which doesn't work—one of those cheap Helbros or some off brand like that, which he probably got for his high school graduation. God, his father must have been glad just to get the son-of-a-bitch through high school, being as dumb as he is—can you imagine?—Probably took him six years. Anyways, he always makes a pretense of taking it off and listening to the goddamn thing tick as if he is diagnosing the problem or something. Well, this morning we are waiting to cross Main Street and there is a bus right next to me and he asks me for the time again, so I said, 'Dowling, let me see that watch for a second.' So he whips it off, it had one of those cheap after market expansion bands on it. You know, the kind that when you throw a baseball the whole watch flies off? So I made believe I was listening to it tick and then I threw it under the right front wheel of the bus just as it took off. The front wheel and one of the back wheels crushed it like a beer can. He just stood there in the diesel smoke and looked at the crushed watch. I handed him a ten dollar bill and said, 'Here, go buy a Timex you brain dead asshole, and don't even think of coming back to the office without it. Oh, and don't ever ask me what time it is again.' Where are you going Jack, that was Tony's we just passed?"

The closest parking space was over in front of Oshman's. Leon started up,

"It's as hot as a Russian musket Jack, we'll be all sweaty by the time we walk over there. It must be 100 yards."

"Tough shit Leon, there is no way I'm valet parking this heap. It's bad enough I have to drive and pay, without being embarrassed by driving something a Mexican wouldn't even own. Just suck it up and quit your whining."

The restaurant was actually cold inside. Typical Houston overkill. They ordered their drinks and Jack picked up the earlier conversation about Volker's testimony,

"I just want to say one more thing about our preoccupation with these Fed numbers and speeches. I don't think anyone knows what is going on and the reason I say that is that we keep changing which number we react to. Are you following me here?"

"Wind it up Jack, will you? This fruitcake will be back in a minute for our order and I'm hungry." Leon crossed his arms hugging himself, looked up and said, "Christ, you could hang meat in this place."

"Look Leon, getting back to the subject. At one point *the number* was money supply—M1 and M2 right? Then some camel jockey, emir gets constipated and decides to cut off our oil and you can't get within 200 yards of a gas station. Then *the number* we all watched was the price of oil. Then it's unemployment. Then it's gold or whatever. The point is that if it really was M1, than why wouldn't money supply always be the number to watch?"

Cannon put his chin on his chest and started a make-believe snore. Jack got the picture and said, "OK, Johnny, but thinking is good. Try it sometime." Leon spoke up,

"Look Jack, a lot of this stuff is beyond our ability to anticipate and figure out. The other thing is that we are so far down the food chain it isn't funny. Germany's Central Bank, all those gorilla Jap banks, GE, Solly and places like them move way before we can. So, I don't worry about it too much. I know where I stand in the food chain." Leon looked at Cannon and changed the direction of the conversation,

"Johnny, got anything going tonight? That may be a stupid question for Johnny "Party of One" Cannon, but Bill Weekly, our branch manager, is having a party and he asked me to feel free to invite any of the traders we do business with. Want to come?" Cannon was a pretty shy guy and hesitated. Jack joined by saying,

"Come on Johnny, I'll introduce you to all the girls who will be there. Couple of them are real nice looking. And don't give me any of that shit about how shy you are. We both know that after two drinks you're all hats and horns. Hell, I'll even pick you up if you want."

"Jack, write out the directions and I'll think about it. I have to check my social calendar." Cannon said this with a straight face and both Leon and Jack laughed.

Johnny Cannon made a big distinction between going over to, say, Jack's house or to Leon's apartment for drinks and going out to a big party with a bunch of people he did not know. For these semi-obligatory affairs he usually had a few bracers while he dressed. With what he had to drink at lunch, the bracers put him in a very mellow and relaxed mood. He thought 'bracers' was a pretty good word.

Johnny had met this guy Weekly a few times and he thought the guy was pretty typical of stockbroker managers, and thought the man should be compelled by law to carry around a couple cans of bullshit repellent.

He downed the last of his last Stoli on the rocks and headed for his Suburban in the driveway. As did all Houstonians, he laid his cord jacket gently across the back seat so it wouldn't look like hell when he got to the party. He had the directions and address of Weekly's house on the paper Jack had given him, but he couldn't read them without his half glasses and he couldn't drive without his sun glasses and he couldn't have them both on at the same time. Since the setting Texas sun was like a nuclear blast, he opted for the sunglasses and suffered with the accompanying error margin as he drove toward the house on Friar Tuck.

There were lots of cars and Cannon finally just parked on someone's nice grass and walked up the first driveway. He didn't want to make a scene so he quietly let himself in. By this time the three Stolies were doing their appointed work of imparting confidence. The first thing he noticed was that there were no partyers around but he figured they were all out around the pool sweating their asses off and he began looking for a drink. There was no bar set up which should have been the first clue for an otherwise smart guy, but he saw a wine rack, took out a bottle with *Chateau something* on the label and found an opener in a drawer. He had his feet up on a coffee table and was enjoying the wine, thinking that he was lucky not to have to be out there mingling with all those flat bellies when he looked over to the staircase and saw a sort of slick looking man in a robe standing half way up the stairs. The man sternly said in a high voice,

"EXCUSE ME, CAN I HELP YOU?" and Cannon replied,

"Yeah, we could use some chips and dip and shit like that down here. It would make it easier to power down this red wine."

"Red wine? Red Wine? What red wine?"

"You know, usually people have like a bar or something for these things. I had to root around for myself and all I got was this shit," holding up his wine goblet to the guy on the stairs.

"THIS SHIT? THIS SHIT? WHO THE HELL ARE YOU ANY-WAY, AND WHAT THE HELL ARE YOU DOING IN MY HOUSE? AND THAT'S COLLECTOR'S WINE FOR GOD'S SAKE!!"

"Hey, you don't have to be a dick about it man. I figured a big shot like Bill Weekly would have a bartender and all that shit, and at least chips and dip." The guy was now at the landing, all red in the face and yelling,

"GET THE FUCK OUT OF MY HOUSE YOU PHILISTINE. I'M CALLING THE COPS!!"

Cannon got up and headed for the door having the grace to at least set down the wine glass. He usually perked up whenever someone threatened to call the police, but he was not alarmed. He hadn't noticed any Dunkin' Doughnuts in the neighborhood as he pulled up, so he figured he had a good half hour's jump on Houston's Finest. As he opened the front door, he yelled back,

"Well up yours you inhospitable son-of-a-bitch. I'm outta here." As he slammed the door and turned to give this guy the finger, he noticed the number on the door was 222 not 212, so his pace quick-ened as he headed across the street to where the party really was hop-ing this guy was not invited. He let himself in and immediately saw Jack in the corner of the first room.

"Hey, Johnny you're a little late buddy! A single, unattached fella like yourself ought to be here early for all this quail, if you get my meaning." Jack gave him a big wink.

"Yeah well, I got a little mixed up on the address. Jesus, I can't believe Weekly lives in a neighborhood with such assholes! I hope they have something to drink besides red wine.

CHAPTER 10

Danny McKay was just finishing up loading his hunting stuff in the back of the Suburban in his driveway. He was pretty careful since he had to leave room for the other guys who were going hunting with him. Nearly every year the muni guys went hunting, usually out by Mason or in South Texas at his deer lease near Pearsall. Danny loved going hunting and getting the hell away from both Houston *and* the bond business. By the time hunting season in the late Fall was in full swing, he hated the bond business with all its year-end pressure to make good profit numbers.

He got into the Suburban and thought that the good news was he never had to get permission to go hunting with the boys. The bad news was that he never "got any", and he was pretty lonely.

First he'd pick up Freddy Brister, then Sammy David Stein, then Cannon who had for some time been living at his mother's house. Finally he'd pick up Jack Armstrong, since he lived the farthest west. About a mile from Cannon's house Danny said to Freddy and Stein, "I got a feeling Cannon is going to be a bit under the weather because I left him at the Sewer last night, and he had a lot to drink. He actually had printed "SCOTCH" on his right palm and "SODA" on his left, so all he had to do was hold up his hands to

86

DAN GILLCRIST

order a drink after his brain waves went flat." Freddy rolled his eyes and said, "God, that is really pathetic, we need to get him some help for Christ's sake. It's like he has a death wish." Stein just shook his head. They all liked Johnny Cannon, he was lots of fun, but he was high maintenance.

Danny pulled up in front of Cannon's house and gave the horn just a 'bip' to make it easy on the neighbors. After a minute he gave it another 'bip'. All three hunters were by now staring at the front door expecting Cannon to come out schlepping all his hunting stuff, when they noticed the thick ivy groundcover to the right of the door start to move. Danny was the first to say something, "Holy shit, he never made it into his house last night!" Just then Stein started to laugh as Cannon arose from the ivy and made his way down his walkway to the Suburban brushing himself off and straightening his tie. He opened the rear door and got in, with everyone but him laughing.

Danny said, "Johnny, are you all right? You need to go back and get all your stuff and your rifle, we've got plenty of time Pal."

Cannon was rubbing his face and said, "Lets get going I'll pick up some stuff to wear at "Monkeys" when we get to Pearsall. Don't they have a "Monkeys" in the pissant town?"

Stein pitched in, "Johnny, it would be easier to just go in and grab all your stuff. We'll come give you a hand with it."

"Naahh, lets ride. She locked me out anyway...said something about tough love through the front door just before I passed out. I could use some coffee. There is a Dunkin' Doughnuts near I-10 on the way to Jack's house."

When they pulled up to Jack's he was already out on the lawn sitting on his duffle bag. He still had some of that 'hurry up and wait' left over from the Marines. Cannon rolled down the right rear window and said, "I need to use your bathroom Jack, OK?" Jake just starred at him and nodded as Cannon headed for Jack's kitchen door. When he was out of sight, Danny filled him in on the story. Jack started laughing and then the others joined him. Just about then Cannon came up to get back in the Suburban when Jack said, "I'm sure glad you wore that suit

Johnny, when we get pulled over by the game warden, we'll tell him you are our lawyer, and we never hunt without our lawyer. Guy would probably crap his pants at the very sight of you." Jack turned to the others and said, "Tell you what though, Cannon's already got his camo thing going with those leaves in his hair and that ivy sticking out the front of his shirt."

They were on I-10 for an hour when Sammy Stein asked Danny, "Wide Load, I've never seen Rapoport on any of these hunting trips, did you invite him this time?"

"Yeah, he told me, 'Jewish guys don't hunt, and don't bring back any of that vile venison.' So, I told him that he missed the whole point. It's not about killing things, it's about comradiere—being with the guuuyyys." Danny started to grin and continued, "He also told me that taking Cannon hunting ought to be a felony in Texas—said his flack jacket was in the dry cleaners anyway." Everybody started to laugh except Johnny Cannon who said, "Fucking schmuck. The reason he doesn't camp and hunt is he can't be without luxuries. He thinks slow room service is roughing it. What an asshole."

Jack turned around from the shotgun seat and tried to make light of the situation, "Come on Johnny, Rapoport was just tooling you around and you know it. He always says shit like that."

Stein evidentially thought it was time for another of his jokes, "This little group of friends from Houston would fly out to hunt in West Texas a couple of times each season and they'd always gas up at Ragsdale's at the Austin airport going each way. One of the guys had a girlfriend in Austin and he'd get out there, and stay the weekend, while the other guys actually hunted in west Texas. Then on Sunday evening, he would get back on the plane when they stopped for gas on the way back. The guy's wife never caught on. Well, one Sunday he's out there waiting for the plane and it's overdue. After awhile they are *way* overdue, and this guy is pacing up and down, sweating like a bull. Finally, the plane lands and taxies over and this guy runs out to the plane, yanks open the door, and shouts over the engines, "Thank God you're here, I thought you crashed without me."

Freddy asked, "What about Leon, Danny, did you ask him on the trip? Although he never struck me as the hunter type."

"Shit, you've got to be kidding, Leon would never think of hunting. Sitting on the wet ground, freezing his ass off and getting ticks and chiggers is not Leon's thing, believe me. His idea of an outdoor adventure is getting laid in the swimming pool."

As they got closer to Luling, where the freeway ended, they could smell the oil wells. Luling was covered with little stripper wells, even on the courthouse lawn, and the oil smell permeated the place.

Stein started on what must have been his tenth joke of the trip, prompted by the oil smell, with the others rolling their eyes. "This Guido was parked behind a big sign in Brooklyn and his girlfriend was, by this time all hot and horny and only had half her cloths on when she said, hoarsely, "Vito, kiss me where it smells" So, he drove her to Secaucus!" Sammy Stein roared laughing. No one loved Sammy's jokes more than he did.

Just outside San Antonio they decided to gas up. Cannon went inside to get some more coffee. Freddy went in and bought a Playboy magazine, something his wife did not permit at home. After awhile he asked, rhetorically, "Where *are* all these women? Is this all made up and air brushed, or are there *really* girls who look like this? How come I never see anyone who looks like this?"

Jack responded, "Think about it Freddy. *You* go to work at 6:30 AM, *they* get up at 11AM. *You* eat lunch at places like Cyclone Anaya's and James' Coney Island, *they* eat at Tony"s and River Oaks Country Club. *You* are, what, 29? and *they* don't even go out with anyone less than 55 years old. *You* live in the suburbs where the best thing that can happen to you is you get Yard of the Month for Christ's sake, and *they* live over by Post Oak in a fancy high-rise, paid for by that 55-year-old guy. You have to be some Hollywood sleaze-bag, or a rich cork sniffer to date racehorses like them. Take my advice and just keep buying the magazines. Those girls might as well be on Mars."

Cannon had by this time gotten over his hangover—having had lots of practice—and he was hungry as hell, "Danny, how about stopping to eat, I'm hungry."

"See that sign up ahead? It's the Bigfoot and Yancy turnoff. We're not but ten miles from Pearsall. Can you wait so we can all go to

Campbell's for lunch?" Just then Cannon saw the sign which said it was 110 miles to Laredo and said, "How about we all drive across the border to Nuevo Laredo tonight—eat dinner and slide over to Boys Town?" Freddy and Stein looked at each other and rolled their eyes. Danny McKay was still driving and said, "Not a chance Johnny. To begin with there's no way you're taking *my* car into *Mexico* and…" Jack jumped in at this point, "Cannon, you better stay out of Mexico son, Boys Town would swallow your ass up like a black hole. I can just see me and Stein retrieving your body from the Nuevo Laredo morgue with some Mexican autopsy doctor saying, 'Son-of-a-bitch got the clap *and* got his throat cut all in *one* night. You bond guys sure know how to party.'" Cannon decided to pass on the idea and looked out the window thinking, 'What a bunch of wimps'.

There was one movie theater in Pearsall and they passed it on the way to Campbell's. Jack noticed that *Amadeus* had finally made it to this little town.

"That was one fine movie, I guarantee you," Jack commented to no one in particular, "What a genius he was. Really unbelievable when you think about it."

"*Armadayus* was a shitty movie Jack, I can't believe you liked it." Cannon put an 'r' in *Amadeus*, "Nothin' but a bunch of queer Englishman running around dressed like women. Liked to turn my stomach."

Jack shook his head thinking that his friend was a complete philistine and totally devoid of refinement, "Johnny, let me explain this to you carefully—I'm only saying it once. First of all, they weren't English, they were Austrian, and the whole story was in Vienna. Secondly, what they wore was the style of the day; no different than the suits you wear to the office or going to something in black tie. Oh, and by the way, you shouldn't talk since your ancestors, the Irishmen of that time, wore skirts while they were killing one another. Hell, they are still killing one another!" Cannon started to say something about kilts but they had arrived at Campbell's and he decided to drop the subject while he was behind.

After lunch at Campbell's they checked into the Rio Frio motel. They had no reservations because, even during hunting season, no one ever stayed there. Danny and Jack always stayed there because it was cheap and because the Mexican couple that ran the place was so damn nice and simple. Also, they never ran into those big shot Houston assholes taking their Wall Street clients hunting. They all stayed at the Porterhouse on I-35.

The place was cinder block, decorated in "Early Montgomery Ward" with an eclectic smattering of nouveau-Mexican black velvet "paintings". It beat camping. They all got settled in four or five minutes and took naps to help dispose of the Mexican plate lunches and the half case of *cervesa* they put away at Campbell's.

Freddy and Danny were roommates and Jack drew the short straw and got Stein the snorer. Cannon, in his usual "missing man formation", was in a room of his own. They all woke about four that afternoon and Jack suggested to Danny that they drive out to the deer lease for a recon to show the new guys the lay of the land.

They were on the lease as the sun went down and started to see rabbits in the headlights. Danny suggested they get out a few guns from the back and the spotlight and drive around for a bit and have some fun shooting at varmints. Jack had the spot light out the right front passenger window and as a result, Johnny, in the left rear window, didn't have a chance to see anything and just looked into the dark.

Jack saw them first on the right side and said, "Three coyotes over under that big mesquite!" Johnny Cannon got so excited that he pulled his borrowed .22 Cal rifle in from the window, swung it across the backs of Danny's and Jack's heads and as the muzzle approached Freddys face, the rifle went off sending a round through the right rear door frame *BLAM!*

"JESUS H. CHRIST, what the fuck was that!!!?" screamed Danny as he hit the breaks. Jack had already dropped the spot light, opened the door and had done a forward roll over a little prickly pear and was cursing something unintelligible. Freddy just sat there, rigid, trying to pop his eardrums. Cannon began to make excuses and quickly dropped back to the more prudent position of offering apologies. Because he couldn't hear very well, Freddy's voice was loud, "Jesus, Cannon, you're radioactive you know that? Rapoport was right."

No one talked all the way back to the Rio Frio, not even one joke out of Stein . When Freddy opened his rear door there was a noticeable metal screech as the exit wound from the bullet scratched against the door. Danny just mumbled "Shit" and went to his room.

It didn't take too long to put the incident behind them. Later they decided to drive into Pearsall to shoot a little pool and drink a few bears at the Rock House. Jack cleaned up at pool and Cannon did the worst. He later complained that he had been unduly distracted by the two local 'split tails' in the tight jeans bending over at the next pool table.

It was still dark next morning when the Suburban stopped at a *cendera,* and Cannon and Jack quietly got out. Danny gave them directions to the deer blind while they got their rifles out of the back and gently closed the doors. The blind was hard to find in the pre-dawn light, but also because it was made of dead brush and limbs, which were lying all over the area. When they climbed into the blind Jack told Johnny to get settled and comfortable and then to sit very still explaining that the deer and turkeys will see you if you move.

Jack was thinking that Cannon was doing pretty well sitting still when he saw the eight *javelinas* off to his left. He watched them for a while. That was really the most fun part of hunting to Jack. If he saw the bull-of-the-woods, something for the Boone and Crocket record book, he'd shoot it, but otherwise he usually just watched the game move around. Cannon whispered, "Jack, look, pigs!"

"They are not pigs, they are *javelinas* spelled with a "j", pronounced with an "h". Spanish word."

"They sure look like pigs to me, Jack."

"Johnny don't question me on shit like this, I've hunted south Texas since I was eleven . . . they're *javelinas.* Look it up when you get home . . . it's under PECCARY in the dictionary." Johnny was still a little hungover from the beer he drank at the Rock House Cafe the evening before. Plus, he was way below his normal quota of coffee. He looked puzzled.

"Wait a second Jack, let me get this straight. *Javelina* is spelled with a "j", pronounced as an "h" and you look it up under "p"? What the hell kind of bullshit is that?"

"Shut the fuck up Johnny, you're scaring away all the game! Do you want to kill a deer or not? Just look it up some time . . . 'peccary'. It's right there in the dictionary between 'pain in the ass' and 'peckerhead.'"

Cannon and Stein both killed a deer. The experienced hunters, Jack and Danny McKay, talked them into butchering the deer right there on the lease and not taking the things home, even though it was slightly illegal. The idea of messing up the Suburban any more than it already had been by the 22. long rifle slug, didn't appeal to Danny. They both thought getting some ordinary deer mounted was stupid. So, Stein and Johnny Cannon watched, proprietarily, as Jack skinned the deer, carved out the backstraps, tenders and took off the hams and put them all into two Igloos. Cannon wanted to know what would happen to the rest of the deer. Jack said that between the buzzards and the coyotes there would be no sign of a kill by next morning.

It always pissed Jack off to see people displaying the deer on their way back to Houston. Pickup truckers propped up the deer so everyone could see the rack sticking up. It was disgusting he thought, and bad hunting etiquette. It always reminded him of that Gary Larson 'Far Side' cartoon of the two bears driving along with two hunters, in plaid shirts, tied across the front fenders. Jack loved the hell out of that cartoon.

CHAPTER 11

Jack and Leon walked into the monthly Houston Bond Club luncheon a little late. It took more time than usual to get Jack's Nova out of the parking garage, and more time to get a parking space at the Downtown Holiday Inn where the luncheon was always held. Leon reasoned that there was probably some wallpaper hangers convention or something going on. Houston was always having conventions.

Attendance was invariably small at these luncheons for two reasons. First, the food was that rubber chicken, political banquet stuff, and second, nothing was ever accomplished with respect to the Houston Bond Club. It was purely a social event except for one meeting a year—this one—where they discussed the Bond Outing.

The Houston Bond *Outing* was the Houston Bond *Club's raison d'être*. The club didn't give wheel chairs away; didn't give food to the homeless; didn't give those $300 scholarships to high school debaters. The Club did one thing, and it definitely was not benevolent—it hosted one of the more notorious, and well attended bond outings in the country.

They had a choice to sit at an empty table and feel like a couple of dopes, or sit at the only table left with two empty chairs. The problem was that the empty chairs were next to Dowling, the world's stupidest bondman.

Jack said, under his breath, "Go ahead Leon, you sit next to Dowling."

"Hey, Dowling what's going on? I'm going to let Jack sit next to you this time. He is always asking me about housing bonds and Cannon told me they were one of your favorites. You two may want to talk shop." Jack looked at Leon and said, "Thanks Leon." and under his breath he whispered, "You're walking back to the office you little shit."

Johnny Cannon was at the table too, and, as was his custom, was holding court over three of his salesmen from G.K. Hill.

Leon asked, "Johnny, has the 'Outing committee' decided on anything yet? Like who's going to drive the vans down this year?"

"I know they need a few volunteers. They have two vans for all the booze, beer and crap tables for our hospitality suite and they need a crew for each one. I volunteered to drive one and I think they want you to take the other one. We'll get Rapoport too. Jack, want to go?"

"Have to check with Mary to see if there are any conflicts. I'll let you know", Jack responded, looking sideways at Leon and waiting for some shit from him about being married or 'kitchen passes'. Just then the Club's current president stood up and hit his empty scotch and soda with his fork and started talking about the preparations for the outing. When he got to the Hospitality Suite arrangements he said, "The committee recommends that Cannon be in charge of one of the vans and Leon take the other one and they drive down a day early." Cannon jumped to his feet, knocking over his empty gin and tonic and, in his very best Senator Joe McCarthy imitation, said, "Mister Chairman . . . Mister Chairman, I demand a recount, I demand a recount sir!" Then Leon stood up and started to say something when four or five guys, led by Jack, shouted, "Leon, stand up when you talk . . . stand up Leon." Then they all said, "Oh, sorry, you *are* standing up!" By this time the whole room was laughing. Leon finally got an opening and paraphrased his all time favorite comedian, Groucho Marks, " Mister Chairman, I wouldn't want to be a member of a committee that would have me as a member!" The laughter started up again with the whole place calling for one more drink

The waiters had, by this time cleared all the plates with the half-eaten rubber chicken, and the "meeting" was basically over. The president stood and said, solemnly, "Before we end the meeting, I'd like to call on Brother Stein to say the invocation." Stein stood up, cleared his throat and told a joke:

"This guy's on his death bed and he asks for his wife,

'Rebecca are you there, Rebecca?'

'Yes Papa, I'm right here.'

'Rebecca, remember when you took the kids to the city swimming pool and one got polio?' She says, 'Yes, Papa, I was there, I remember.'

'Rebecca, remember when the factory burned down and you'd let the fire insurance laps and we lost everything?' She says, 'Yes, Papa, I remember.'

"Rebecca, remember when your brother sold us all that real estate and it went down and down and down?' She says, 'Yes, Papa, I remember.'

'Rebecca, remember, you took me to the docta's and he gave me six months to live and today is the last day?' She says, 'Yes Papa, I remember.'

'Rebecca, you know something? I think you're a fucking jinx!'

Leon and Cannon decided to leave at 8AM on the Wednesday prior to the Outing, and caravan the two vans from Houston down to Brownsville. They had asked Rapoport and Jack to ride shotgun. The evening before they had loaded up the cargo so there would be no delays. The plan was to meet for breakfast at Mi Tierra in Richmond, then continue on Highway 59 for points south.

Marc Rapoport decided to take the first shift and let Leon have his coffee. Leon had apparently gotten a little jump on the Outing the night before at The Cellar Door and needed a little recuperative time. As they pulled into the parking lot of Mi Tierra they saw the other van. Apparently Jack and Johnny Cannon were already there. Leon said,

"God it's great to get away from that office and the hell out of Baghdad on the Bayou, and into the country." Marc responded,

"Leon, Richmond, Texas ain't exactly "the country". We're barely out of Houston. Christ, I hope you're not going to be asking, 'Are we there yet?' all the way to Brownsville." As they opened the door to Mi Tierra's, Leon said,

"You know something Marc? We haven't gone 40 miles and you're already getting on my nerves." Both of them were still laughing as they sat down across from Jack and Cannon.

"What's so funny?" Jack asked. Rapoport said, "I'm already getting on Leon"s nerves. Of course it's a little easier to get on his nerves after a night in the arms of Bacchus."

"I can't believe you were drinking the night before the caravan Leon. My God, if you ever crashed that van full of booze, they'd have to get that state toxic waste team, or what ever the name is, out here. Shit, they'd have to shut down the highway."

"Now *you* are starting to get on my nerves Jack. Stop worrying for Christ sake. I feel fine now. Lets eat."

Cannon said, "Marc, if Leon gets out of hand, signal us and we'll all pull over. I brought a roll of duct tape and we'll tape the shit out of him and throw him in the back of the van with the booze and the crap tables."

"Duct tape, my ass." Leon chuckled.

"Now there is an idea!" Jack said.

They decided to meet for lunch at a seafood place on the docks in Corpus Christi that Jack really liked. He told them that they had all sorts of stuff right off the fishing boats, and it was terrific. He remembered the place from when he did his flight training in Corpus, back in the Marines. As they pulled up near the fishing boats, Jack was the first to notice the new billboard and started to howl laughing. Rapoport said, "What's so funny?" and as Jack pointed, Marc saw the billboard and had to stop the van. It was an advertisement some wag with the local fisherman's association came up with, saying,

SUPRISE HER WITH CRABS

Marc and Jack had tears in their eyes as Marc attempted to park the van just under the billboard. They went into the place, got a table by the windows overlooking the fishing boats and waited for the waitress.

She paid no attention to Marc and said, "What will you have handsome?" as she looked straight at Jack. He figured she was a military wife, or some camp follower. Jack still looked like a Marine just home on leave.

Marc said, "Yeah, handsome, what's it gonna be? I'll tell you what, the Outing officially starts now and I am having a drink."

"Do you think that's wise Marc? We still have 125 miles to go and I don't want to be awarded the club's "Man of the Year" posthumously, if you know what I mean."

"Wise? Wise? hell its brilliant!" Rapoport turned to the horny waitress and said, "Gin and Tonic." Jack was wavering and said he'd need more time to think about it.

Marc could see the waitress, over Jack's shoulder, heading for the table "Say, handsome, Miss Horny 1979 is on her way over here, so make up your mind on the beverage of your choice." The waitress just stood there this time and Jack said, "Dos Equis" She left with a bit of a wiggle.

"You must give off some sort of a scent or something," Marc said as he took a sip of his gin and tonic.

"What."

"Don't give me, 'What,' you know what I mean. You've got a gift. Women want to screw your brains out. I've seen it plenty of times. Leon told me that the girls in the back office actually smell your tickets."

"Hey, I can't help what other people do. Besides, if I'm ever going to twist off, and sleep with another woman, it ain't going to be the bimbo of the month over there. She is going to have big tits, a face like Gina Lolobrigida and own a chain of liquor stores. Otherwise, forget it. And stop listening to Leon. We both know he's full of shit half the time."

Marc took another sip and said, "Speaking of Leon, where are those two?"

"After four hours in a van with Leon, Cannon probably pulled over back there somewhere to beat the shit out of him." Jack smiled. He loved sitting around bullshitting with friends. He really didn't get to do it as much as his single friends did.

The door opened up and in walked Leon and Johnny Cannon laughing. Marc guessed they too had seen the billboard. They spotted the table and as they made their way over, Leon gave a 'drinks' wave to the waitress. The seafood was really good after all. They watched the drinking and got back on the road.

The outing was at La Posada Resort and Golf Club outside of Brownsville, this was the second year there. Normally it took about three years before the Houston Bond Club outings were banned from a particular resort. It varied depending upon the economy. If business was good, the places would not let them back after the first year. If business was lousy, it depended upon how much pain and suffering the management could handle. It usually averaged out at three years. The net result was that the quality of the venue declined over the years. La Posada, or as the attendees referred to it, *the* La Posada, was sort of a big Holiday Inn with a golf course. It was fine for a bunch of muni guys. Those pointy shoed, investment bankers from the carriage houses in New York wouldn't be seen in a place like *the* La Posada. It was The Breakers, Greenbriar or the Broadmore, or nothing for those people.

The caravan crew was pretty tired after checking in and stocking up the huge hospitality suite. They had brought the club's own crap and blackjack tables as well as the booze and beer. After a nap and a shower, they all assembled in the resort's bar for drinks before dinner.

Since all this was either directly or indirectly paid by their respective firms, the caravaneers let it all hang out, or at least to the extent one could do such a thing in a semi-dump like *the* La Posada. So, by the time dinner was cleared away from their table, they were waxing philosophically, and about one drink away from a cure for cancer. This is when Marc Rapoport, who was not as accustomed to drinking as the others, decided to make a toast. He waved pontifically at the waiter,

"We will have a bottle of Sambuca, four glasses and please turn down the lights in this area." In a few minutes they all had their glass full of the vile stuff and Marc stood up wavering, and began his slurred toast,

"You guys are the best, I'm not shittin' ya. There is an old Jewish custom, at least I think it's Jewish, anyway, to light the Sambuca and toast your friends." With that he lit his drink and began a disjointed effort at a toast, while his glass burned pale blue in the darkness. "I never had such good friends (blah, blah, blah). The business is a great business (blah, blah, blah)." He went on and on until they shouted, "All right Marc, for Christ's sake get on with it!" He had been waving his drink hand about for emphasis and the burning Sambuca was running down his bare arm and dripping blue flaming drops off of his elbow on to the tablecloth. Jack and the rest were, by this time, laughing and Leon shouted, "Enough with the fucking toast already!" At this point he had spilled half of the Sambuca and the rim of the glass was red hot. Rapoport put the glass to his lips and everyone heard a SSSSSSS sound as the glass rim stuck to his bottom lip, at which point Marc involuntarily, because of the pain, blew the remaining napalm out of the glass and all over Leon who jumped up screaming, "What the fuck! Jesus Christ Marc." The glass fire was now out, but the glass was still stuck onto Rapoport's lower lip and he was saying, "OH, OH, OH Gwowd!" Jack and Cannon were of no help whatsoever because they were afflicted with 'laughing body' syndrome. Meanwhile, Leon was standing to one side swatting the fires with his napkin.

Jack and Cannon were doing their best, under the circumstances of riotous laughter, to do some damage control for Rapoport. He had not yet gotten the glass completely off of his lower lip and, apart from no eye brows, a screwed up lower lip, blisters in place of hair on his right forearm, Jack figured Marc was 'good to go', and pre-disastered for the outing.

CHAPTER 12

Kitty McDonald had a big smile on her face when she said, "Pardon me sir, is this seat taken?" Stein had been sitting there, near the back of the plane with his half glasses perched on his nose paying no attention to who was boarding. He always hoped that the flights were not full and that he'd have a vacant seat to spread out, and no irritating old lady who wanted to talk to him all the way. He even had a few tactics to encourage his fellow passengers to sit with someone else. First, he tried to make himself appear large which was pretty easy considering he was six foot three and overweight. He'd also leave his attaché case open on the adjacent seat and if an unusually unattractive candidate came down the aisle, he'd start his very best, phlegmy coughing spell. As a last resort, he would be forced to start picking his nose just as the prospect was ready to sit. The problem with that tactic was that *if* the person sat down anyway, he felt like a complete moron for the rest of the trip.

Stein looked up and as his finger headed toward his nose, he recognized Kitty "The Dipper" McDonald in all of her six-foot beauty and quickly stuck out the same hand and said, "Kitty, what a pleasure! Yes, please join me. I was afraid some jerk would sit next to me and spoil the flight." She shoved her bag in the overhead bin and sat in the aisle seat.

As she sat down there was a little rush of expensive perfume, which Sammy took pleasure in. The bond guys all tried to treat Kitty like one of the boys except she was so attractive that it was difficult.

They were both heading to Harlingen for the outing. The resort was actually closer to Harlingen airport than the one in Brownsville, plus the Southwest flight schedule there was better than Brownsville's.

"I didn't realize you were going to the outing Kitty, frankly I am a little surprised. It gets a little wild down there you know."

"Well, Sammy, I figured that this is the first outing since I came to Texas, and I thought I'd make an appearance, you know, go to the dinner, play golf with Jack Armstrong, but generally stay out of sight. In fact my boyfriend Paul, is meeting me there on Saturday morning and we plan on doing some stuff on our own, shopping in Matamoros, things like that."

Sammy said, "Phew." he was clearly relieved.

The stewardess asked, "Would you like something to drink?" Even in her hot pants uniform she wasn't half as good looking as Kitty, Stein thought. He let out one of his signature guffaws and said, "Is the Pope a Catholic? What do you want Kitty?"

"Bloody Mary for me." Kitty said looking up at the too tan stewardess with the Farrah Fawcet hairdo. Stein held up his hand with a five between his fingers signaling two and said, "It's Paul Clements isn't it? Works for Vinson, Elkins? I do a lot with the bond attorneys over there and I've heard good things about him."

Kitty nodded and said, "I know you manage the muni department over there but don't you do the underwriting too?" *Traders* make markets in the "secondary" market, which is to say older bonds, which have, for a variety of reasons, come back into the market place. *Underwriters* price and bid on new issues.

Stein was thinking how pleasant it was to be sitting next to a beautiful, nice smelling woman who could carry on an intelligent conversation and the conversation was about *his* business. "Yeah, I'm the underwriter and Marie Skipper helps with most of the syndicate stuff . . . she's a big asset over there."

Changing the subject Kitty said, "I hear your daughter got married recently."

"OH GOD! Did you have to bring that up?" Stein said laughing. "In the Marines, we used to call events like that Chinese Fire Drills". Sammy looked at Kitty thinking he may have lost her and said, "It's an oxymoron. You see the Chinese . . ." Kitty said, "I got it, I got it. My brother is a Marine, keep going." Stein continued thinking he really liked this girl, "Anyway, it was like organizing a visit by the Pope and almost as expensive." The drinks arrived and he took a big sip and said, "Aaaahhhh. I was telling Cannon awhile back that between my wife, who wanted this big shindig and Becky, who wanted this 'hippie' thing in the goddamn woods, it was awful."

"What did *you* want?" Kitty asked, already having heard the whole, hilarious story from Cannon.

"Well, I just wanted a simple wedding ceremony . . . it's a sacrament for Christ's sake, not a social thing."

"Johnny told me that there were four priests on the altar . . . sounded like it wasn't very simple Sammy. Don't you just need one of them for a "simple" ceremony?" Kitty said with a big smile.

"Saying four rosaries is better than saying one, right? Plus," he said pointing up, "the more smoke you have the better. You know, you get their attention more, right?" Sammy laughed, but it was an uneasy one if Kitty was any judge. In fact she wasn't much of a judge about Catholics at all since she grew up not knowing any.

"Sammy, tell me something. What is it with the Catholics and some of those names of churches and stuff? They have all those, "Our Lady Of's". I lived in Boston getting my MBA and there were churches all over the place with names like Our Lady Of Perpetual Guilt or something like that. They seem to love those Roman numerals too—St. Pius X and St. Louis XIV and St. Henry . . . no no, there was no Henry XIII. I'm wrong there, but I swear there was a St. Louis XIV." Sammy just looked at her, trying to keep from laughing. He thought she was right though, with some of those names. The one he could never figure out was Sts. Cyril and Milosovic . . . he figured it was just another Polack thing.

"Where are they living, what do they do? Didn't they both graduate from Berkley?" Kitty was back on the subject and Sammy's mind was still back on the Catholics.

"You mean Sonny and Cher? They are staying with us for the moment . . . between successes if you get my drift. Becky is trying to figure out what she's going to do when she grows up, and the groom thinks he's working on the great American novel. His father has a very successful garment business in New York City, and he told me at the wedding that he's pressuring his son to move up there. I don't know why they don't go back there, but I don't think that's in the cards, they like it here in Houston, can you imagine?"

"Has she thought of getting into the business?" Kitty asked as she looked out the corner of her eyes for a reaction.

Stein did not move, nor did he say anything for a moment. The thought was so alien that a Berkley hippie would consider getting into the muni business, that it never occurred to him. "You think anybody would want her? I mean she took all this weird shit out there. Both of them eat stuff like tofu and use words like karma. You ought to see our refrigerator for Christ's sake. My bottle of vodka is always hidden by stuff like goat's milk and herbal sun tea. Try living with some flower people some time, it's a bitch."

"Look, we both know that there basically is no curriculum that prepares a person for this business, so it doesn't matter what she took out there. The fact is, that it's a great school and she is plenty smart to have graduated. What was your major Sammy, English or some Humanities thing? Then you go into the Marines. Then munis. So, what's the difference between you and Becky when it comes to the business?"

Stein thought for a minute and said, "Now that I think about it, I don't know the majors of anybody in the business, except the ones I've hired. I know where all the guys went to college, whether they played ball, stuff like that, but not what they studied."

"That's because it really doesn't matter. I'll tell you what seem to me to be the common traits we all possess. Everyone is fairly bright, but they all seem to have a certain street smarts, you know, chutzpah and good bullshit. Do you know what I mean? Look, have her call me some time. I'll take her to lunch and between the girl talk, I'll feel her out to see if there's interest and see if maybe Johnny and I could use her on the desk somewhere. What do you think?"

Just then the over-tanned stewardess asked if they wanted one more Mary. Naturally Stein said yes. When the stewardess had gone, Kitty said, "If she keeps laying out in the sun her body is going to look like the face of the moon after they carve off all the melanomas when she is 50. I just finished this big article in *Scientific America* on UVRs and skin cancer. Very interesting stuff." Sammy started to get depressed and thought, 'Where were girls like this when I was dating? She's good looking, a good trader, I know she's very athletic, and reads *Scientific America* for Christ's sake. Here I am with a receding hairline, a gut, I've got to wear reading glasses. If I ever had to chase a burglar, I wouldn't make the first block. I look like I should be doing some lounge act somewhere. Leona is even getting to be more of a pain in the ass than ever.' He just then remembered a sign he had in his office when he was a platoon leader back in the good old days in the Corps. It was a take off on the 23rd Psalm:

> "Yea, though I walk through the valley of the shadow of death, I will fear no evil,
> For I am the meanest son-of-a-bitch in the valley."

Stein thought, 'Yeah, *right*', and got a little more morose thinking, 'Shit, I feel like I'm trapped, like I've got one foot in the fucking grave. As soon as I get back from the outing, by God, I'm going to' start running and working out. This time I'm fuckin' serious!' He nearly shouted OOOOOORRRRRRAAAAAHHHHHH!!!!! into the cabin, but caught himself just as they gave that soliloquy over the P.A. system about the position of his tray table and the rest of that shit. Besides, only Marines knew what OOHHRRAAHHH!!! means.

Harlingen Airport was the home of the Confederate Air Force, and as they taxied past the P-51, the B-29 and all those great WWII airplanes, he thought about his promise to himself a little earlier and resolved to get in shape again as soon as the outing was over.

Stein and Kitty carried their luggage up to Jack's van and Kitty gave him a big hug and said, "How you doing, you big hunk of man you?" Stein looked at Jack's flat belly and thought, 'That's it, goddamn it, just as soon as I get back to Houston, I'm gonna start working out—kicking ass and takin' names again. Loose my stomach, get in shape. Just as soon as the outing is over . . . *seriously!*'

They climbed into the van with some guys from J.J.Kenny in New York and waited a minute for a bunch from Chicago to put all their golf bags in the back. The Chicago people were young. The big banks like "First Chicken" in Chicago, always sent their young salesmen, the ones who covered Texas dealers. The older bankers generally had better sense than to attend. They were a bit wary of Jack and gave him a wide birth for the entire outing as it turned out. Jack had caught them eyeing Kitty's formidable rear end as she got into the van and he leaned close to one of them and quietly said, in a rather menacing tone, "Don't *even* think about it fella." Jack got into the drivers seat, pointed out the Igloo full of beer and there were cans popping before he even cleared the arrival area.

Kitty asked Jack about how the trip down in the vans had been. As Jack filled them in, she and Stein started laughing, while the Chicago boys just sat there drinking their beer. As they pulled up to the hotel lobby entrance, Jack waved at Marc Rapoport, sitting in his golf cart. Marc's job was to supply and operate the bond club's refreshment golf cart. It was an extension of the hospitality suite. The Houston Bond Club did not wish any guest to go thirsty, either in the hotel or any-where on the grounds. So, Rapoport cruised the golf course and the tennis courts all day with igloos full of beer and bloody Marys, which he naturally enjoyed as well.

As they got out of the van Kitty said, "I see Marc Rapoport got a jump on us and is already playing golf."

Jack explained, "That's a mobile hospitality suite, a bar on wheels and Marc runs it. He insists on having that job each year. It's perfect for him. He gets to give away free beer and booze all day, so everybody gets to know him. He loves the lime light part. When all these out-of-towners go home the only one they'll remember is Rapoport."

Jack asked, "You two up for an eye opener?" Pointing toward Rapoport he added, "The bar is open!" and started to walk toward the golf cart. As they got closer Kitty made a little face and asked

Jack in a whisper, "What's wrong with Marc's lip? UUGGHH that's awful. His face is all red Jack." Jack was smiling by this time remembering the Sambuca toast the night before and said, "Kitty, I'll tell you later."

With Kitty's bags in one hand and a Bloody Mary in the other, he headed toward the registration desk. Jack grinned broadly as they chose the shorter line. Kitty asked him what was so funny and Jack said, "Last year your fellow worker and associate and captain of industry, Johnny Cannon walked into the lobby, set his bags down next to those potted trees over there, and went right up to the hospitality suite because he thought the line was a little long. Well, he started drinking and playing Black Jack and having fun with all his friends. Anyhow, time sort of slipped by and Sunday noon checkout time rolled around. Cannon says good by, and I asked, 'Where are your bags Johnny?' He said 'I never made it up to my room, I just left my bags over next to those Ficus Aunt Jemima trees in the lobby.' He never even checked in, never opened his bags! What a piece of work."

After dropping off the Dipper in her room, Jack headed to the hospitality suite to have a beer and see who had arrived. He noticed Leon over at the crap table with his buddy from Searl in New York, Frankie Rizzo.

Rizzo was a syndicate guy and he and Leon had lots of dealings and had become friends over the phone. Frankie was on the desk a year before Leon actually met him at a traders meeting in New York. It was at this meeting that Leon did what Jack always thought he did best—invent nicknames. From that meeting on, Leon called him "Retro". He reminded him of that host guy on *The Twilight Zone*. Frankie was stuck in the 50's. He wore narrow lapelled suits and chinos to work, and dirty white bucks for all other occasions. He had a flat top haircut, loved the Kingston Trio, Harry Belafonte, the Brooklyn Dodgers and the New York (Football) Giants. He must have had a ton of 45rpm records with those big holes. He thought Frank Gifford hung the moon. His hobby was restoring cars, and he had a cherry red mint condition, lowered 1953 Mercury with duals, which he drove to Jones Beach on the weekends. Frankie "Retro" Rizzo was an anachronism. He was also a hell of a lot of fun to be with and Jack was delighted to see him.

"Frankie, how are you doing? Glad you could make it buddy" Jack was totally sincere. He loved this stuff.

Frankie said, "Too bad Louie couldn't make it. We both can't be off the desk at the same time—my turn I guess."

"Leon, let's get a little group, you, Retro, me, maybe Cannon, and drive to Arturo's for dinner tonight. What do you say?"

"Fine with me. You know who I just saw in the lobby a while ago? Milo Thompson. He's a pisser, let's get him too. Let's go early so we can come back and gamble."

Frankie, standing there in his 50's outfit looking like an extra for the movie *Grease*, said, with a totally straight face, "Am I dressed all right for this place Leon?"

Jack had hunted in the Rio Grande valley often enough to remember how to get to Progresso, home of Arturo's. Leon was in the shotgun seat of the van with Rizzo, Cannon and Milo Thompson were in the back. Cannon had made a few too many visits to Rapoport's mobile bar during the day and was pretty drunk. He had made the point at least eight times since he had gotten into the van, that the Irish were the best writers in the world. He was humming "Danny Boy" when he said,

"Leon, have I mentioned that the Irish . . ." Jack shouted over his shoulder, "goddammit Cannon, cut it out! You're starting to piss me off with that Irish shit. Now shut the fuck up. Do you hear me? Say that one more time and I'm throwing your sorry ass out of the van! Jesus you are a pain in the ass sometimes."

Milo piped up to change the subject directing his question to Jack, "Chester, do you know where you are? I feel like were driving across the Outback. I don't see one damn light."

"Milo, Arturo's is in the middle of nowhere. Walk out the kitchen door and you have to watch out you don't fall into the Rio Grande."

Leon looked at Jack and asked, "How come Milo called you Chester? What's that all about? I thought I knew all about you big fella." Milo started to laugh in the back and said,

"Jack and I were on this float trip down the Green River, put on by some Denver bond dealers and there was an underwriter from New York City there. Anyway, we camped on the riverbank the first night and as we were picking out places to throw our sleeping bags, this dopey 'cliff dweller' looks at his friend Jack here and asks for some guidance. He had never slept under the stars in his entire life, can you believe it? . . . typical New Yorker. So Jack says, 'Well Bob, me and Milo here are going to sleep on this special rubberized tarp I brought along—it keeps the snakes away. You know they hate rubber, right Milo? Too bad there's only room for us. The cowboys always laid a lasso on the ground around them. I heard snakes hate rope. Look around, see if you can find one, although I doubt the guide brought one along.' So this Bob guy says, 'Snakes? What snakes? Nobody said anything about snakes.'"

Jack was starting to laugh at Milo and added, "Leon, it took Milo all of a half second to pick up on my bullshit, and he says, 'Well shit Bob, this the West. We're in the middle of the Rockies for God's sake; it ain't Central Park, although it's probably a lot safer. New Yorker like yourself, you know, used to muggers and shit like that? ought not be afraid of a few Chesters.' This guy Bob says, his voice is a little louder now, 'Chesters? What are Chesters?' So Milo says, 'Bob, they are big assed rattlesnakes—only find them out here as a matter of fact. Most regular rattlers, as you probably know, strike you on the ankle or calf. These suckers are so fucking big, they hit you right in the middle of your chest. You can forget all that first aid bullshit with tourniquets, cutting those little crosses and sucking out the venom. With a Chester, your toast, hell a Hoover couldn't suck out all that venom!' So this guy Bob looks at Milo and says, 'WILL YOU STOP WITH THE SNAKES ALREADY."

Instead of going back to do some gambling as Leon had mentioned earlier, Jack suggested going across the border to Matamoros and Blanca White's. Leon and Cannon, who had sobered up considerably from Arturo's food, had completely forgotten about the place and were delighted that Jack had remembered it. Since the bar was only a few hundred yards inside the border they decided to leave the van inside the good old US of A and walk. Jack figured loosing his old Nova to Mexican thieves was one thing, but getting a rented van stolen was not something either he nor the Houston Bond Club would want to risk. He never read those rental contracts, but felt sure that there was a fine print clause which read, "Don't even THINK of taking our van into Mexico." Jack thought also that since they had no automobile, the Mexican street kids, who shook down *nortoamericanos* under the rouse of 'watching' their cars while they shopped, would leave them alone. That was one good thing about Blanca White's, they always had a bad ass, Pancho Villa looking bouncer at the door who the street kids steered clear of.

Rizzo went nuts with the style of the place. It was rustic with lots of old wood, a bit like the inside of a barn. The cool thing was that there were no windows. Big tall shutters covered the openings onto the street so, for the bond group, they had the benefit of a great bar and a view of the street happenings, which in Matamoros were considerable.

Jack said to the barmaid, "*Cervesas por cinco por favor*", as they settled in. She promptly returned with small galvanized buckets half full of shaved ice with ten opened half sized beer bottles called splits, stuck into the ice. Everyone was relaxed and talked and drank beer until they began to get hungry again.

Milo asked for a menu and Leon said, "Don't bother Milo, the barbecued shrimp here are worth dying for, so let's just get a half dozen orders, OK?" When the shrimp arrived they stopped talking until the food was all gone, except to say a few, 'Oh my God!'s and 'This shit is great!'s. The waitress could barely keep up the *cervesa* supply. They did this virtually all night, and when the bill finally came, Rizzo grabbed it. The sign for pesos was the same as the dollar sign and Retro wanted the bill to hand in to Louie when he got back. Since the peso then was on its ass vs. the dollar, the bill was something like $11,000. "I want to see Louie's face when he sees that number, by God!"

Rizzo looked at his watch and was trying to figure out New York time and realized the sun was about to rise there so they all decided, reluctantly, to go back to the 'resort'. Both Milo and Rizzo decided that they now could die as completely happy men.

CHAPTER 13

It was the Tuesday following the outing and Leon and Jack were almost fully recovered from the 72 hours of partying. They had both come in Monday and gotten caught up on paper work, but stayed clear of anything resembling trading commitments. Leon learned early in his career never to trade bonds unless he had all his wits about him. It was too easy to get "picked off". But today was Tuesday, and both of them were ready to get after it. As Leon walked into the bond department Jack shouted out the words of a bumper sticker he'd seen the day before about the disgraced Nixon which he evidentially thought appropriate, "He's tanned, he's rested, he's back, Walla in '78." Leon sat down at his desk and answered, "Close Jack, as usual, but all I can say is that I have a gamblers tan, and I'm back. As for the rested part, it's going to take a week of hard work here to recover. It's a damn good thing the outing is not but once a year." One of his lines rang…it was Frankie Rizzo back up in New York.

"Now that was fun Leon. I loved Arturo's, but if we could throw a cable around Blanca White's and drag it up from Matamoros to New York City, we'd have us a gold mine. That's got to be the best bar on earth. There'd be lines around the goddamn block Leon. And the best part would be that we both could get rich and leave this chicken shit business."

"I know why you're calling Retro, so lets get started. I've got this idea on the State of Texas deal that I've been thinking about for a while. We just may be able to blow the goddamn doors off of this thing and leave Solly, and the rest of the gorillas in the dust." Salomon Brothers, Goldman, Morgan Stanley and a few others were, because of their enormous capital, considered "gorilla firms".

There was a competitive new issue for the State of Texas, selling on Thursday, which was huge. The potential for profit was correspondingly very big. Of course the potential for loss was also there. If interest rates moved against the winning bidder right after the sale of the bonds, or if that firm did a lousy job of quickly marketing the bonds to the institutions, than profits could disappear. Leon and Frankie Rizzo had decided, along with their big boss in New York, not to syndicate, but to bid the issue alone this time.

"So, what's this idea Leon?"

"OK, the preliminary official statement (POS) where the conditions of the bid are laid out, does not address couponing. They simply left it out. I've read it three times Frankie, and that numbnuts over in Austin in the Treasurer's office, failed to pick it up. And of course the bond attorneys missed it as well. The point is that since they did not stipulate coupon limits, we can bid using anything we want, including zero coupons."

Each new issue's POS states how many bonds mature each year and the range of coupons, which the issuer will permit. It might say that the bidder has to use coupons within 2% of each other. So, all the coupons must be between 4.00% and 6.00%, or 5.00% and 7.00%. Since they failed to stipulate, Leon saw an opportunity to bid big coupons such as 8% and 9% on the shorter bonds, and 0% on the longer maturities, thus improving his bid. He knew that lots of underwriters, through sloppiness, being too busy or not being too familiar with "zeros" yet, would likely miss this point.

Frankie was thinking and finally said, "Hmmmm. The problem is, where do we sell the 'zeros'?"

Leon had thought this through, "The life insurance company actuarial dweebs say that in the year so-and-so, so many geezers will die, and they will be needing x dollars to pay off the policies right? The company buys bonds now to offset that future liability. We need to get our salesmen to call their accounts with the idea of buying 'zeros' now at, say 40 cents on the dollar, which mature in the needed years. This way they don't need to put up nearly as much capitol to offset their future death benefits—they can use the money for other investments. What do you think?"

"Everybody thinks you are a bit of an asshole Leon. I happen to agree with them incidentally. But the good part is, that you are a very smart asshole *and*, more to the point, you are *our* very smart asshole! It's a great idea. I smell a big bonus here Leon, if this shit works."

Leon spent the next two days hunched over the IBM computer near his desk used exclusively for bidding new issues. It had software written just for this purpose, which was light years ahead of the old adding machine method he once used. Mainly, it was very fast and it allowed Leon to change the couponing over and over to see which arrangement produced the lowest bid consistent with the underwriting spread they wanted to make. During this time he talked to all the institutional salesmen to get a feel for what their accounts would buy.

Jack had volunteered to drive to Austin to "cover" (hand in the bid) the 10AM sale. He had a couple of banks there to see and he had spent the day before talking to them about buying the shorter, non-zeros in the Texas deal. He was really excited because he had gotten big indications of interest if they bought the deal at the yields he had discussed. He called in to Leon in Houston ten minutes prior to the cut off and Leon kept him holding while he went over the bid figures once more.

"OK, Jack fill in the form as follows", and he went through the couponing, total interest, the net interest cost and so on. "Read it back to me Jack". Jack thought that was stupid in light of the impending cut off time only a couple minutes away, and said so. "Goddammit Jack, I've busted my ass on this one and I don't want it fucked up because you're a little busy. READ ME THE FUCKING NUMBERS JACK!" Leon was standing now, which he always did when he got excited, and everyone in the bond department was looking his way. Jack read back the numbers to Leon's approval, hung up, and raced down the hall to the Treasurer's office to hand in the sealed envelope addressed, Treasurer of the State of Texas.

Jack didn't hang around for the official opening of the bids; rather, he headed for Searl's Austin office to get on the phone with his accounts. After the cut off time, the various bidding syndicate underwriters called each other up to compare bids to see who won. They seldom waited for notification from the issuer. They knew within ten minutes who was "high" and, except for an occasional bidding error, they were nearly always right.

Leon knew, after a two calls that he had done it. He was sitting there stunned with a big time adrenaline rush going on when Jack called and, attempting to control his voice, said, "How are we doing Leon?" Leon said, "We're buying this puppy Jack!" He could hardly control his voice, and then he jumped up and actually stood on his desk, raised an arm and, with everyone staring at him, shouted into the phone, "Rommel, you magnificent bastard, I READ YOUR BOOK!"

Several people around the muni desk smiled at Leon's quote, but Jack on the other end of the phone laughed like hell. Jack knew that Leon watched the movie *Patton* at least once a month. He loved that movie and, if threatened with having his feet shoved into a bonfire, he could probably recite most of George C. Scott's lines. Sitting at his desk he would often, absently, whistle the haunting French horn part of the sound track.

The fact is that Leon loved the military. It was one of the reasons he liked Jack and Stein so much. He admired warriors and loved heroes. It didn't seem to bother him that he never served in the military, or at least it never showed. Back when all those construction workers in New York and the other big cities came out in support of the troops in Vietnam by sticking American flag decals on their hard hats, Leon thought it was great and put a decal on the side of his Monroe Trader 'Compucorp'.

Jack called Mary from Austin to tell her the good news, and to say he'd be home by 7P.M. or so. Mary said, "You got a call from that girl you went through flight school with, the one who lives in

Seattle now, Britt Eagland. She is going to be in town over the weekend and wants to take us to dinner." Britt and Jack became friends in flight school and had kept in touch while they were both still on active duty, all way before he met Mary of course, but they had lost touch after the military. He had told Mary all about her before. Their relationship had been professional and Jack had great admiration for her abilities as a pilot, in fact she had graduated number one in their class.

Jack was a happy guy on the drive back to Houston. He'd sold nearly 10 million bonds and while he did not know exactly until he talked to Leon, he figured he'd make about $80,000 gross. He thought, 'Not bad for a hair lip.'

He was so busy thinking about his big trade and the reunion with his old friend, that he had forgotten about lunch and he was starving by the time he pulled into La Grange. There was a butcher shop on the south side of the square named Prueses, which cooked great barbecue in the back. The best barbecue in Texas was to be found throughout what the muni guys called "The Hindenberg Line", a string of counties, running along the Lower Colorado River, between Austin and Houston, which had been settled by German immigrants a hundred years earlier. The meat was always cooked in a screened in shed in the back of the butcher shops, and invariably prepared by aging black men. They were gifted, and no doubt underpaid. The shops weren't even close to being restaurants; you never could get a beer in any of them. They were simply a place to pick up a sandwich, or take home food.

"Howdy, how you all doing today?", Jack said to the entire, empty butcher shop. Jack thought to himself, 'Hot dam I'm feeling good!' The butcher smiled back with, "What'll you have friend?"

"I'll have some of your world famous barbecue, that's what I'll have sir . . . to go, and a brisket sandwich to eat here. Have you got a Big Red too?" An old black man came out from the back and smiled at Jack in his suit, "Yes sir, what can I get you?" He'd already made up his mind to bring some of this stuff home to the kids; they'd love it, "A brisket sandwich, half a chicken, 2 pounds of pork ribs, a pound of sausage and a pound of brisket." The black man got to work and Jack was halfway through his sandwich when the old man called over to say the 'to go' order was ready. Jack settled up the tab, shook the black man's hand with a $5 bill folded into his palm and said goodbye. As he got into the Nova he thought, 'Life doesn't get much better than this…why do people commit suicide for Christ's sake?' The engine coughed only once as Jack started the Nova. It was all he needed to hear. Out loud he said, "By God, I'm getting rid of this piece of shit. Leon's right. Now I'll have the money to get something decent."

As soon as he got rolling again Jack started to think about Leon being the architect of his financial good fortune, and decided to take him out to a top of the line dinner soon. Then the thought occurred to him that since Britt was in town, he would include her. Leon would really like Britt he thought. He'd check it out with Mary when he got home—she had a lot of sense when it came to stuff like that.

He wished he already had the new car he'd promised himself, instead of the station wagon. Taking the Nova out on a festive night like this simply was out of the question, so it was the station wagon. He and Mary were on their way to the Warwick Hotel to pick up Britt, but first they had to pick up Leon at his apartment. Mary said to Jack, "You know, I'm sort of surprised Leon would go out on a blind date like this."

"Honey, this is not a blind date and please don't use that term tonight. Both of them would cringe if they heard you. 'Blind date' is strictly 50's. We did stuff like that when we were kids."

"Speak for yourself, big boy," Mary allowed, who never went out on a blind date in her life. The idea sounded dreadful to her. She considered blind dates either a necessity or a favor. Since she was very good looking and popular growing up, there had been no necessity, and going out with a friend's goofy brother was a favor she was totally unwilling to grant. Driving a getaway car for a friend, maybe, but not a blind date.

They pulled up in front of Leon's apartment complex and he was waiting under a live oak tree in a blazer, adjusting his tie and looking a bit nervous. Leon got into the backseat and Jack headed for the Warwick.

"So, tell me about Britt. Have you ever met her Mary?" Leon

asked. Mary knew where he was headed with this question, but didn't have a chance to answer before Jack jumped in,

"She and I went through flight school together and became friends Leon. She helped me quite a bit—real smart, boy she knew that stuff cold. She was top of the class and got to go jets and I," Jack lowered his voice and said officiously, "subject to the needs and requirements of the Unites States Marine Corps, was ordered to helicopters." He swerved suddenly and gave another of his fellow Texans the finger. Mary shouted, "Jack! Jesus we could be shot doing that. You know they all carry guns . . . God!" Jack looking over his left shoulder said,

"Oh, yeah? That bearded, Saab driving SOB better bring his lunch if he wants a piece of me!" Jack said this a little too loudly, as if the other jerk could hear him. "Anyway Leon, because women can't fly combat, they sent her to NAS Miramar in San Diego where she trained new pilots in F-4s, you know the Phantoms, before they went to the fleet. She didn't stay in because it's a dead end for women. I even remember her call sign—*Glands.*" Mary and Leon glanced at each other with raised eyebrows, and Mary, with a big smile, said, "You go first, Leon."

"So Jack, what's with that name Glands. I mean, where do these things come from, these pilot call signs?" Leon probed.

"Hell Leon, you name people all the time. I never saw anyone as good at it as you, as a matter of fact. Her last name is Eagland, what can I tell you?"

Mary spoke up and patiently said, "Leon, Britt happens to be very good looking and has a fabulous figure. Are you following me on this Leon? You have to understand that the testosterone level among naval aviators is quite high and is of course," and she said this slowly and dripping with sarcasm, "inverse to their maturity level. The name didn't seem to bother her though, did it Jack?"

"Hell no. She was the best in the squadron, and would kick their asses during air combat maneuvers on a regular basis. She even wore the call sign on her flight jacket, right above her aaahhh. You know, on the front." Leon thought to himself, 'So, she's smart, tough as hell, drop dead good looking and she couldn't possibly like somebody like me, no way...the longest shot in the winter book.' But he was resolved to have a good time with none of his usual romantic expectations, and he was determined not to show his nervousness.

Jack turned toward Mary, "I never heard Wingnut complain about *his* call sign."

"Wingnut? Who was Wingnut?" Leon asked.

"H. Winston Ensenat," Jack pronounced it in a ring announcer voice like that radio show he listened to in the car, *The World Tomorrow, With Garner Ted Armstrong.* "Win Ensenat is a buddy of mine from the Marines. We went all through OCS, The Basic School and Jacksonville together, Leon. Then we ended up flying helos in Vietnam in different squadrons but still out of Danang, so we spent a lot of time together. He is a great guy and a very close friend."

Mary wedged into the conversation at this point, because Jack always described people from a masculine, military point of view and it invariably left civilians with an incomplete picture, "Leon, Winston came from New Orleans, his parents were quite wealthy. His Dad died while he was over here going to Rice and left him pretty well off, I think. His stepfather is Gator McCully. He's in the oil business and a big Republican here in Texas, and Win works with him now in the oil business."

"Well Mary, more to the point, where did that name come from, you know, 'Wingnut'?"

"Leon, have you heard of that guy Ross Perot from Dallas, the guy in the computer business up there?" It was Jack with that 'male answer syndrome', talking over the top of Mary again.

"Seen him in some magazines, why?"

"Well Leon, Win looks like a big, handsome version of Ross Perot, if you can imagine such an oxymoron. See, his ears are pretty big and he doesn't help the matter any because he wears his hair pretty close to the old 'high and tight' like we did in the Corps." Just then the car came to a halt in front of The Warwick

Britt was waiting just outside the front door. Jack was a little embarrassed driving the station wagon, particularly since, in a few days, he'd have a real man's car—the new Bronco he was determined to buy. Britt wore a pleated, navy, gabardine skirt, well above her knees and a khaki blazer over a starched white blouse clearly under some strain. She had high heals at the end of a pair of stunning legs which, Leon felt sure, went clear up to her gorgeous ass. Now he was really getting nervous, since, on top of being this killer fighter pilot, she looked like a damn movie star. Mary was, as usual, sensitive to Leon's discomfort and got into the back seat after hugging Britt.

"Britt, meet Leon. Since I owe both of you a big favor, Mary suggested we take both of you guys to dinner, thereby, as the saying goes, 'killing two birds with one stone'. Have you ever been to Tony's Britt?" She turned around in her seat just ahead of her pageboy hair.

"Hi ya Leon, nice to meet you." Looking over to Jack she answered, "Actually I ate there once, the last time I came to Rice for this doctoral thing I'm doing." Leon looked across the back seat to Mary, rolled his eyes, and bent his head forward with his chin on his chest. He thought, 'Jack how could you be so fucking inconsiderate? I've never felt more uncomfortable in my life, and this dinner is supposed to be some sort of treat for me? What's the next surprise, a fucking Nobel Prize?' Mary grabbed Leon's hand, squeezed it and said,

"Britt, Leon is here because he just made Jack a bunch of money on a trade idea. He's just about the best muni trader in the South."

"Mary, I wasn't exactly out of the room when that trade occurred, you know." Jack said defensively. "But she's right Britt, Leon is a bit of a legend." Turning back to Leon and beginning to laugh at his up coming joke, Jack said, "Leon, you're a legend in your own mind, you know that?" Turning back to Britt he continued,

"It's amazing really. Leon remembers every trade he does—I mean for years! I forget where I left my umbrella, and Leon remembers one of my accounts buying 300M UT 5.5% or something three years later." Leon was beginning to feel a little better about the evening now and a little less pissed off at Jack for this blind date with Miss 'doctoral thing'. Just then she turned toward the back, pageboy flying, and cut Leon a killer, Ipana smile causing him to give up all of his gains. He thought, 'God she's beautiful.' He just then decided to stop worrying and just have a good time. He thought, 'Christ, I'm not marrying her. Lighten it up Leon.'

Jack parked in Tony's lot. He hated valet parking because either he drove a car he didn't want to be seen in, or, in a week he'd be driving a car he didn't want some asshole in sneakers parking for him. To support his position, he imagined that valet parking guys always changed both the radio pre-sets, and the seat position.

After three rounds of cocktails and plenty of interesting, catching up between Britt and Jack, their slick, Gentlemen's Quarterly waiter arrived and began taking orders. Leon was having trouble deciding from a menu which was bigger than the *Daily Bond Buyer*. Mary looked over and suspected that Leon had probably had a couple of bracers before they picked him up because he was doing too much smiling. The waiter was being patient and stood a little behind Leon's chair when he finally appeared to decide on his entree. He slammed shut the menu, handed it back over his shoulder to Mister G.Q. and grandly said,

"Bring me something flaming."

CHAPTER 14

Leon and Jack, along with nearly all the muni guys, looked upon the typical stockbrokers in their respective firms with considerable disdain. It was almost like the feeling Jack had as a varsity football player toward the members of the high school newspaper, or the radio club. The bond department was separate and apart from "the boardroom" where these dopes sat around all day staring at the stock "ticker" running green dots across the far wall. This condescending attitude basically came from the notion that stockbrokers had a dozen or so products which they sold and about which they generally knew enough to barely get by, while the muni guys had only one product, which they knew inside and out. The 'stock jockeys', as Leon called them, would come back to the bond department all the time looking for help with munis and showing their ignorance in the process. Both Jack and Leon were friendly and always helpful, but they never really respected most of these guys. They also both knew their bias was pretty unfair, but they couldn't help themselves. Some of the brokers had a system like a Las Vegas gambler. Whenever X happened, they did Y. When the price of a stock fell by X% they bought—always a formula. One broker told Jack the key was that he was, "totally unemotional"—just the numbers.

Jack was not surprised when this same guy became very emotional when Bill Weekly, the manager, fired his ass for lack of production.

There were two or three stockbrokers who really stuck out. One of them was a snake of a guy who sold his mother mutual funds, never giving her the benefit of the price break at the 'net asset value' given to family members. Bill Weekly had to watch him like a hawk so the broker wouldn't churn his own mother's account. Leon thought one of the guy's problems, apart from character, was that he completely fell for all of the Research Department's buy and sell recommendations. His clients, like those of most of the younger brokers, were invariably the last few up-tick trades just before the stock went south. One time the advice did work out for him, and he had a huge day. At lunch, he bought himself a Patek to replace his fake 'gold' Rolex. Leon and Jack had a bet about how long the guy would be in the business before he was either thrown out, or thrown into Club Fed in Allenwood, PA.

Like all board rooms, the one at Searl, Patrick and McNulty was a large, open area full of desks, surrounded by glass offices for the big producers. The open part of the boardroom was for the rookies and the older brokers who didn't have very good production numbers. These guys usually shared a Bunker-Ramo quote machine with someone else. Production was everything in a brokerage firm. If you were a big producer, you could do almost anything. You could be a little cavalier with the many rules of the SEC and the NASD and get away with it, if you were a big producer. This was a fact that Jack and Leon disliked about the stockbroker community in general—not just at their firm.

Bill Weekly was the manager of the stockbroker side of the office and was the quintessential "big producer's manager". He was one of those nervous, high energy guys who's knee vibrated up and down at a rate of four strokes a second all day long as he sat at his desk, and who simply was bored if he didn't have at least seven crises going at once. His supervision was directly related to commission numbers. If you were a rookie he paid no attention to you, whereas, if you generated lots of commissions, he was all over you like a cheap suit. If a big producer wanted another machine, or more secretarial help, he need only ask.

Leon walked up to the trading desk, sat down and said to his desk-mate, "Jack, you are not going to believe what I just saw out in the boardroom. Bill Weekly's got a new secretary."

"And?"

"And? And she is gorgeous, that's 'And'? Come on and go to the kitchen with me and get a load of this."

As they walked past Elvira's desk she gave them both her patented stern, disapproving look, which bothered Jack. Evidently she already saw Weekly's secretary, or she overheard Leon talking about her. Leon never gave a shit what Elvira thought of him. As they approached the new 'girl's' desk, Jack knew right away what Leon was talking about. She was dressed, nominally, like all the other secretaries—a blouse, skirt and heels, except that hers, with the exception of the high heels, were about two sizes too small. She was way beyond nubile. The comparison was even more pronounced since the other secretaries were, in Leon's words, "a bunch of trolls". She looked to be 35 or so, Jack thought, and just oozed sexuality. As they passed her desk she was leaning across the desk to get a quote on her Bunker Ramo, with her skirt raising to mid thigh and the buttons of her blouse were under a strain leaving little windows between them.

Jack really did not want any coffee, but they had to go to the kitchen for appearances. Leon said, "What did I tell you?"

"The word 'arresting' comes to mind Leon—arresting. She's got that sunken cheek, hungry, predator look to me . . . very, very sexy indeed, and completely the wrong image for the firm. I probably ought to say something to Weekly."

"Don't open your goddamn mouth Jack! This is the best thing that's happened to this office in years. Personally, I'm going to be drinking a hell of a lot of coffee. Just shut up. Besides, who the hell are you to be commenting on the dress code out in the boardroom or anywhere else for that matter? So, you'd prefer she came to work in a schmock?"

"Leon, the word is sMock, not sCHmock. A smock is a fully cut tent of a dress, designed for fat ladies. A schMUck, on the other hand, is a man much like yourself Leon . . . you can ask Rapoport."

"And another thing Leon, she's way too much woman for you anyway, in case you had any ideas. Women like her go out with good-looking, rich, powerful men. Plus old, yeah, they are always older too. You sort of have to be old to be rich anyway. Don't you think they go together?"

Leon thought he saw an opportunity to set a trap for Jack and said,

"So, Doctor Freud, which of the categories do I lack?"

"All of them."

"Jesus Jack, what an asshole you are! That's insulting, you know that?" Leon then dropped his head and tried his best to look hurt, "You really know how to hurt a guy."

"Leon, are you rich, powerful or old?" (out of charity Jack left out good-looking but added a pause). " Yeah, then I rest my case."

Leon didn't answer because he knew what Jack was saying. She was extremely sexy but would be far too high maintenance and, based on Leon's romantic record, she'd be screwing some tennis pro within a week.

"One more thing Leon, if she ever came on to you, you'd probably pee your pants anyway. So, don't even think about it."

They headed back to the bond department with their unwanted coffee right past Bill Weekly's office and she was still stretched out toward the quote machine. Weekly yelled out of his office, "Hey, come on in!" They both turned, went back into his office and sat down. Weekly asked, "So, what do you think?"

Leon went first, "Let me guess . . . your new secretary?"

"Of course that's what I'm asking. By the way, she is very able and talented . . . tons of experience." Weekly's attempt at seriousness was obviously weak and, as usual, insincere.

Jack looked over at Leon on the other end of Weekly's couch and they both raised their eyebrows. Neither would argue the "experienced" part. Jack said, "Strong as a garlic malt Bill, she is some kind of strong." Just then Weekly's phone rang and he put it on speaker. He was a big shot and always had his calls on the speaker. It drove his clients nuts, but he did it anyway.

"Bill? Listen Bill, this is Bob. I want to know how to make out this check."

"What check is that Bob?" Weekly said holding up his thumb and forefinger a little bit apart signaling he'd only be a second, so Leon and Jack just sat there and waited.

"Listen Bill, I've decided to send you a check—you personally you understand, if you agree not to call me any more."

"What the hell are you talking about Bob, I'm your stockbroker for heaven's sake. I'm not following here."

"Look Bill, each time you call me you recommend I buy some stock—your pick *du jour*, and every time, the fucking thing goes down and I loose money. Then you call me later, and we sell that shit for another looser. So, I figured it out for all last year and I lost an average of $860 per month. I figure if I send you $200 a month, providing you agree not to call me with your cockamamie ideas, I'll be $660 a month better off. Are you following me Bill?" Bill Weekly followed him all right, and his mouth went slack. Leon and Jack on the other hand began to laugh uncontrollably—this was vintage Bill Weekly. The scene was like at church when they were kids and not allowed to laugh. Pretty soon they could not contain themselves and started roaring.

The client said, "Bill, who is that laughing? I'm serious about this. Who the fuck is in your office Weekly? Turn that fucking speaker off for God's sake! Can't I have a conversation without an audience?"

Bill Weekly hit the button and picked up the phone as Jack and Leon made their way out of his office with their hands covering their mouths.

As they passed the new secretary again, Jack thought she was a truly sexy woman indeed and said, "Leon, it looks like her body is having a war with her cloths. Man those there are some serious tits—I guarantee you."

Elvira gave them another dirty look as they walked in, still laughing from Weekly's office. The only muni guy around was Freddy Brister who didn't look too happy. Jack sat down and said to Freddy, "What's wrong Freddy? A big hitter like you should always have a smile on his face, particularly with the account package you managed to get out of this august institution, and all the commissions you rack up every month."

Freddy said, "Sometimes I hate this business. Remember that banker from Midland, the one who never buys anything from me? Well he just did another tap dance on my groin. I don't know why I even call on him."

"What's that asshole's name and his number?" Leon asked looking at Jack as he said, in a deep, theatrical voice, "This sounds like a job for 'Sunshine Phillips'." They both knew that whenever Leon wanted to tool some one around, he'd call them up and pose as this hippie named Sunshine Phillips.

"Oh my God Leon, don't do that. No way." Freddy pleaded.

"What do you give a shit Freddy, you're never going to do business with this asshole anyway. He probably does all the bank's bond business with his old queer roommate from college or something. It's hopeless and you know it. So what's his name and number?"

"Oh, hello is Mister Wirjacks in the bank? This is Sunshine Phillips calling." They put him on hold for a bit.

"Wirjacks, may I help?"

"Yeah, Mister Wirjacks, my name is Sunshine Phillips and I need to talk about a small business loan, you know that government thing where they give money away? You know, for this t-shirt business me and my friend Wally want to expand. We'll need some money, know what I mean?"

"I'm sorry Mr. Aaahhh, Sunrise was it? That's a name I'd remember Mr. Phillips. Do you have an account with us?"

"No maaannnn. Are you kiddin'. Hell, if I had a bank account I wouldn't need any money."

"Yes, well perhaps you would tell me a little about this business of yours Mister, aaahh excuse me, Sunrise. Oh, and by the way, the government doesn't *give* money away."

"Oh yeah? Whatever. Anyway, we have this '65 VW van and we go to football games, you know, like in the parking lots? and make up t-shirts in the back. Two weeks ago at the Texas-OU game we did real good. Must have sold six dozen."

By this time Jack and Freddy were standing next to Leon trying not to laugh. Even Elvira had caught on and walked over for the show.

"Hmmm. Yes. Well, Sunrise, how much of a loan were you

expecting for this little expansion?" By this time the banker was getting a little snotty and condescending, since he had figured by this time that Sunshine Phillips was no DuPont black sheep heir.

"Half million dollars" There was a long pause. Everyone figured that this dopey banker was catching on to the gag.

"That's a lot of money Sunrise, what sort of collateral are you prepared to put up?"

Leon jumped up from his chair. He was starting to take this interview a little too seriously, "Well, fuck, that van's got to be worth somethin'" With this Jack burst out laughing, heard clearly by the "lending officer", and the rouse was up. Leon just hung up on the jerk.

There was a smile back on Freddy's face once more as he went back to his desk.

Leon announced to Jack, "Get out the board!" and pulled open the top drawer of the two-drawer file cabinet between them for Jack to lay out the backgammon board for their late afternoon gambling.

As they set up the pieces Jack said, "Had lunch with Stein earlier. What a piece of work he is. He told me his latest Jewish joke. It's hilarious. There was this cab driver . . ."

Leon interrupted him, "Hold on Jack, a Stein, Jewish joke should only be told by Stein. No offence, but you'd probably ruin it. I know you're funny and all, but your death on a good joke. You even screwed up that old one about the prison with the joke books with all the jokes numbered. You remember Jack, when the new prisoner yells out in the cafeteria 'NUMBER 78' and nobody laughed? "

"Yeah, yeah, yeah. Just play the game will you Leon?"

Jack just then rolled double six's and trapped Leon. "I'm going to crush your little ass like a dung beetle Leon", and turned the doubling cube to two and got back on the subject. "Leon that's a bunch of bullshit and you know it. Trouble is, you see your self as some kind of Henny Youngman or, what's that other son-of-a-bitch's name? . . . anyway Leon, you aren't any ball of fire on the joke telling either. The difference is I'll admit it!"

Leon rolled a four and a five, which he did not need since he was still stuck behind Jack and said, "Christ, just stick a gun to my head and get this shit over with."

CHAPTER 15

Bill Weekly strutted into the bond department in one of his six-hundred dollar suits and started to hand out commission checks to the salesmen. This month's check to Jack was a whopper, due to the State of Texas bond issue, which Leon was clever enough to buy. Jack had promised himself a new car but dreaded the buying process. He and Leon were reading the *Journal*. They always swapped sections.

"Leon, I know you will be profoundly disappointed, but I'm getting rid of the Nova. I know you've become attached to it over the years, but my decision is final, so don't try to talk me out of it. Gonna' trade it in on a new Ford Bronco. They are great hunting trucks, plus I can do all that homeowner stuff with it too. Of course a renter like yourself would not appreciate that. Leon, do you even own any work cloths? You know, paint pants and stuff to wear in the garden—shit like that?"

"Look, Jack," Leon put down the Markets Section, "I live in an apartment precisely so I don't have to do any of that kind of shit. I don't paint, fix drips, do windows or mow lawns. And if I ever have a house, I'll just hire a couple Mexicans to do all that. The Wallas were a proud race of warriors, they never did windows either."

"Warriors my ass," Jack loved it when Leon pitched him a slow ball like this. Leon did it all the time just to start some banter.

"They were more likely a bunch of thieving, sneaky Gypsies if you're any representation. Hell, it's why you're such a good trader Leon, screwing people in trades in genetically imprinted in you. Which brings up something I want to propose."

Jack leaned closer to his deskmate, "You know how I hate buying a car, all that transparent bargaining bullshit at the dealers. I honestly dread buying this Bronco, I'm not kidding. I know I'm going to get screwed and pay too much. Those assholes know I'm a sucker when I walk into the place and probably start to salivate when they see me. So, I've got a proposition for you Leon. I'll pay *you* $400 to buy *me* the Bronco that I pick out, at the best price you can get. What do you say?" Jack's eyebrows were raised in anticipation of a "Yes".

"What are you going to do with the Nova, donate it to the Ugly Car Museum up in Lake Tahoe?"

Jack ignored him. "Well, what's it going to be?"

Leon made a face, "I'll think about it."

"Come on Leon! You know you love buying cars. You'll be great, managing to look offended at getting you're low-ball offers rejected, getting all huffy and threatening to walk out of the place. I can see it all now. Hell, I'll even throw in a little "Oscar" statue on top of the 400 bucks. Plus, I'll be your best friend"…Jack paused and waited, "Don't make me beg, you bastard." Leon had a big grin on his face. There was never any doubt he'd do it. Leon loved sitting across from some bozo car salesman with a wide tie and yanking the guy's polyester pants down.

A week later they were on their way up to Houston Intercontinental Airport in the new Bronco. Jack had picked Leon up on the way and was showing him all the features as he drove and, in the process, weaving all over I-45. They were on their way to "Toppers", the New York City Outing. The guys on the desk in New York, as well as Leon's two trader pals from other firms, Dominic Mortabella and Charlie Stonebreaker, had been after him for years to come up for it.

It was a noon flight, which would get them to La Guardia in time to get to their hotel, eat, have a few drinks and turn in. The first event was a breakfast at 9 A.M.

"What would you like to drink?" asked the stewardess. She was asking Leon but peeking at Jack.

"Is the sun over the yardarm?" Jack responded with a big grin.

"I beg your pardon?" she said, not having a clue about what that meant. They gave her their orders and as she moved to the next row Jack looked at Leon,

"Why do my little jokes and light banter always go over women's heads? I swear to God Leon, it happens all the time. They are in a different Zip Code."

"Have you ever tried just saying, 'Scotch and water', instead of all your engaging bullshit? Who do you think you are, Sean Connery?"

"Tell you what Leon," Jack said leaning out into the aisle as she moved forward taking orders, "That there, is close to a Boone and Crockett ass on her . . . damn." Just then the stewardess found a bag which belonged in the overhead bin which she evidently had missed before takeoff, and in a flash, she cleaned and jerked the bag into the overhead like she was at Muscle Beach, and in the process showed a little more thigh than the airline would have liked. Leon heard, "OOH LA LA" from Jack, but couldn't see because he had picked the window seat. Jack loved the aisle seat. Actually the stewardess wasn't that great, he just liked to mess with Leon.

"Jack, we're not even to cruising altitude, and you're already checking out the women. I'll bet we're not even out of Harris County airspace. You ought to be ashamed of yourself, you know that?" The drinks arrived and they tried to clink their plastic glasses to toast what promised to be a good time in the Big Apple.

They were on approach to La Guardia and the stewardess passed by collecting empty glasses. Jack again checked out her fanny at eye level, as she passed by heading forward.

"What is it with this 'seatbacks in the upright position' nonsense anyway?"

"What?" Leon, once again, had no idea what Jack was talking about or where he was going with this one.

"Your seat back . . . in the upright position. It's a stupid policy Leon—doesn't make sense. In military planes everybody sits facing backwards so it's safer when you crash. Well, not the pilots naturally."

"Where do you come up with this shit Jack?"

"I'm serious, think about it Leon. If we ran into something wouldn't you rather be sitting facing backwards with the seat to support you? Face forward when you hit, and all you've got is a seat belt across your stomach. It wouldn't make a shit what position your seatback was in. Do you follow me Leon?"

Leon said patiently, "Jack, what are we doing right now . . . 350 or 400 miles an hour? They could wrap your ass in a hundred yards of bubble wrap and you'd still be dead if we ran into something. Relax for Christ's sake. You think too much." Leon watched the rooftops of Queens go past for a few moments and added, "You also talk too much."

Leon had arranged to meet Dominic Mortabella at the Westbury Hotel on Madison Avenue for drinks. They had timed it beautifully because he was standing in the lobby as they came back down after dropping their bags off in their rooms and tapping a kidney. Mortabella looked like some Puerto Rican who just dropped off a cardboard box full of buttered rolls and coffee. He had on a t-shirt, jeans and running shoes. Jack had been forewarned about Dominic, who the hotel's manager had been eyeing with suspicion, thinking that any minute, this guy would either rip off the hotel or break into a number from *West Side Story*. The night manager of the Westbury had no way of knowing that this New Yorker in the jeans and t-shirt, made several million dollars a year and could almost buy the hotel.

Leon had told Jack all about this eccentric guy—he was legendary in the bond business. His firm insisted that he be on the board, which he had resisted. He finally relented and showed up at his first board meeting in his usual jeans, t-shirt and running shoes. Two of the old, blue-blooded widows of the company's founders nearly swallowed their tongues when he walked into the room, in a t-shirt, which said JONES BEACH. He was approached afterward by the firm's CEO who begged him to at least wear a jacket to future board meetings. The last thing they wanted to do was run off a guy who generated huge profits for the firm. So, Mortabella stopped off at the St. Vincent DePaul shop on his way home, and paid $9 for an old, black tuxedo jacket with wide satin lapels and hung it on the back of his office door. When he first wore it to a board meeting, the firm's president gave the two old, widow ladies a disapproving look as they put their right hands over their hearts. They each thought they were having massive coronaries . . . Dominic thought they were saying The Pledge Of Allegiance and stood up and put his hand over his heart too. Leon told Jack, "You gotta love a guy with balls like that!"

The night manager appeared relieved when two guests in suits greeted the 'mugger' in the running shoes. To this stuffy guy, suits were the key. He would probably prefer someone hold up the hotel in a suit rather than jeans and running shoes.

When the drinks arrived, Leon asked Mortabella about the next day's schedule. He lit another of the 80 or so cigarettes he smoked each day, and began,

"Get a cab to Pier 38 and I'll meet you there. Be there at 9 A.M. The first gig is put on by the Port Authority—a breakfast followed by a boat ride around Manhattan Island counting bridges. They like to show off all their bridges and piers and all the other shit they control. It will be fun. I'll introduce you to the good guys, which shouldn't take too long. They always have about six tons of shrimp and oysters on the boat, and naturally all you can drink. They have to use a low yield nuclear device to clean the toilets after a whole day of use by liquored-up muni guys. Stonebreaker will meet us there."

It didn't matter where on the planet Leon was; he woke up at 5 A.M. local time. Jack, on the other hand, had to be artificially awakened, regardless of where he was. Leon decided to let him sleep in, since they were not due at the Port Authority piers until 10 A.M. He decided they'd skip the Port's breakfast, so he had breakfast downstairs, read the *Journal* and went for a walk along Madison Avenue. He loved Madison up in that part of town.

At 9.30 A.M., Jack got off the elevator in khakis, a blazer and cowboy boots, and they went out to try to flag down a cab. It was Friday and it took awhile. As they headed down town, Jack leaned over and whispered to Leon, "I don't know whether this guy's hack license is "last name, first name, middle initial" or the other way around. I've never seen any of those names before. What ever became of Anglo Saxon cabbies, or at least Europeans? Every time I come to the City, another immigrant group is driving the cabs."

Leon said, "In two generations, their grand kids will be lawyers. This is America Jack . . . Vaat a kuntry! Remember that guy Yakov Smirnov, the Russian comedian, the one on Carson all the time? I heard him say that the best thing about America was warning shots! Isn't that hilarious?" As he said this, Leon noticed the cabby smile in the rear view mirror and figured the guy must be a Russian too.

"God," Jack thought out loud, "how depressing. Can you imagine being hated in your country, then emigrating to America and in just two generations your grand kids are hated in *this* country because now they are lawyers?"

They staked out a couple of benches on the main deck in the forward part of the boat—Leon, Jack, Dominic and Stonebreaker. Leon barely sat down when he said something to Dominic and turned around to see that Stonebreaker already had a drink in his hand. Dominic asked, "So, Charlie, how many drinks are you going to have today?" Charlie thought for a minute, as if he were actually doing some math in his head, and finally said, "Fifty or sixty" and then polished off his gin and tonic and headed for the bar again. All three had seen Charlie in action before and knew his capacity for alcohol was legendary, but they doubted such a large number . . . no way 50 or 60 drinks!

While Stonebreaker was gone to the bar, Mortabella, the gambler, said, "Let's get up a drink pool on Charlie. We get ten guys at $100 each; pick numbers from 51 drinks to 60 drinks. Winner gets a grand. What do you say?" Leon, also a gambler, brought up the problem of verification, "We would need a counter to follow Charlie around all day." Just then Mortabella saw Sean Molloy, a young trader he hired to work on the desk, walking aft, and grabbed him by the arm,

"Sean! I need a favor. We need someone to follow Charlie Stonebreaker around all day to count how many drinks he has. We have a little bet going. Well, not so little really. Anyway, we need someone reliable, you know, somebody without an ax to grind. You'll need to watch what you drink though, because your count will determine the winner."

"I don't drink Dominic."

"Oh, yeah? When did you stop?"

"I never started. I never drank"

"*You never drank in your life?*" Dominic marveled, "You went to Boston College, your name is Sean and you don't drink? . . . amazing! NYU ought to put you in a big jar at the Med School with a label that says "Sober Irishman".

Jack piped up and said, "Yeah, they'll put it right next to the jar that says, "Celibate Italian", only they're still looking for that guy."

Dominic paid no attention and continued, "Well, anyway, will you do it Sean? There's a hundred in it for you."

"Of course I'll do it Dominic, but I don't need to get paid. I'll do it for nothin'."

"No, no. You get a C-note, plus you'll have fun. Following Charlie will be like following Jane Mansfield. You will be the center of activity I promise. Here he comes with drink number two, so get something to write on and get started and don't fuck it up."

The boat was now underway as Charlie sat back down, "I just heard that some Ginny Mae trader at Goldman jumped in front of the IRT at Grand Central this morning. Guy took 'chapter eternity' on his way to the job for Christ's sake . . . Jesus" He shook his head looking at Dominic and added, "Can't blame him though, can you imagine trading that shit?"

Leon had a macabre sense of humor and quipped, "Yeah, they took him to the hospital and put him in rooms 341, 342 and 343." Nobody laughed; they all just looked at him. So he said, a little indignantly, "Pardon the hell out of me for not getting all misty eyed over somebody who kills himself because the average life of the mortgage pool was shorter than he thought."

Jack put his Lucchese boots up on the bench across from him, and admired the scenery. The Circle Line boat trips were really interesting. The infrastructure of a city this size, and in this geographic location, was fascinating and better viewed from the water. It was a beautiful, sunny, late-Fall day, and the City was very impressive from the surrounding rivers. Jack thought it was a whole lot nicer than being *in* the city, since you didn't have to smell all that urine, and have soot blowing into your eyes.

Just then some wag got on the boat's PA system to announce that the food was now available—all those shrimp and oysters Jack and Leon had heard about. "OK fellas, our generous and benevolent host, the Port Authority of this august metropolis, has made food available in the main cabin. Please help yourselves and remember, you can't throw up if you don't eat."

Dominic was right when he said it wouldn't take long to introduce the 'good guys' to Leon and Jack. A lot of the bond people aboard were public finance bankers with names like C. Harrison something-or-other, with numerals at the end, and wives named Buffy or Bittsy. They were way too Ivy League for the tastes of Dominic and his circle of friends. In fact, the business seemed to consist of the ones with the numerals on the one end, and the colorful, free spirited characters, who looked like they could have been in the Witness Protection Program, on the other. There were few in between.

As the day wore on, everyone got progressively drunker and more sunburned, and their cholesterol levels rose dramatically from eating shrimp all day long. Sean Molloy had a 3 x 5 card and a Cross pen with which he religiously kept Charlie's stats. Nobody fell over the side this outing, to the delight of the Port Authority staff responsible for the excursion. The four guys stayed in their section of the forward deck, while they alternated holding court and entertaining visitors

The betting pool had agreed to meet for lunch at Harry's on the following Monday to hear the final, official drink count from the rookie Sean. He was also the banker holding the $900 net prize (Sean had already taken his $100). Leon and Jack had even rescheduled their flight home for late Tuesday so they could be there. They made believe that they had stuff to do at the main office, but all they really accomplished that day was to show up at Harry's for *the number*.

Sean was there at the trading desk when Leon and Jack walked in and looked expectantly at him, hoping for a hint. He made that sign little girls use when they keep a secret, turning an imaginary key in his lips, and then got back on his phone.

"Leon, what's your number? Want to go joint account with me on this thing? We'll pool our two tickets and improve our chances." It was Dominic Mortabella, the numbers man.

Leon Walla, also a numbers man, thought for a second, "Tell you what Dominic, I'll *sell* you my ticket for $250. How about that?" Mortabella made a face and said,

"Here's my final proposal Leon, because we gotta go to Harry's soon. OK, Jack has 53, Leon has 59 and I've got 51. Leon, how about I *short* you a particular number, lets say 55?"

Jack said, "Hold it, hold it! What are you talking about?"

"I'm offering to *sell short*, number 55 to Leon here, even though I don't have it. You remember short selling from your Series 7 exam? I just told you I have 51, right? I'm simply betting 55 won't win—are you with me Jack? If Leon has any balls at all, he will pay me $150 for number 55."

Jack Armstrong, the people man, but nevertheless not stupid, asked, "So, what if 55 *is* the winner Dominic?"

Leon jumped up, with a big smile and a gleam in his eye, "Then Mortabella gets screwed. He has to pay *me* the $900, which we all know will be easy, since he is as rich as three feet up a Jersey bull's ass. Plus, don't forget the price of his ticket, minus the $150 I'll pay him for the short sale. It's simple Jack, if 55 is the winner, Mortabella just stepped in his messkit."

On the elevator, Leon agreed and Dominic shorted him number 55 for $150, which he stuffed into his jeans.

Louie Napolitano was the last of the ten to arrive. They assembled at the bar near the front door of Harry's, ordered drinks and heard Mortabella propose a toast to Charlie Stonebreaker, who they had neglected to invite, "Here's to Stonebreaker. May his liver outlive this bond rally." They all took a gulp and looked at Sean Molloy like he was with Price Waterhouse on Oscars night.

"Well, I want to say that I followed Charlie all day and counted each gin and tonic. We got off the train in Freeport at around 11:30 P.M. You know that big cannon across from the station? Well, Charlie went down on one knee and held on to the cannon. But it was only a little sinking spell, he was doing fine really . . . considering."

Dominic, expressing everyone's feelings, said, "Come on Sean, cut the bullshit. *What's the fucking number?*"

"55" answered Sean.

Leon shouted, "YES, YES, THERE IS A GOD AFTER ALL."

CHAPTER 16

After lunch at Harry's Leon told Jack he was going to walk Dominic Mortabella back to his office on Broad Street, and they agreed to meet later. Leon was delighted to have picked Mortabella's pockets for $900. It wasn't the money so much as it was winning a bet with a friend. There was always a little extra pleasure derived when you won from friends. Dominic, on the other hand, couldn't have cared less about the money. He had fun betting on Stonebreaker's drinking and the short selling, and that was all he needed. In many ways he was quite simple. If he made a zillion dollars he would still wear sneakers and a Jones Beach t-shirt to the office.

It was 1 P.M. on a beautifully cool and dry Fall day, and Leon thought there must have been 100,000 people out in the financial district. Being there was always exhilarating, but he knew he could never live like these people. They had just turned onto Broad Street and were weaving in and out of the crowds when Leon heard a bloodcurdling scream, "A a a a a a a a i i i i i a a a a a a a a a a!" He turned toward Dominic to see what had happened only to discover that it was Dominic screaming. Veins were popping out of his neck, his face was red and his head was back like he was looking up at about the 14th floor across the street. He'd later tell Leon that you scream better with your head back like that. After four or five seconds he stopped and Leon yelled,

"Holy shit Dominic! What's the matter with you?" Dominic started walking again with at least 300 people watching as he sidestepped a newsstand and answered,

"Nothing. Every once in a while I've got to get it all out of my system Leon. You know," and he waved his arms at the Wall Street anthill around them as they walked, "all this shit."

Leon, who had never been more embarrassed in his life said, "Yeah? Well the next time you want to pull a stunt like that, at least have the courtesy to give me a few seconds to sort of drop back like 50 yards so nobody associates us. Does this happen often with you? We are friends Dominic, but I've got to tell you, that you're about two side dishes shy of a Blue Plate Special, you know that? That's the weirdest thing I've ever seen."

Even the rent-cop in his own building lobby gave Dominic the once over as they got on to the 20th to 44th elevator. The back office was on the 29th, so there were a few pretty strange New Yorkers on the elevator coming back from lunch, but none as strange as Dominic Mortabella. Leon thought, 'What a piece of work.'

"I need to call the office, can I use a phone Dominic?"

"I run a full service shop Leon, ask and it shall be given unto you. You can use mine, come on in." Leon sat at Dominic's desk while Dominic lay down on the floor near the door and did some stretches. Just then a girl in a mini-skirt casually stepped over Dominic and dropped a couple of new issue scales on his desk. She then turned, stepped back over his head and disappeared out the door. Leon thought, 'Jesus! Stuff like that never happens to me. I'll bet Dominic didn't even look up her dress.'

The phone in Houston rang only once before Elvira answered, "Bon Apartment". Leon figured, correctly, that there wasn't anything going on back there since he and Jack were gone. He thought that Elvira and her covey of secretaries were probably plotting against him . . . a *coup d'etat*. "It's Leon, do I have any messages?" She read off seven pink slips and Leon said they could all wait. He then asked for Freddy Brister.

"Howdy Leon, what have you guys been doing up there?"

"Sameo, sameo . . . just whipping it around the infield Freddy. Anything new down there? Incidentally, we'll be in the office Wednesday morning. Oh, and Freddy, you need to come up for this outing next year. The guys on the boat ride were straight out of Central Casting. It was hilarious. We had a great time"

"Leon, where are you?"

"I'm up in Mortabella's office. At his desk actually. He's over lying on the floor, looking up girl's dresses at the moment. Only Dominic could get away with shit like that."

Mortabella, who had not even noticed the girl step over him said, as he pulled his knee toward his chin, "What?"

"Never mind Dominic, go back to whatever that shit is you're doing."

"Freddy, let me tell you something. This is a weird city, full of weird people and Dominic Mortabella is the strangest of the lot. I'll fill you in on all the details when I get back. See ya."

Stonebreaker had told Leon and Jack that he'd pick them up at the Westbury in the morning. He didn't want them schlepping all that luggage down to the office and then again when they left for La Guardia airport that afternoon. A limo pulled up and the hotel doorman, in his Admiral Nelson uniform, yanked open the rear door thinking there was a big tipper inside only to find Charlie Stonebreaker in the back seat and he didn't look like he was about to get out. Jack was the first to figure out that this was the ride and he and the driver threw the bags in the trunk.

Jack got in beside Charlie and Leon took the jump seat across from their host.

"Nobody said anything about a limo. This is the way to go, right Leon? Although a couple of bigshots like us deserve the treatment. Thanks for the lift Charlie."

Leon settled into his seat and looked up at Charlie and was a bit startled, "Jesus Stonebreaker, you look like shit, you know that? Are you OK?" Jack had not noticed and leaned forward for a look and raised his eyebrows and thought Charlie really did look bad.

Jack changed the subject and asked about the limo and Charlie told them that with the job of syndicate manager, he had quite a bit of latitude on expenses. At any given time he might have four or five deals going with all the accompanying meetings all over town, and each had an allowance for expenses he incurred, such as printing the bonds, legal services and entertainment including closing dinners, all supposedly associated with that particular underwriting. "When you think about it, you couldn't eat enough or drink enough or take enough limos to put a dent in all those fees. The expenses I rack up, nobody questions. So, I do what I want—anything I want . . . right, Owen? Owen's my driver." Leon turned around to see a big smile from the front seat underneath a chauffeur cap and nodded to Owen.

"Sounds like a license to steal Charlie." It was Jack, "Charlie, are you OK? You're sweating like a bull." Stonebreaker's chin went to his chest and he closed his eyes, "Maybe it was that brandy after dinner. That shit always gets me. I ought to know better . . . Lord knows I've had enough experience," Charlie said with a feeble smile. "On the other hand, my arms are a little numb . . . Owen, I think I'm having a heart attack. Take us to Beekman Downtown Hospital, will you?" Owen stomped on the gas as if he'd heard this request before and they were off and running like a Roman cab.

Leon braced himself and Jack held Charlie's hand as Owen did his thing. Charlie was not the only one sweating by now. Jack and Leon were very concerned. Jack knew that if worse came to worse, he would be the only one in the back of *this* limo to give mouth to mouth to poor Charlie as he passed into that big bond outing in the sky. Leon was definitely not a mouth to mouther. He would probably do the external heart massage or run for a doctor but no way on the mouth to mouth, no matter how close the friend. Jack knew Leon would kiss women every chance he got, but Leon drew the line when it came to men, no matter how dire the straits.

The ride reminded them both of that scene in *The French Connection* with Owen driving on sidewalks, into oncoming traffic and running red lights. Leon saw one Con-Ed worker actually dive down a manhole as his little tent was mowed down! Owen finally said, "It's OK Boss, we're getting closer." That's when Charlie opened his eyes and lifted his head. He was starting to feel better. By the time Owen screeched to a stop in the front of Beekman Downtown, Charlie appeared fine. The sweating had stopped; he had feeling back in his arms. He smiled, looked up at Leon and said, "Lets get a Bloody Mary Leon. Owen, just drop us off at Harry's will you?"

The bartender looked up at Jack in that sort of Italian way, with all five fingers on each hand held together at the tips and facing upward and a shrug to his shoulders. He didn't actually ask, "What will you have?" but that is what he meant with the fingers.

'Bloody Mary. Wait a second . . . a Bloody Bull instead . . . know how to make them?"

The bartender said, "Lemmy guess, you're not from here, right? Just tell me how you want the drink. This ain't Jeopardy, know what I mean?"

"Just substitute beef bullion for the tomato juice part . . . it's all you got to do and you've got a Bloody Bull. A very popular drink in Houston."

"Yeah? Well we don't have bullion. So pick somethin' else." the bartender then turned to Stonebreaker for his order. In a couple minutes he was back with the fingers.

Jack asked, "You think they might have some bullion in the kitchen?"

The bartender started to laugh and waved the four guys in toward the bar as he looked around conspiratorially at the empty bar.

"This guy reminds me of the joke about this rich old woman from Park Avenue. She all of a sudden had a craving for some ice cream so she tells her chauffeur to stop at some Baskin and Robins. She goes in to the place with a full-length fur coat, you know, all tits n' diamonds, and the place is full of some Cub Scout pack. The kid behind the counter is working his ass off but he stops to ask the rich lady what she wants.

'I believe I will have a hot fudge sundae with chocolate ice cream.'

'We're out of chocolate lady, can you pick another flavor?'

'Then I will have a milk shake with chocolate ice cream, please.'

'Lady, I just told you we are all out of chocolate . . . probably be in this afternoon. Pick somethin' else.'

'Well, in that case just give me a chocolate cone please.'

The kid has at least 50 cub scouts givin' him shit and standin' on the chairs, and this rich nut-case, he don't need. So he says,

'Lady, do you know how to spell the 'straw' in strawberry?'

'Why yes, S-T-R-A-W.'

'OK, do you know how to spell the 'ras' in raspberry?'

'R-A-S-P of course.'

The kid says, 'Good. Now do you know how to spell the 'fuck' in chocolate?' The lady thinks for a second and says,

'There is no 'fuck' in chocolate.' The kid yells,

"*LADY, THAT'S WHAT I'VE BEEN TRYIN' TO TELL YA*"

Leon had just taken a sip of his gin and tonic, which he promptly blew into a fine mist out over the tables and started choking, the lime burning his nostrils. Jack had to wack him on the back a few times before turning back to the bartender and saying, "Lets stick with a Bloody Mary."

Charlie, who was feeling a whole lot better now asked, "What time is your flight?" Leon pulled out his ticket and told him it was 3:25 P.M.

"Good, we can just stay here, have a couple of their world famous gin and tonics, have some lunch and I'll have Owen drop you two at La Guardia. We'll get Mortabella and Louie to join us. Dominic can provide the entertainment."

"Charlie, don't you have to go to the office?" Jack asked, checking his watch.

"If they want any of my Solomon like decisions, they know where to find me." Charlie answered, pointing to a phone on the wall like the ones in people's kitchens.

"You mean you've got your own phone here? . . . in a bar?" Jack was astonished.

"Yeah, it's a direct line to my trading desk. You know, in case I'm here doing the firm's business." Charlie had a big smile on his face as he continued, "Besides, they are having another meeting for the office personnel this afternoon and I refuse to go to them. I think that the big boss has attended one too many of those seminars . . . all that touchy-feely bullshit, you know, the workers holding somebody up in the air, or falling backwards into your team's arms . . . what a crock of shit."

Leon turned to Jack, "Incidentally, when I called in awhile ago, there was a message from Rapoport. He said that his buddy at Solly told him that they want to talk to the two of us. Lets talk about it on the plane."

Owen and his limo were waiting across Hanover Square in front of the building housing EF Hutton's brand new gothic (in more ways than one) bond department. He had not been able to get a space closer to Harry's front door. Of course there were no "spaces" anywhere, they are *all* illegal around Wall Street, it is simply a matter of degree. There is a jungle of signs saying what you can and cannot do, when you can and cannot do them, who can and cannot do them and under which circumstances. Stonebreaker once told Owen that he was going to replace him with a lawyer. Owen and all the other drivers knew the system was completely ungovernable, like much of their city, and so parked and waited where they liked. If a cop showed up he'd just give the driver the thumb to move, and he would drive around the block. Leon and Jack walked to the limo and got in the back like a couple of bigshots. They had not bothered to transfer their luggage after the "medical emergency" trip to Beekman that morning. They were ready to go.

"It's La Guardia, right Mr. Walla?"

"Yes, La Guardia, and Mr. Walla was my father Owen . . . Leon will do just fine thanks."

Jack settled in as Owen headed for the East Side Highway, "Leon, you know for a sawed off little redneck from Pasadena, Texas, you handle your self quite well up here with the swells. I didn't hear you once ask what the fish fork was for."

"Don't start up with me Jack, OK? As I recall, you have often reminded me of your humble origins in some jerkwater mining town or whatever it was. So where do you get off talking about social graces? It's a mystery to me where you got the few you have, unless *Leatherneck* magazine carried Emily Post's column."

"Fill me in on the Solly thing Leon. Why the hell would a gorilla firm like them want to talk to the likes of us?"

"We'll have to wait and see, if we want to bother going up to see them. I suspect that they want to begin covering second tier banks in addition to their regular huge clients and the easiest way is to hire someone like you who already has a book full of those accounts. All they have to do is to hire you and they are instantly in the new business—they have no risk. Besides, Solly deals in real risk, you're no risk at all Jack. You are a proven producer who would bring all your clients along with you."

Jack thought about the whole Solly idea as he looked out the window at what had to be the world's largest hospital for the criminally insane. When Leon had asked Owen what that huge, and very ugly building was, he had filled them in on the whole depressing subject as if it were an attraction for the city—some chamber of commerce thing. Leon thought, 'That is the most depressing fucking thing I've ever seen. They must deliver the Thorazine in friggin' tanker trucks. I can't wait to get back to Houston.'

"So, Leon, what do you think?"

"About that nut-house back there? I think it's awful. Most depressing goddamn thing I ever saw!"

"No, no, I'm talking about the Solly thing Leon, try and keep up! Do we want to go to Dallas to see these assholes or not? My gut feeling is that it's a waste of time."

"Jack, do you know Tim Dunn, the intermediate government bond trader over at First City Houston? He told me a great Solly story one time that pretty much says it all about their culture."

"I've seen him a few times."

"Well, First City was part of this humongus loan, involving offshore oil rigs, with some foreign country. You know, those rigs that are like ships? I don't understand it completely, but it was gigantic, involved several big banks and the loan was collateralized with Treasury bonds. First City held the collateral and for the loan to be paid off, part of the process was to finally sell the bonds securing the loan, you know this collateral. At any rate, Tim all of a sudden has this huge position of $500 million of whatever the bond was. I forget, but I think it was the two-year note, which he is told to sell. Tim figured that this is a shitpot of bonds and to do this in an orderly fashion, he would have to sell into the bid at, like, $25 million bonds at a whack, and as he kept selling, the price would probably fade and he would end up averaging 15 or 20 trades to get the job done.

"So he figures he'll start with Solly and he calls them and says,

'What's your bid on the 2 year treasury?,' Solly's trader thinks Tim is some pissant from the bowels of a second or third-rate bank and says, in the most condescending, arrogant voice,

'Par and 5/8ths.' so Tim says,

'How many bonds is that bid good for?'

The Solly guy laughs and *actually* says—and I'm not making this up Jack—'This is Salomon Brothers asshole, you can't own enough bonds to matter to us.' Can you imagine telling *anybody* such a stupid thing Jack? It's unbelievable!

"So, Tim says. 'Yeah? So my size (position) doesn't matter to you?' and the Solly guy laughs again says, 'I'm a par and 5/8ths bid, stop wasting my time. What do you want to do?'

"Tim says, and I'm not shitting you on this, 'You just bought yourself $500 million bonds, and don't ever call *me* an asshole.' Tim told me that he could actually hear the guy's Adam's apple fluttering as he hung up. Can you imagine going to your department head to tell him you just committed a half billion dollars of the firm's capital?" Leon smiled and thought to himself, 'Couldn't happen to a nicer bunch of guys.'

"Why don't they just send somebody down to talk to us Leon, you know, take us to dinner instead of us schlepping up to Dallas? It would be a lot easier."

"Not Solly's style Jack. They always want you to come kiss the ring."

"Well Leon, the more I hear about them the more I feel like telling them that they can come kiss my ass."

CHAPTER 17

Leon got off the elevator and walked into the bond department thinking that it was Wednesday already and the week was shot. He had no regrets though about staying in New York an extra day. He had a lot of fun hanging out with Mortabella, Louie and Stonebreaker, and he convinced himself that he hadn't missed much back here in Houston. As he approached Elvira's desk to get his stack of pink, 'While You Were Out' slips, she said,

"Nice to have you back Leon, how was New York? Did you have fun?" Leon strongly suspected that she was more than a little disingenuous and really didn't give a shit if he had fun or not. He always had the feeling that she either didn't like him, or that she hated men in general. So they kept at arms length, which was easy for Leon because he always thought she was homely enough to turn a funeral up an alley.

"It was great Elvira, Jack and I had a lot of fun. Jack had never actually met some of those people up there, so I think it was productive." Leon headed for his desk, which, predictably, was piled high with new official statements, and the usual stuff passed out all day long at brokerage firms. As soon as he sat down the direct line from Marc Rapoport lighted up,

"House of Value. What, do you have a spy over here or something?

I haven't even sat down and I'm already being harassed by chiselers." Leon always enjoyed Marc because they always seemed to get a lot done but still had some fun in the process.

"Value my ass. What the fuck does a gentile know about value? So, what are you two going to do about Solly?" Marc was a very nosey guy and had a compulsion about knowing *everything* that took place on 'the street', particularly in Houston and Dallas.

"We talked about it some on the plane and Jack is sort of lukewarm. As you can imagine, he has a low threshold for arrogance. Those guys are a little too pompous don't you think?"

"Leon, it can't hurt to go up to Dallas and check out the prospects, you know, see what you're worth these days."

"We'll talk about it at lunch and I'll let you know what is going on Marc." Leon hung up as Jack dropped his smelly gym bag next to his desk and asked,

"Let me guess, that was Rapoport already asking about our plans. You know Leon, if I didn't know better, I'd figure," and he held up his thumb and forefinger about a quarter inch apart, "he was about that far from being queer. For a straight male, he is the biggest busybody I've ever seen." Just then the speaker between their desks came alive. It was Leon's fellow trader from San Francisco, John "No Relationship" Glenn.

"Houston, pick up."

Leon picked up the squawk box phone and said, "Bullwinkle? Is that you?" Leon was the only one to call Glenn by that name. It was just another of Leon's tagging someone with a nickname. Everyone else was easier on the poor guy who had to go through life explaining that he was no relation to the astronaut.

"Leon, Wells Fargo trust department is asking about a new deal down there called the Houston Sports Arena. Do you know anything about it?" Leon loved to jack "Bullwinkle" around whenever he had the chance, so he pushed the button on the 'laugh box' he had on his desk, which he bought at a trick shop, and put the receiver next to it.

"HA, HA, HA, HA, HEE, HEE, HEE, HEE, HO, HO, HO,

HO," after five seconds he turned it off to hear Bullwinkle say, "You wouldn't have turned that stupid thing on if you didn't know the answer, so I'm calling you on an outside line."

Jack laughed and shook his head and said to Leon, "You know Leon, you've got some pair of balls calling poor Dominic Mortabella weird. *You* are the one who is weird."

The phone rang and Jack picked it up, "Armstrong". It was the expected call from Bullwinkle, obviously asking for Leon.

"He's right here John. He is a little busy though, he is practicing for his origami class this evening out at the Community College." Leon got on the line and brought Glenn up to date on the new deal Merrill Lynch was bringing for a sports arena to be called *The Summit*. Jack was about to say something about having lunch to talk over their plans when Sammy David Stein called and asked Leon to have Jack pick up too.

"Leon, is Jack on the line? Oh, Jack hi. Listen I want to take you two to lunch today. I'll meet you at the Houston Club. Lets go early, say, quarter after eleven? I need to talk to you about this Solly thing. Both of you are real good friends and I don't want to see you do something dumb." Leon and Jack were so shocked that they just mumbled agreement on lunch and hung up.

Jack leaned his reddening face closer to Leon and, trying to control himself, attempted a whisper, "I have an idea Leon. Why don't we just take out a FUCKING AD in the *Daily Bond Buyer,* or maybe a tombstone in the *Wall Street Journal*, just in case there is some asshole out there in America somewhere who doesn't know about OUR FUCKING DEAL WITH SOLLY!" Leon chose to let the moment cool down a bit and said nothing. He knew Jack Armstrong was some kind of pissed off.

They were a block away from Rusk Street where the Houston Club was before either of them talked—Jack broke the ice,

"I can't believe we let Stein talk us into lunch to discuss something which is none of his business. We have not even talked to anyone at Solly and the whole street has us already there! I wouldn't be surprised to start getting calls from realtors wanting to sell me a house in Dallas. Jesus Leon, this is way, way out of hand."

"Look Jack, lets just have a nice lunch. Dave means well. He's a good friend and I don't want to hurt his feelings. We'll just tell him we can't discuss the matter."

"Yeah, right Leon", Jack sounded real sarcastic, "that ought to go real smooth. The reason Stein is one of the great salesman of all time is that he won't take no for an answer. You'll look like road-kill after you tell him we can't discuss it. Look Leon, let me handle this, OK?"

The Men's Grill was a left off the elevator and they knew that's where they'd find Stein. Predictably he was at the entrance end of the bar with a drink in his hand and a big smile on his face. He waved them over, shook hands and signaled the bartender.

"What will you have Jack?" Jack started to laugh remembering the episode with the bartender at Harry's the day before and he told Stein the whole story including the 'chocolate ice cream' joke which was one of the few jokes Sammy had never heard. When Stein laughed everyone in the bar looked over his way. He had a raucous, uninhibited, infectious laugh. Ordinarily he was fun to be around.

"Let me tell you guys one, then we can go to our table;

There is this Jewish cab driver in New York who is very devout. All his life he has wanted to go to Jerusalem and pray at The Wall, but he had kids, and had to educate them and everything, so finally one day, he has the money for the trip.

He checks in to his hotel over there and goes right over to the concierge to ask the guy if he is dressed properly and where the Wall is, and stuff like that. The concierge says that the cabby looks fine and gives him directions to The Wall. Then he tells him to work his way up to The Wall and rock back and forth and say his prayers.

He gets up to the Wall and he's next to a little, gray bearded old man in a black hat and overcoat who is rocking back and forth. Finally, they stop praying and the cabby introduces himself to the old guy, 'You look so devout praying there sir, do you come to the Wall often?'

'Often? OY. Every day for thirty years I'm coming to The Wall.'

'That's wonderful, just wonderful. Tell me, what do you pray for?'

'Vell, I pray I should live a long life. That my wife, she should be healthy. That my daughter, she should marry a docta. That my son should get through dental school . . . things like dat.'

The cabby asks, 'Oh, that's wonderful, have your prayers been answered?'

The old guy says, 'It's like talking to a wall!'

"That is a good joke." Jack began, "Look Dave, let me shorten this up. Number one, we have not even spoken to Solly. Number two; I don't even want to go up there because I hate Dallas. Number three, I don't want to work with those guys and I have something going on in my life at the moment, which would prohibit me from considering the thing anyway. Number four; I am led to believe that they want both of us. It's an 'all or none' thing . . . both or neither of us. Sooooo, it's as dead as Kelsey's nuts. End of story. Let's order."

Leon was staring at Jack, and Jack knew why. Leon concurred with every point except he was puzzled with the " . . . something going on in my life" part.

Stein held up his hands and said, "Look, it's none of my business, but this rumor went through the street like a dose of salts yesterday and I wanted to give you two the benefit of my opinion. You are my friends and I want you to be happy, that's all."

Every time Leon went to lunch at the Houston Club, he ordered the shrimp remoulade and he said the same thing *every* time, "These shrimp are huge Stein. Where do they get these things, out of the cooling pond at the South Texas Nuclear Power Plant?" Then he would laugh, yet again, at his little joke. This time they all laughed uneasily and attempted to change the subject. The food was so good that was all they discussed the rest of the meal.

Stein's office was conveniently located in the Houston Club's building, so they said their adieus at the elevator. As they left through the garage exit of the Club and hit the street, Leon could no longer stand it,

"Jack, I need to know what you meant when you told Stein that you had other things going on, which would keep you from doing this Solly thing'.

If you can't talk about it, I'll understand but *I* can't consider any changes until I know what's up."

"You've heard me mention my Marine buddy Win Ensenat and his colorful, oil man stepfather 'Gator' McCully? Well, Mr. McCully is a big contributor to the Republicans, and is wired in pretty tight. He is particularly close to our governor . . . a confidant you might say, and our governor is a *very* close friend to Ronald Reagan. They were just outside the Cellar Door when Jack stopped and said,

"Leon, I don't want to talk about this in the office, so let's stop in here for a cup of coffee and wind this up." There were a few of the hard core still there from lunch, but it was way too early for the Happy Hour crowd, so they could sit anywhere. The coffee was delivered and they got back to business.

"Mr. McCully wants to do something in D.C. I gather it is a combination of his being tired of just making more and more money in the oil business, and Win's mother's desire to make the canapé circuit up there. But I am told that he is being appointed to something significant . . . he paid his dues, he is very smart and experienced in business and the right people like him."

"Jack you are a typical Irishman, you know that? Ask him what time it is and he builds you a watch. Get to the point. I don't give a shit about these people, I want to know how any of this effects you."

"I got a call from Win while we were in New York. The Governor and McCully want to talk to me as soon as I can get over to Austin. I think they want me to go up there with McCully, you know, to Washington. They are getting their ducks in a row. Leon, that is all I know at the moment and a lot of it is speculative as hell. I am taking Friday off and driving over for a meeting. I haven't even told Mary any of this. And Leon, this is secret. I don't want another Solly fiasco. So say nothing."

Leon looked out over the dusty cafe curtains at the next glass building and sipped his coffee. Jack let it all sink in. When enough time had gone by, he said, "There are a number of issues which could queer this thing Leon, so I am a long way from renting the U-Haul. First, I go to Austin, then I talk with my wife, then I'll give you a call or maybe you can come over the house Sunday for lunch. But let's put this thing away until then . . . what do you say?"

CHAPTER 18

Gator McCully sat in his office on Congress Avenue looking out the window at the pink granite Capitol a few blocks to the north. He had no appointments other than his meeting with his stepson Win's friend Jack Armstrong, followed by the two of them walking to the Governor's office. It was one of those rare, quiet moments when he was going over his life. What prompted this little retrospective was the opportunity he was soon very likely to have presented to him—working in the new Republican administration in Washington. It was true that he was getting sick of the oil business, but this was a big decision and he needed to think it through.

William Fredrick McCully had been born in Midland, Texas. He entered the Marine Platoon Leaders Course (PLC) right out of SMU, just in time for the Korean conflict. If anyone bothered to make the effort, and plied him with good whisky, he just might regale them with his experiences with Chesty Puller up at "The Frozen Chosin" reservoir. Nobody could recall if he had been tough before the Marines, Korea and the battle of the Chosin Reservoir, but nobody doubted it anytime since.

When he left the Marines he went back to get a masters degree in petroleum engineering and went right to work for a New Orleans based drilling company. Most of the work was on shore, but considering the fact that the highest landmass in all of Southern Louisiana is the Achafalya levee, it was wet work. All the roustabouts thought he was the 'meanest son-of-a-bitch in the swamp' and began calling him 'Gator" . . . but not to his face. Actually, he liked the name and before long even the rough necks stopped using 'Mister McCully'. The men liked him because he was fair as a level and not a bit hesitant to get his hands dirty. Half the time you couldn't tell him from the drillers.

One evening while waiting to be seated at his favorite watering hole, Galatoire, a buddy introduced him to Ruby Ensenat. She had been widowed for a couple years and McCully privately always thought that her first husband must have been one dumb son-of-a-bitch for killing himself with a hang glider. Gator often thought, 'This guy had the most charming, beautiful woman I've ever seen and the dope takes up a hobby of jumping off cliffs hanging onto a big coat hanger, wrapped in toilet paper!' He would have crossed it off to the theory of natural selection, except for their young son, who appeared to be perfectly normal and, whom Gator would grow to love and cherish as his own.

So, the question he asked himself on this particular afternoon was, 'I've got a great wife, a damn good marriage, a fine stepson and I've got all the money and stuff I want, so why the hell am I considering moving to Washington with a bunch of over-educated, pencil-necked, lawyers and bean counters?' He couldn't believe that he was about to put the full court press, about going to D.C. and all that "giving back to the country" stuff, on his guest, Jack Armstrong, while *HE* himself was not yet convinced! He started to psyche himself up for the meeting with Jack, admonishing himself for being a comfortable whimp, and recalling freezing his ass off at the Chosin Reservoir.

"Jack Armstrong, how in the world are you? And how is that fine little family of yours? Two beautiful little girls, THREE excuse me— forgot to include Mary! How I envy you Jack."

McCully never let Jack answer, so he was a little lost with how to answer, so he just shook his hand and said, brightly, "You're looking mighty fit Mr. McCully. It's nice to see you again."

"Stop the bullshit Jack, you know I'm a good 30 pounds over-weight. Goddammit Jack, if I didn't have so much fun seeing my friends and playing cards over to the Austin Club at lunch, I'd be my fighting weight." With a big grin he continued, "As it is, they force me to go there every day and eat rich food, drink good whiskey and sit on my ass for two hours playing poker! It's just *awful.* I hope you're sympathetic." Jack began to laugh and thought to himself, 'Jack me boy? You've got a finite number of hours left in your life. Spend as many of them as you possibly can with colorful people—like this guy Gator and your bond buddies—and as few as you can manage with all those bland drones out there.'

"Have a seat Jack. Can I offer you a adult beverage?" Jack declined wanting to keep his wits about him. There was no point in waiting so McCully began,

"The Governor called awhile ago and asked if we could forego the meeting in his office, and just meet for an early dinner over at the Austin Club in an hour. I told him that was fine and that I would give you all the preliminary stuff.

"Reagan's people have approached the Governor with the idea of appointing me to an undersecretary post at Treasury. He is all for it. We're good friends and I've been a supporter of Republicans from the Governor all the way down to Dog Catcher, and they want to reward me and frankly I'm inclined to take them up on what should be a gener-ous offer."

"Sir, I am sure that they want you because you'd do a good job. There must be lots of big supporters who they couldn't give an important job like that to."

"Thanks for that comment, and you are right Jack. In fact, they do reward those people, but not with *real* jobs. They make them ambassadors to places we never heard of like Tobago or Inner Something or Other, where they spend their time in a Cadillac with flags on the front bumpers driving over water buffalo shit. You couldn't pay me to do that. In fact, I don't think they pay them at all. They are all rich as hell, and are more than willing to pay any and all the expenses they incur, just so they can be called "Ambassador" the rest of their lives. It is really a corrupt system which State is gradually shedding. At least that is what I'm told.

"Getting back to the subject, I am going to need someone I can trust to come along. Jack, I don't know who they will saddle me with up there, but I am going to hold out for the right to bring along my long time secretary, who you just met, who happens to know the good guys from the bad ones and where all the bodies are buried. Also, I'll need someone who is real smart, familiar with finance and who has all the social graces to run in the circles I'll be in up there. What I'm getting at Jack, is that you're the man I want . . . simple as that. In fact, having known you since I proudly witnessed the two of you boys graduate from OCS at Quantico, all of my initial feelings about your character and many qualities have been confirmed. Jack, you're a fine American and I want you beside me up there with those Treasury Department pencil-necks. Will you do it?"

Jack didn't answer right away and Gator knew better than to press the question. He had very good instincts when it came to negotiating. It is one reason he looked forward to the Treasury job because he figured that what they needed up there was a few more old horse traders. Gator McCully knew that Jack was thinking about the money and abandoning the business he had worked hard to build.

"Look Jack I know what you're thinking. Government jobs don't pay much and you're right about that, but you need to look a little farther down the road. You spend four years at Treasury, and you'll make more contacts than you could shake a stick at . . . I promise. Corporations love to hire people who are wired into the loop in DC. Jack, I am going to make a prediction, and I am pretty goddamn good at this, that your future after leaving Washington will be far and away better than the one you've got now. The question is, 'Can you afford living up there for four years, or maybe even eight, on government wages.' That right there, is the crux of the thing Jack.

"The money comes and goes Jack. Life is really about the experiences you have and the people you love and who love you. They can't take that away from you. All the rest is bullshit Jack. You could go to work in the Post Office and have no risk. You'd work for peanuts;

take all sorts of shit from people inferior to you. You'd think about sticking a gun in your mouth about twice a week for the rest of your life, *but you would be secure.* I've had several friends in the oil business who've gone from rich to broke and back a bunch of times. Now they laugh about getting evicted from their homes by bankers who told them 'It's nothing personal'.

"Hell's fire, I remember the first time I made a whole bunch of money." He smiled broadly, looked out the window at downtown Austin and was away somewhere in thought. Then he was back in the office, "Yeah, Jack I remember I spent a bunch of it on beautiful women; a bunch of it on good whisky," and with a twinkle in his eyes continued, "and I pretty much wasted the rest." He quickly added, looking over the tops of his pulpit half glasses, "This was, of course, before I married Win's mother, you understand."

Gator had in fact not let Jack answer. He just went into his soliloquy and in so doing, he bought Jack some time to think and he lightened things up a lot. Jack thought to himself, 'Gator, you cagey bastard, you are one smart, colorful son-of-a-bitch and I think I'd like to work for you.'

"Well Mr. McCully, I am flattered to be considered and particularly by you. I really am. It sounds exciting and interesting, but I'll need to gather some more information and think about the money side and talk it over with my wife"

Gator got up from his desk, "Well of course you do Jack. You take all the time you need on this." McCully grabbed Jacks shoulder, looked him in the eye and added, "I want you to know that I'm not asking anyone else Jack. I am utterly convinced that you are the man for the job, and that it would be in your best interest. I am so sure that I am not even considering an alternative plan. Lets head on over to The Austin Club Jack, we don't want to keep the Governor waiting and I damn sure need a drink."

As they left, McCully introduced Jack to his secretary,

"Jack, I want you to meet the most organized person east of the Pecos. Lupe Anaya, meet Jack Armstrong. If it was not for her, this office, and my affairs would look like a Chinese fire drill." They shook hands and chatted it up for a few seconds until Gator broke in with,

"Jack, where are you staying? My wife is a little angry with me for not thinking to invite you to stay with us."

"I'm at the Driskill, but Mr. McCully don't worry about it I'm fine there but tell her thanks though." McCully waved a hand dismissively and turned to Lupe,

"Lupe, call over there and have them pack up Jack's things, have them waiting in the lobby so we can pick it up after dinner and charge it to our account and send the concierge a tip."

"That is really unnecessary, I'm fine over there."

"Bullshit Jack, you're staying with us. If you don't come home with me I'll never hear the end of it. Win's mother has adopted you as a surrogate son, whether you know it or not, and she can be as tough as a steak about these things. Actually, she never gets mad because she does those affirmations each morning."

"Affirmations, Mr. McCully?"

"Yeah Jack, you know, where someone closes his eyes and says he has unconditional warm regard for some son-of-a-bitch he can't stand. Or that he loves the way he looks just as he is, even though he's ugly and the dope weighs 350 pounds. My wife does this stuff every morning. Hell, I guess it must work—Lord knows she's always in a great frame of mind, even putting up with all my shortcomings. I often wonder if she says one for me. Probably a good thing she doesn't say hers out loud. Personally, I think it is all a bunch of bullshit."

Lupe smiled broadly thinking that this young man reminded her a lot of William Fredrick McCully twenty years ago when she first went to work for him . . . that is before he got all independent and crusty.

There was a black Ford in front of the Austin Club, which was obviously the Governor's since it must have had a half dozen antennas, and it was illegally parked. The plainclothes trooper with the earphone, standing on the Club's porch confirmed that he had arrived ahead of them. It was easy to find the Governor since he was surrounded by members saying hello. The Governor stuck out his hand and said,

"Mister Armstrong, Gator here has told me a little about you and I'm delighted to meet you. Why don't I call you Jack?"

"Delighted to meet you Governor and Jack's just fine with me. My dad always said, 'Call me anything you want, as long as you call me for dinner'."

"That is a good one Jack. An old one for sure, but a good one. I'm trying to identify your accent, where in the world are you from? I'm usually real good at this but yours stumps me."

"Well, Governor, I was born on Oahu. Actually, my dad was a Marine at Kaneoe. It's over on the north shore. We moved around quite a bit so I guess that explains it . . . I've been sort of homogenized." Gator broke in excitedly and asked,

"Your old man was a Marine Jack? You don't say . . . you don't say." McCully then went silent in thought and he seemed far away when the Governor stepped back into the conversation,

"Now Jack, a homogenized man like yourself, may not understand this, but when I went to Princeton, my friends up there would actually buy me a beer just to hear me say 'winda' and 'evathang' . . . no shit! Never saw the likes of it, a beer to say those words. Of course they'd make me say it in a sentence, 'Be so kind as to open the winda Billy Bob.' Or, 'Show me evathang you got'. It all wore off by Halloween of course, since they lost interest in buying all those beers. The funny thing is that they never stopped smiling whenever I said, 'fixin ta'. Went on for the entire four years. I've often thought that if I took those Yankees on out to Mason, Texas for barbecue, Shiner Beer and a sunset, they'd never leave." He began to laugh at the upcoming joke, "So, since I didn't care to take such a risk, I never invited them!" The entourage laughed heartily.

"Actually, I have taken some of them hunting south of San Antonio—most prolific game I've ever seen. Ever hunted around Pearsall Jack?"

"Yes sir, I've hunted that area since I was about 14 or so. You know Governor, I don't want to sound like some tree hugger on this, and I completely agree with you about the game, but it's a whole lot better than when I was a kid. I attribute it all to the good offices of your Parks and Wildlife Department, good game management on everyone's part, and of course the eradication of the screw worm."

McCully's head jerked at the word screw, and he came back from his daydreams. His intention had been to get the Governor and Jack bullshiting with each other to show Jack 'on his feet' and it appeared to have worked. The old and very reserved black waiter appeared for another drink order. Without a word, McCully pointed his raised index finger downward and scribed a circle. The waiter disappeared like he was in a Disney movie.

"Jack, tell me, did you go to college here in Texas? Our host Gator here failed to send me your resume." He turned to his pal Gator with a smile and asked, "You are picking this up aren't you?"

"A&M Governor, then into the Marines. Best two decisions I ever made . . . except marrying my wife of course."

Gator's face lit up, "Nicely said Jack, nicely said." He turned to the Governor and continued, "See what I told you? This is the man for the job up there Cookie, he is the guy I want goddammit, so start leaning on those Washington bastards, and get the show on the road!" McCully never called his pal the Governor, Cookie, in front of others, but he had gotten excited. "Can you imagine a big, good lookin', decorated, former Marine pilot like Jack—slick as owl shit—up there at those parties in DC? Hell, after a month or two the invitations would probably start coming in addressed to *him* instead of me, with a note not to forget that old son-of-a-bitch."

The new drinks arrived and the Governor leaned across to Jack, "Jack you've got the job and you're perfect and I'll, by God, get it done, believe me, but there is an element here that particularly appeals to me and let me explain, partly for Gator's benefit.

"Texas and its political subdivisions—all those towns, cities, counties, school districts and the like—are collectively the second biggest issuer of municipal bonds in the country behind California. Our ability to borrow billions of dollars each year in the tax-exempt credit markets for public works is vital. There are two schools of people in Washington who, from time to time attempt to, pardon my language Jack, screw up a good thing, by trying to have the tax exemption attached to municipal bonds rescinded. First there are those knuckleheads on the Hill, and second is The Treasury Department! There is one man in particular at Treasury—one of those rich, up east, Ivy League sons-of-bitches, who's got some of what I call *noblese oblique,* who has got it in for municipal bonds. Incidentally, I define that as "rich and obligated *not* to personally give anything back to the community, but to make sure *all the other rich people* do. Like most of those bastards he is rich by virtue of birth, and wants those who are rich by virtue of hard work to pay for everything. What I am excited about is having a man up there who is intimately familiar with the process and the instrument, so we can be forewarned. As a personnel favor to me, and I am assuming you will take the position, I want you to keep a mental list of those whom you detect are philosophically opposed to the idea of tax exemption for municipal bonds. In other words the goddamn enemy. They are all big government and control freaks, and I want them the hell out!"

On the way home McCully counseled, "Jack, this thing is picking up speed so talk to Mary and try to come to some decision, and remember these points; you're the guy for the job, no question about it; it's in your own best interest in the long term, and I think you'll see, the short term as well; I want you and look forward to working with you; you've got the blessing and backing of one of the most influential Republicans in the country; and finally, I predict that Mary will love the move . . . end of speech"

CHAPTER 19

Jack never flew back and forth between Austin and Houston. He figured that by the time he drove from the house down to Hobby Airport, waited around for the flight, flew to Austin, rented a car and drove to his appointment; he was better off simply taking his car in the first place. It was probably a bit more time but, for him it was not worth the effort to fly. Besides, he liked driving and seeing the Texas countryside, particularly between Houston and Austin. He also enjoyed being in the car by himself so he could think.

The route followed the Lower Colorado River. In fact you crossed the river a number of times, and it was very pretty. Often he would stop in Columbus to have a slice of homemade pie at the cafe on the square where the old county courthouse was surrounded by huge 100-year-old magnolia trees. He always found something special on his road trips around Texas.

After a sumptuous breakfast with the McCullys, Jack took off for Houston and immediately turned off the radio—he had to think about the sea change going on in his life and he didn't want to be distracted. Of course, McCully was right about this move being in his long-term best interest. All of his points were unassailable . . . the man was just flat right about all of it. One thing that was becoming apparent was that McCully had Jack's best interest at heart. True, he wanted him to take the job so that Jack could help him, but Jack felt strongly that McCully would not have pursued the matter if he were not convinced that it was best for Jack and his family. He decided then—at that moment—that he wanted to work for a person like this, and that he would take the job. All the rest was incidental; quitting the business; moving and finding a place in DC; the salary; schools for the girls. He was now, as a bond salesman, not really working for anyone, it was not the nature of his job. He was more like a sole proprietor. In this new situation he would certainly be working for someone in the traditional sense and, by God, he was not working for jerks again, as he had twice in the Marine Corps, and often in his part time jobs as a youth.

After he had thought about it and made his decision, he felt great and turned on the radio and sang along with Mick and the 'Stones' . . ."Let's spend the night together. Now I need you more than ever." He was never sure of the lyrics and faked them a lot when he sang in the car, but he was never unsure with the melody. One of the reasons he liked road trips was that he could let it all out, singing in the car. You couldn't do it in Houston for fear the guy next to you at the traffic light would notice and think you weren't taking your Thorazine. So whenever he drove to Austin, he listened to Dewey Compton's Garden Show until he got to about Columbus where the traffic thinned out, then he'd listen and sing along with the likes of the Mamas and the Papas and of course Mick Jagger.

About the same time Jack was having his third cup of coffee earlier that morning with Gator McCully and his wife, Leon Walla was getting off of the elevator on the 47th, floor of One Shell Plaza in Houston. His ears had not popped as usual, or if they had, he had not noticed. He was pretty hung over and he was preoccupied with the aspirin and Alka-Seltzer he was about to have, just as soon as he reached his desk. He did not however miss the lousy elevator music on his way up. This morning's treat to the ears was a synthesized version of *Guantanamara*, which was unusually bad. He thought it was only marginally better than the night before when he left the building to something the Carpenters had once done. He would have gotten off to avoid hearing it except he was on an express elevator, so he just covered his ears while some law firm intern looked at him. He recalled telling Louie Napolitano his theory about Musak—it was the Mob's way of getting back at American Society for putting them out of business.

Normally, Leon would have already taken care of his remedial, post-merriment hangover cures at the apartment, except that for the first time he could remember, he ran out of both Alka-Seltzer and aspirin. He had been furious with himself when he discovered he was out, and shouted "JESUS H . . ." into the bathroom mirror but failed to finish, instead grabbing his temples. He would often run out of other stuff, but never the basic necessities of life, as he knew them, like Alka-Seltzer and aspirin. Running out of things like toilet paper, shampoo and tooth-paste was nothing by comparison. He thought that it must be something from his youth, though he never seemed to run out of milk. There was always an unopened, very, very plump quart of milk in his refrigerator. He was convinced that the grocery store was way off on their "sell by" dates, since they always seemed about a month behind. Since he had his coffee black, never ate at the apartment and never had anyone spend the night, much to his disappointment, he seldom *actually opened* the milk cartons. Instead he simply threw them out once a quarter, at least. It was a health thing with him.

Leon walked into the bond department and headed right for the little kitchen to get water for his Alka-Seltzer and coffee for his central nervous system. He had not even bothered with his pink "While You Were Out" slips.

At about 11AM the phone rang and Elvira picked up, "Bon Apartment . . . Leon, it's Jack."

"Leon, I'm at a gas station in Katy, anything going on?"

"Naaah, just ridin' around . . . same shit, different day. What happened in Austin?"

"Tell you what Leon, meet me at Cyclone's for lunch and I'll fill you in. It ought to take me 40 minutes to get there. OK?"

Cyclone's daughter had put on a little more weight Leon thought, as she approached the table, "Something to drink?"

"There will be two of us, the other guy isn't here yet. How about a Tecate?" Leon sat there looking at the duck shooting machine but not really seeing it. He had an ominous feeling in his guts. Jack had sounded pretty upbeat on the phone. Leon knew he was about to loose his buddy to the Feds and it pissed him off as he thought, 'Fucking Treasury Department. They tax about half of everything I earn, they are constantly trying to do away with tax exempts, and put me out of the only business I know anything about, and now they are going to hire away my best friend. The only fun I have is screwing around on the desk with Jack and they are fixin' to take that away too. Maybe I ought to do something else for a living . . . shit.'

"*Una ves mas, por favor*", he said to the daughter. Leon over the years had built upon his high school Spanish through trips to border towns like Matamoros and Nuevo Laredo. He called it "Boys Town Spanish". "*Chips y salsa tambien.*"

For some reason Cyclone's always left the empties on the tables and Jack noticed as soon as he walked in that Leon had obviously gotten there plenty early since he was on his third beer. That was all Jack needed to decide not to go into the office after lunch. He needed to get home to square everything with Mary and besides, what would he do in the office now that he'd decided to leave the business?

"How long have you been waiting?" Jack asked a little too sternly, looking at the now three empty Tecate bottles and the half-eaten basket of chips.

Leon ignored the question, "I've got a good idea what you are about to tell me Jack, and I'm not sure I'm going to like what I hear. So, I decided after the second beer, to blow off the afternoon . . . I'm going home after we're done, so get on with it."

Jack ordered the chicken enchilada plate and a beer and began telling Leon all about what went on in Austin. He did it in great detail, leaving nothing out because he thought Leon deserved the whole story. When he was finished he took a fork full of his now cold enchilada and made a face, "Shit, they ought to be more careful picking these chickens,

I think I just got a rotator cuff or something." It was so nasty that he spat it out onto his plate.

"That's disgusting Jack! Jesus, you're supposed to sort of squirt the stuff onto your fork and then put it on the plate."

"I know what I'm supposed to do for Christ's sake Leon! Hell, I was about to swallow when I felt this thing—I was in the middle of breathing and I didn't want to choke to death, so I just spat the stuff out. Gimme a break it's Cyclone's for God's sake! Plus, your the last son-of-a-bitch I want around when I need the Himlick Maneuver done to me. You're great at getting another round and stuff like that, but forget about Himlick maneuvers, CPR and especially mouth-to-mouth resuscitation."

"You're the wrong gender for me to do the Himlick Jack. Show me a good-looking lady with a 38 D-cup and I'll show you some serious Himlick. How did we get onto this shit anyway? We were talking about your career ending decision."

"Yeah, well that's it. I'm going to do it Leon. I am getting tired of the business and I think this will be an exciting phase of my life—a shot in the arm. I need to go home and explain the whole thing to Mary and try to work out how we can afford the job change."

Leon looked at his watch, waved to Cyclone's daughter and signaled for two more beers.

"I ought to get going home Leon." Jack's voice having little conviction to it.

"Oh, come on Jack it's not but 2:30! It only took you 20 minutes to tell me the whole nine yards. Mary's going to say, 'Fine Jack, whatever you want honey', anyway. She'll give you a big kiss and tell you what a big strong man you are. Hell, you may even get lucky."

Jack waved at his perfect neighbor as he pulled the Bronco into his driveway. Bob Welton was mowing a lawn that did not need mowing, at least by Jack's standards. The guy was a great neighbor but Jack thought he was way too anal about the appearance of his house and yard. He'd miss Welton when they moved to DC since he was a resource to Jack. Every time some thing-a-ma-jig in a door lock or the stove fell off, Jack would bring it next-door for a diagnosis. He remembered once, in a flash of creativity and energy, attempting to change a washer in the kitchen sink only to discover as he peered into the dismantled faucet, a square hole in the middle of the valve seat. It obviously required a special tool . . . Welton naturally had one.

"Hey Jack, I've been giving your idea about a deck a lot of thought and I have a pretty neat design in mind." He then proceeded to talk about it, but all Jack heard were unfamiliar words like 'pressure treated', 'lag bolts' and 'footings'. His mind was on what he was going to tell Mary and he had to get into the house without offending Welton. He didn't have the heart to tell the guy that he really didn't give a shit about his deck ideas. He thought to himself that you had to watch what you said to this guy—he was starved for projects since he had already done every renovation/fixer-up permutation possible to his own home. Jack thought, 'Welton's worst nightmare probably was having another perfectionist move in next door after the Armstrongs moved out.'

"Great Bob, but I'm putting that on hold for the moment, plus I need to take a leak. I'll explain it to you later."

He remembered the bottle of that crappy Korbel sparkling wine someone left them and decided to open it up for his little talk with Mary since it was the closest thing to a celebratory beverage they had in the house. So he stuck it in the freezer and went looking for her. He was excited and a bit apprehensive at the same time.

They both sipped the stuff while Jack went through the whole thing, from Gator McCully and what the job would entail, to what it would be like for Mary and the girls, and how he was going to quit. At the very end he said, "The only thing about this is that I don't think these government jobs pay what we are accustomed to me earning. I'll find that part out soon, but I know it will be a pay cut. Housing is the big nut up there. We could probably get by except for the housing." This made Jack laugh. 'Get by *except for housing*'.

"I don't think that's a problem Jack. I've got something to tell you too. First of all, I am delighted for you. I'm very excited and you deserve this opportunity. You'll be great at all that political stuff, and it will be neat for the girls to grow up in Washington. Plus, it won't be long before I can go back to work."

"So, what's this secret Mary?"

"I've got some money I never told you about. Aunt Lydia and Mother have been gifting me money for years. They can do it tax exempt up to $10,000 a year each. It's really an estate tax dodge their CPA got them into. Maybe they had doubts about our marriage, who knows? They set up an account in the bank in Portland with the understanding that I leave it alone and only withdraw it for the purchase of a house. We didn't need it to get this place so I just left it there."

"Come on Mary, out with it! What's the number?"

"Are you asking how much money is there?"

"OF COURSE, what do you think?!"

"Well, the last time we discussed it which was earlier this year, Mother told me it was something like $275,000."

"HOLY SHIT MARY! Holy shit. What nice ladies." That was all Jack could think to say . . . 'Holy shit'. He jumped up and said 'holy shit' again.

"Mary, let's go out to celebrate. Can we get a sitter? A good place this time, like Tony's or that great steak place . . . what's the name of that place? It's way in on Westheimer...remember? Goddamn Mary, do I feel GREAT! Holy shit."

CHAPTER 20

Jack looked up at the ceiling to see that little stain in the shape of a Rhorshak that had greeted him every morning since he had bought the house. He was pleasantly surprised that he felt pretty good in spite of drinking that awful Korbel the night before. He wondered if it really was the effect of that high-end cabernet at the steak place and not really the cheap sparkling wine. Anyway, he felt good and lay there going over the things he had to do, now that all systems were go on the Washington move. Mary could get the ball rolling with movers and realtors, but he had to call Gator McCully first thing.

After Jack accepted the job and expressed his gratitude, McCully said, "That's great news Jack. I could not be more delighted—really. Now Jack you need to get up to Washington and get the process moving. Show your smiling face to the powers; fill out forms; give them your fingerprints and all the rest. You could do all that from here of course, but you'd be better off getting the lay of the land. Additionally you can drive around the residential areas like Arlington and get a feel for housing. I've contacted a realtor and I'll have him give you a call."

"Incidentally, Jack, I am told that your title will be Special Assistant To The Deputy Secretary Of Treasury for whatever it is they have me do. Since titles in Washington appear to be inverse in length to their importance, this puts you way down on the pecking order." They both laughed a bit uneasily since neither had a grasp of just how Byzantine it really was east of the Potomac River. Jack again thanked his new boss after getting instructions concerning where to go and who to see. The second call was to Leon.

"Bon Apartment." It was naturally Elvira with her signature greeting.

"Hi, it's Jack, where is Leon?" She hand signaled Leon.

"Make it quick Jack, I was just about to call Dowling to offer him your job. I want to keep the average I.Q. up here at its historic levels." As usual Jack ignored Leon's attempts at humor, realizing Leon was funnier when he didn't try to be funny.

"Hey Leon, I've got an idea. I have to go up to Washington, why don't you come with me. You have never been there and we'd have some fun—sort of a farewell thing. What do you say?"

"What?"

"Leon, don't start jacking with me. You know that I am immune to your jacking. Just call Louie and tell him you've got to go see McBain in the Bethesda office. Tell him you need to go over a few things, you know, better relations, going joint account on bonds…bullshit like that."

"I don't want to see that guy Jack. It's bad enough I have to see him once a year at the muni conference, and incidentally, that's exactly what Louie will say to your stupid idea—it's bullshit."

"Look, Louie doesn't give a shit Leon. All you need to do is a cameo appearance at the Bethesda office. Besides, I thought you had the hots for his secretary, remember, the one with that deep sexy smokers voice? I really like McBain by the way. I never did get why you had a problem with him. Another thing I never got Leon was how come you go out with smoking women." Leon responded,

"If they've got big enough tits, I'll go out with them even if they are on fire!" Leon thought this was hilarious and laughed so hard, he began to choke. Jack was not giving up,

"Anyway, the expenses come out of your profit center. Plus nothing is going on in the muni market and you know it. It's the perfect time to travel. A watched pot never boils Leon. You're sitting there isn't going to make things happen. So make the reservations for Christ's sake. I'll call you later with the number of my flight. Hell, I'll just make the reservations for the both of us—I don't trust you."

As was their custom whenever they flew together, Jack picked up Leon on the way to Houston Intercontinental. Leon bought a Playboy magazine on their way to the gate, and as he sat down after stowing his gear in the overhead, Jack started up on him,

"Leon, aren't you a little embarrassed reading that stuff in public? I mean what if a woman or some kid sat down next to you and you had that thing open to some vagina shot." As he said this Jack was looking at the opened magazine, which Leon promptly slapped shut.

"Unfortunately Jack, some lady failed to sit next to me on this flight. Instead I got a former Marine hairyleg, hypocrite, busybody son-of-a-bitch who is going to ask me for this magazine as soon as I am done with it. So don't get all uppity with me. Of course I would not read this shit in front of a lady or some kid! You think I'm some sort of a Philistine Jack, you know that? You're Gary Grant, and I'm Ernest Borgnine or someone. That's what you think." Jack knew when to quit and didn't respond. Besides he didn't want to screw up his chances of reading the magazine later.

"Ladies and gentlemen, this is Captain Mulroony. Aaaaaahhhhhh, there is a big weather system over Nashville with tops up around 45,000 feet. We've been cleared to skirt around the storm on the southeast. It may get bumpy, but we'll be well clear of the cell all the way. I'm asking the flight attendants to secure the drink cart and have a seat. So, if everyone will return to their seats and buckle up, we'd appreciate it."

"Oh shit Jack!" hissed Leon. His knuckles got white as his all American red blood cells got squished away somewhere. He had a death grip on the armrests.

"Relax Leon, we're going *around* the storm, not through the damn thing. Piece of cake." Jack wanted to reassure and distract his friend. He scanned his memory bank for an entertaining weather story. All pilots have them.

"Leon, I was at the Marine air base at El Toro for transportation to

Vietnam. I had my orders and everything but there was some problem. They had a '46' they needed to ferry to N.A.S. New Orleans and saw that I was available." Leon interrupted,

"What's a '46', and where the hell is El Toro? Jack, you need to remember, I'm no war correspondent. I'm not Dan Rather, I'm a muni trader, remember? If you're not going to finish that vodka tonic, I'll take it off your hands." Leon did not wait for approval, but simply gestured for Jack to continue and poured Jack's drink into his empty plastic cup.

"El Toro is in Southern California; and a '46' is a twin rotor helicopter—a lot bigger than a Huey. Can I go on now? Dan Rather my ass. So anyway, were heading east right along the Mexican border. We go all across Arizona and New Mexico. We're scheduled for an overnight and pit stop in El Paso, but there is this humongus storm cell moving north out of Mexico and it's between us and El Paso. I didn't have the fuel to loiter and I'm not about to land in the middle of some ranch.

"Well, I figure—I mean who the hell is going to know that I crossed into Mexican air space to skirt this storm, right? The last place the Mexicans need surveillance is the U.S. border for Americans trying to sneak into that fucked up country, so they can get robbed and abused. Know what I mean Leon? So I skirt around the storm to the south over some *patron's* ranch, come up north and land in El Paso. I taxi over to the place they want us to park. My crew chief and I get out and there are these two guys in crew cuts and suits. Now, you've got to remember this is in the 60's when everyone had a doo like John Denver or Ringo. These two flip open their wallets and show us that they are F.B.I. The short one says, 'Follow me'. No please or anything. So we follow them into the airport office there and the little one says, 'What's you name?' Leon, this guy is a full foot shorter than me—no offense, but he is as short as you. I want to sort of lighten it up a bit so I answer, 'Who's askin'?'

'Don't get smart with me, just answer the question.' No please again—this guy is starting to get on my nerves. Know what I mean? Plus, my name is on my flight suit and Sargent Friday here fails to notice.

'What's this all about, aaaaahhhh—what's your name anyway?' This guy is stupid enough to answer me, and I hadn't even given him mine yet.

'Polanski—Special Agent Polanski.' I figure, 'Oh Christ a Polak. We'll be here all night with this dope, right?'

'You flew in from Mexico Lieutenant…' He finally had the sense to read my name and rank off my flight suit. 'What were you two doing in Mexico?'

'I was coming from the Coast and we had to skirt that storm on the south, or probably wreck my helo out there in your local boonies. You remember that storm? It probably only dumped a foot of water on this airport in the past two hours.'

'We're searching your aircraft for a drug shipment.'

'YOU'VE GOT TO BE SHITTIN' ME!!! Hey, you got a warrant or something? You're messing with The United—by God—States Marine Corps, you know that? You don't know what pain is!'

'Don't give me a hard time Lieutenant or I'll cuff you to that radiator over there.'

Now I'm getting really pissed off Leon. They even hassled my crew chief. So I blow up. I mean this guy is a real prick evidentially full of Napolianic complexes—not at all like you Leon, believe me. So I tell him,

'Do you really think you can intimidate me Mister Special Agent Polak? I've got orders for Nam in five days where I'll probably get my young ass killed, and you're threatening me with keeping me here in the safe, good old U.S of A. Go ahead and arrest me asshole!' Leon, this guy is stunned and just glares at me. So, I lean a little harder and I'm enjoying myself.

'You got a case Agent Polak? Than arrest me—shoot or drop the fuckin' musket.'

'DON'T YOU DARE GIVE ME ANY LIP LIEUTENANT.'

'Lip? You want some lip? How's this for lip Agent Polak…FUCK YOU!!' Leon this guy turns the color of a stop sign and lunges at me he is so pissed off. His partner grabs his arms and pulls him back and whispers something to him. Probably that they didn't find the ton of marijuana they expected in my chopper.

'You know Leon, I'm going over there to get shot at for a year, and I don't need any shit from people—I don't care who it is—*on my way over there*—for God's sake! Plus, I know I'm right on this and he's wrong. So I say as he is heading out the door straightening his skinny tie,

'Say hello to J. Edgar Hoover for me the next time you see him at one of your costume balls.' In one second, he turns into that green guy on TV.—The Incredible Hulk, and comes at me again. Lucky for him his partner stops him once again and I yell,

'Let the little son-of-a-bitch go! I'll tear off his head and crap down the hole!'

By this time they had skirted their own storm and Leon was feeling pretty good, waving to the stewardess for more drinks. One of the things he liked about his good friend Jack Armstrong was that he seldom took any shit from people. He also told a hell of a story. Leon wondered if this was some kind of a Marine thing since Sammy Stein was also like that.

"Key Bridge Marriott," Jack told the driver. National had plenty of cabs so they had no wait. "Leon, this is National Airport. They ought to get rid of it because it's dangerous, old and in the middle of town for God's sake. But they wont because the Members of Congress don't want to schlep all the way out to Dulles. So the pilots have to fly down the river dodging buildings so these assholes don't have to have some staffer drive them another 30 minutes. It's pathetic really—selfish. They have enormous power in this city, but I still like it here. Plenty of memories for me here."

As they pulled up to the hotel, Jack saw the familiar, though up-dated, Marine Corps bus over to the side. There were still some O.C.S. candidates hanging around in their tell tale buzz haircuts trying to decide what to do. Whenever they were given liberty, the bus drove the "candidates" from Quantico, Virginia to this particular hotel. It was convenient to Georgetown just across the river, but Jack suspicioned that it was also because it was also just across the highway from the Iwo Jima Memorial. In fact while he loved the Corps, he was always a bit suspicious of their motivation concerning the men. He thought they messed with the minds of Marines more that the other services.

They grabbed their luggage right out from in front of a disappointed bellhop and headed for the check-in desk. But not before Leon made an observation of the 'candidates' outside,

"Was that you in an earlier life Jack? Don't they feed these guys? They remind me of some Holocaust movie."

"Yeah they feed them. Of course they feed them. I mean food is available and everything, but sometimes the DIs will mess with you Leon," Jack slipped into the first person. "We had one who would dismiss the platoon in front of the mess hall to eat lunch, and then walk around to the back where the exit was and expected us to be there! I mean done with lunch. So, we'd run like hell through the mess hall, grab two slices of bread, put a huge glob of peanut butter between them and haul ass out the exit. We looked like a bunch of chipmunks with our cheeks bulging out. Plus they ran way more calories off of us than we ever could possibly ingest in thirteen weeks here."

"Leon let's just check in, throw our stuff in the rooms and walk over to Georgetown. It's great over there. We'll eat have some drinks and turn in. What do you say?"

"Jack, I made plans to meet McBain for a drink—it will be our 'meeting', and it will be a quickie believe me. He doesn't want to spend any more time with me than I do with him. Then I'm meeting Coughing Squaw at a haunt of hers across the river. I think she lives over there." Leon had a big grin on his face, obviously expecting to get lucky that evening.

"Coughing Squaw? You mean the smoking lady in McBain's office?"

"Yeah, she's part Indian. Didn't you know that Jack? It's on page 123 of *Tough Minded Management* Jack. Know your employees—basic management stuff. You must have been absent that day."

"You actually call her Coughing Squaw?…I mean to her face?"

"Well not while we're knocking boots or anything, but in lighter moments, yes. She thinks it's funny…not the sex, I mean the name. With sex she is as serious as a heart attack, you know, a regular Israeli fighter pilot."

Jack and Leon didn't see that much of each other in Washington as it turned out. Leon's squaw took a couple days off for their romping, and Jack spent more time than he had anticipated at the Treasury Department endlessly filling out forms and doing pictures and fingerprints.

Early on the last day in Washington, Jack did his morning run along the old Barge Canal in Georgetown that ran along just above the Potomac River. He ran across the Key Bridge and then dropped down to the path alongside the canal. He had some running routes he considered comfortable and even special. In Houston the Buffalo Bayou run he did nearly every day wasn't really that special, but the Barge Canal path was beautiful. During the entire run he thought of various special runs he had had. While he was in Europe once he ran through Hyde Park in London, the Bois de Bologna in Paris and the Vienna Woods. Whenever he went to San Francisco, he ran around the Marina. Jack Armstrong loved to run.

CHAPTER 21

As usual, the manager Bill Weekly was on his phone when Jack knocked on his open office door. He waved him inside and held up his index finger and thumb signaling, along with his trademark conspiratorial wink and nod, that he'd only be a minute. With Weekly you never knew. Every time Jack went in there it seemed Weekly was having some sort of a conflict or blow up with a client. He couldn't understand this since he, Jack, never had these sorts of things happen with his clients and knew he couldn't stand to have such relationships. He knew that Weekly was a bit of a high roller and figured that he probably burned up his book of clients every few years with his aggressive selling and market recklessness. Jack could still recall as a new salesman, when some old timer in the business had given him some advice, explaining the expression "burning up a book".

'Don't ever lie to a customer; always do what you said you were going to do and never push someone into something inappropriate. Remember, tomorrow is another day. There are a ton of people in the stock business who will do almost anything to make a commission including jamming inappropriate stocks down client's throats. About the third time they screw their clients, the client finds another broker.

It's an unbelievably stupid way of doing business and surprisingly, some of these jerks are the biggest producers . . . figure that one out. Can you imagine how well they'd do if they were on the up and up?'

Jack knew that he would always conduct himself properly and didn't fear "burning up" his book, but he nevertheless accepted and followed the advice from this old broker.

Weekly finally hung up on the client he was arguing with. It appeared to Jack from the phone call, that he had sold some flaky tax shelter with a 4 to 1 write-off to this poor sap a few years earlier and now the IRS was denying the write-off and bouncing his return. Jack knew what that meant. He'd seen it over and over where these broker's clients paid $10,000 for a tax shelter and wrote off $40,000 against that year's income and figured that they'd made a killing at Uncle Sam's expense. What actually happened was that the shelter was so crappy that it was now worthless; the IRS 'denied the write-off'. Then they wanted the taxes on that $40,000 phantom income, plus interest and penalties for the four or five year interim. The whole, cumulative effect was often huge. That taught Jack, a) never to listen to tax shelter people and, b) screwing with the IRS was like playing Russian roulette with six rounds in the cylinder.

"So, what's up Jack? What can I do for you?"

"Bill, I've decided to leave the business. I'm not going to another firm or anything and what I'd like to do is to stay a week to wind things up and introduce Freddy Brister to my clients. I'd rather he have them than to risk them going to the competition. It's just better for the firm and everyone else." Jack immediately saw that Weekly was, probably for the first time in his life, completely at a loss for words. Jack had wanted to present this resigning thing as a *fait accompli,* so as to avoid Weekly's inevitable lecture about how great this business was. It seemed to work because Weekly just sat there speechless. He had never seen a good producer leave the business before. Jack felt a little guilty and explained the circumstances briefly and left to go back to the bond department. He never felt so good in his life.

It was still pretty early and Jack was going through his day's agenda in his mind as he headed for the kitchen and his second cup of coffee. Bill Weekly's sexy secretary was in there and was bent at the waist as she peered into one of the lower shelves in the refrigerator. Her already tight gabardine skirt was being put to a tensile strength test probably on the order of one of those Underwriters Laboratory jobs. Jack's eyes involuntarily locked on to her shapely rear end like a Sidewinder missile as he walked straight into the Coke machine with a bang. She straightened right up and turned around,

"Oh, Jack, you scared me! Oh dear, what did you do to your nose? Jack it's bleeding! How did that happen?" Jack was embarrassed and mumbled something about not watching where he was going, which was an understatement. He tore off a corner of a paper towel and stuffed it into the bleeding nostril,

"What a dope. Sorry. I'll be fine. My nose bleeds a lot." Jack said with little conviction. She looked sympathetic as she attempted to tuck in the blouse that had come out in the back. She was using her thumbs and the effect on her chest was scintillating to say the least. Jack decided to forgo the coffee and headed back to the bond department. As he walked in he heard the phone ring and saw Elvira pick it up,

"Bon Apartment." Leon could always tell it was her husband since she spoke really low whenever he called. Just then Bill Weekly walked into the bond department and sat down at Leon's desk handing him a manila folder,

"What do you think of Jack leaving? He'll probably be back don't you think? I mean where else can you make this kind of money?" Money was truly everything to Weekly. "Say Leon, look this one over for possible tax swaps, will you?" Leon opened it up and immediately recognized the bonds.

"We just did this one at the end of last year Bill. Rates have not moved off enough for tax swaps to make much sense to the client. I can tell you that without even looking at this."

"Leon, look. The guy hates paying capital gains taxes to the Feds— he hates paying all taxes. I mean it's visceral with this guy—know what I mean? So he loves it when I show him losses to offset all the gains I generate for him." Leon just looked at Weekly thinking that Jack, the second smartest guy in the whole office, was leaving him all alone to deal with knuckleheads like Weekly for the rest of his life. 'All the gains I generate for him my ass', he thought. He felt like telling Weekly to go fuck himself, and just head for the Sewer for a drink with some people with scruples.

"OK Bill, let me explain this one more time. Each time I help you on this portfolio, we've had to drop down in quality and extend this guy's maturities just to make the swaps work. Bill, we are degrading his portfolio just to get a few measly tax losses, which don't warrant screwing up his portfolio. Hell the transaction costs are greater than the losses, let alone the tax advantages! Are you with me here Bill? It's bad for the client." Weekly just looked at him and shrugged. Leon remembered the punch line from Stein's Jewish joke . . . 'It's like talking to a wall!'.

"Bill I remember helping you put this portfolio together a couple years ago. It was beautiful then, all laddered out with high grade bonds maturing each year. The way things are going, this poor bastard is going to end up with an entire portfolio of BA rated Puerto Rico Sugar Cane bonds out in the second coming of Christ!" Weekly looked at his gold Rolex with the diamonds and got up from the desk,

"Look Leon, this client doesn't give a shit about all that technical stuff. The only reason he even has a muni portfolio is because his CPA sold him a bill-of-goods about asset allocation. He is a gambler for Christ sake! All we do is options and commodities. Just do the best you can for me, OK?" The last sentence was said over his shoulder as he made his getaway.

Jack had not said a word during the exchange. Having just resigned from the business, he found it hard to get too worked up. Leon looked across at him in disgust,

"You got any more openings up there at Treasury? I can't stand this shit anymore Jack. This business is getting on my nerves. Maybe I should start my own firm. I already have a name picked out, Cuthroat, Pillage, Byrne and Walla—what do you think? The brokers here either have room temperature IQs, or they are scumbags."

"Look Leon, you need to lighten it up or you'll have the big one right here at the desk. I can just see it. You're working late into the night on Weekly's stupid tax swaps. Elvira finds you the next morning, slumped forward, with your face all crunched up on the Compucorp keyboard with O V E R F L O W on the screen. Hey, I need to talk to Freddy."

Jack got up and headed over to Freddy Brister's desk and sat down,

"Freddy, I just now resigned. I'm leaving the business entirely and I want to introduce you to my better accounts so there's a smooth transition and the client will feel comfortable. I'd feel bad just leaving them high and dry, and I know you'll do a good job for them. I think the smaller accounts are going to be split up by Louie in New York, but I told him I was giving the better ones to you and he agreed."

"Hey man, I really appreciate you thinking of me Jack. Your better accounts will make a big difference in my business. Goddamn! This is great! Of course I'm sorry to see you leave—it goes without saying. Do you think you're going to like it up there in Washington?" Jack didn't feel he had to answer that last part,

"Look Freddy, making a phone call isn't going to guarantee you get all their business. All I can do is sort of anoint you in a phone call to each one of them, you know, say some nice things about you, and the rest is up to you. Here are my holdings pages with their names and numbers and everything, just stick them in your book. I'll give them a call right now." Jack headed back to his desk and began to smile at an idea he just got.

He always remembered a phone number for a thing called "Dial-a-Prayer" in Houston. He never forgot the number because it was so dumb—"dial ACT HOLY", they used to say it on the radio. He knew Freddy would be listening from across the room—that was the whole point. He dialed ACT HOLY . . . it rang once,

'Thank you for calling, Praise Jesus! Today's reading is from the boo . . .©' Jack slide the ear piece down under his ear so he didn't have to listen to this Bible pounder, and started talking to the phantom client loud enough for Freddy to hear every word.

"Hi, Mr. Bell please." Jack smiled and nodded conspiratorially at Freddy as if he were on hold. "Hey Mr. Bell, Jack Armstrong. Listen I wanted to let you know that I will not be covering the bank anymore.

I've resigned and I'm leaving the bond business. The reason I am calling is to introduce my replacement, Freddy Brister from here in the office. He'll seem like a nice guy at first, but you'll need to watch him like a hawk of course. I always wondered when I was at my previous firm, how he managed to live over in River Oaks with the swells, and now I know the answer." Freddy's face had gone white and Leon and Elvira both turned toward Jack in disbelief. "So, I gave him the names of you and my other clients and he has added them to his 'List of Fools', you know," Jack laughed here, "that's what he calls his customer list. Ha, Ha, Ha. Yeah, and thanks for all the business Mr. Bell" Jack then hung up on Dial-a-Prayer and asked Freddy, "Who is the next one on that list?"

Leon thought that if anybody was going to have 'the big one' up there it looked like Freddy's was already underway. Of course Leon saw through the rouse almost immediately and decided to pile on,

"Freddy, what's the matter with you? You're pale as a ghost. You look like you're coming down with a case of the dreaded Chinese Arthritis that's going around." In Leon's Texas accent it come out as, Chaaneese Arthur Itis. "You know, that's the one where all the iron in your blood turns to lead in your ass." Freddy had gotten a bit of the old color back in his face and by now had figured out that he was being had, but found it hard to laugh along with everyone else. Instead of "ha, ha, ha" coming out, it sounded more like he was about to puke. All he could say was, "Very funny, very funny."

Jack stood up and announced, "I'm buying. I've about had all this bond fun one man can stand. What time does the Cellar Door open for lunch Leon? Call Stein and Wide Load and maybe Rapoport—see if they want to join us, I want to tell them the good news. GODDAMN!! it feels good to be out of this fucking business." As soon as he had said that he regretted it and looked over at Elvira only to get her standard stern, disapproving look in return for his use of the 'f-word'. Jack didn't feel too badly though, because he had a feeling that, away from the office, she was probably pretty profane herself. He had a mental picture flash into his head of Elvira and her husband—Mr. and Mrs. *American Gothic* con Budweiser—down fishing for channel cats off the Galveston jetty, when her husband Frankie the sheetrocker, after the first six pack, makes a bad cast putting a #6 treble hook and some smelly bait into the back of her neck. His mental picture didn't have a sound track, but he could just about read her lips as she screamed, "WHAT THE F U C K !!"

"They already know you're leaving." Jack came back from the mental image of Elvira to hear Leon. "The whole street knows, or at least everybody in Houston." Jack was not surprised and didn't even bother to respond. He thought, 'Typical!'. He had long believed that secrecy, and all this Chinese Wall stuff on Wall Street was a bunch of bullshit. There certainly were no secrets in the muni business.

Since there was no one else on the elevator except the two of them, Leon decided to mention something, which had been on his mind all morning,

"Jack I don't think it is a good idea, nor very charitable for that matter, to be dumping all over the muni business now that you are out of it, while the rest of us are still in it. I know you're excited about the new job but we're all stuck here, so don't rub our noses in it."

Jack dropped his head down, shaking it from side to side, "Is that how I sound Leon? Jesus man, I apologize. That is so rude. I'll watch it Leon. Thanks for pointing it out."

On their way to lunch Leon remembered something and started to laugh, "Mortabella called earlier. You're not going to believe this shit Jack. He just got back from Mexico and was going on and on about how great it was in this place, how great that town was—you know the usual shit. I mean the guy never travels. Anyway he starts talking about how great the food was compared to all those cheesy Mexican joints up in New York. So I asked him, 'Did you get any cabrito?' and he says, 'Hell no Leon, I was with my wife for Christ's sake!'"

There was no wait at the Cellar Door for lunch since they got there pretty early. So, they joined McKay and Stein at the bar. Stein had already reserved a big table for the guys he knew were coming. He grandly asked both of them what they were drinking and nodded to the bartender who had been listening.

Stein smiled and leaned toward Jack and said in a conspiratorial tone, "Jack, you luck son-of-a-bitch. Getting out of this chickenshit business— God, it must feel great!" Jack was fresh from being taken to the woodshed by Leon, and was not about to 'dump' on the business, so he answered diplomatically,

"Well I'm sure going to miss all you guys. My new boss refers to the people in Washington as pencilnecks. I've got a feeling they'll be a bunch of bland, pasty bureaucrats, all covering their asses. Not like the colorful sort of zany guys in this business."

"I'll tell you one thing Jack" Stein announced as he took a big sip of his drink, "At least we are well paid. We make more money than 95% of our contemporaries. The business sort of sucks but we're paid for it at least. It reminds me in a way of that book, "The Peter Principal"—remember that one? Look at Dowling for instance. I don't know what he makes, but it has to be 100 grand, right? And the guy ought to be a fucking usher in the movies. Where else . . . in what other business . . . could a dopey bastard like him make that kind of money? The business if full of people who have maxed out their potential Jack. A bunch of them started out in the back office, or they were gofers on the trading desks. I guess that's good in a way."

"Wait a second Sammy, Dowling is exceptional in his stupidity, don't you think? I mean he is not typical at all. Plus his father was in the business—he is a legacy. At least that's what the colleges call the second generation."

"Some legacy! The problem with that Jack, is that his father was just as stupid as this guy is—I remember the guy. I mean he ran himself over with his own car for Christ's sake. They're still trying to figure that one out." Stein took time out for another big sip of his 'Mary'.

"Look, Sammy, there are lots of smart guys—I mean look at the two of us. We're both former Marine captains—officers and gentlemen—college graduates for Christ sake."

"We volunteered for the Corps. Jack. Think about it. We *VOL-*

UNTEERED for the goddamn Corps. For both of us it was in the middle of a fucking war no less! Some people would think that was pretty stupid. My hippie, Berkley daughter calls it Darwinian. Then, to make things worse, *you* volunteer *again* for helicopters so you can fly all over Vietnam sitting on a manhole cover so thousands of five foot guys in pajamas shooting up at you wouldn't give you the seven millimeter enema. And we call Dowling stupid? You're over there getting shot at while this guy is trying to get the bra off of the new girl in the dairy department. He's probably got flat feet and the draft didn't take him. By the way Jack, if you ever want my opinion, just ask me." They both laughed and took big sips so they didn't miss any of banter—they were both in their element. Jack thought to himself that he would really miss this sort of thing.

"You're being pretty cynical Stein. I like to think that our joining the Corps was a standup thing to do—sort of noble. I don't want to get all misty eyed and use the word heroic—patriotic is closer—but referring to it as stupid is a bit offensive don't you think?"

"Yes I do Jack—of course I do. But that's because we are Marines—we're part of a special brotherhood of warriors. We all share a common experience, which was a sea change in all or our lives which we'll all take to the grave. The problem is that nobody else really understands that. The press writes stories, Hollywood makes movies, but none of them were Marines and none of them gets it Jack—they don't understand—they're all feather merchants. We stand up for the Marine Corps Hymn at some ball game and people just look at us. I'll tell you Jack, that our wives come the closest to understanding us, and of course, other elite units—you know, Airborne, Seals, submariners and people like that."

Leon was now listening to their conversation and said, "My eyes started to glaze over as soon as Stein started all that John Wayne shit. What we need to talk about is Jack's going away party." Stein just looked at Jack and said, "See what I mean?"

CHAPTER 22

The table had been cleared and Sammy Stein had already ordered a double Irish Coffee, as if the three Bloody Marys and the two Heinekens he consumed before and during lunch were not enough. Leon took one look at the steaming mug and waved the waitress over. He ordered the same thing, saying to no one in particular, "Well, that will cover two of my food groups—caffeine and alcohol." Everyone chuckled politely since they had heard him crack that joke about a thousand times before. It was exceeded only by his joke about the big shrimp caught from the South Texas Nuclear Power cooling pond. Jack got the distinct feeling that nobody had any intentions of going back to their offices, and that this "working lunch", as Cannon had referred to it, was going to be an all-afternooner. Johnny Cannon's theory of expense accounts was that the size of the check was inverse to the likelihood of returning to the office.

Stein as usual took over the meeting pulling a yellow legal pad out of his attaché case. "Ok, I'm going to make notes on all your ideas for this party. Who wants to start?"

Leon opened it up, "Let's don't forget to include Napalitano, Stonebreaker and Mortabella from New York. Oh yeah, and Retro Rizzo too. They will come, and they are a million laughs. Sammy, have you ever met Mortabella? What a piece of work."

Johnny Cannon brought the table talk to an abrupt halt with his contribution;

"We need to have a fat lady sing at the end of the party. Wouldn't that be hilarious?" Everyone just stared at him blankly. He looked at each one of them and determined that, somehow, for some strange reason, these normally funny guys didn't get his little joke. So he went on;

"You know, a fat lady. As in Yogi Berra? . . . 'It ain't over 'till the fat lady sings'? What the fuck is the matter with you guys? Jack's leaving, and it is finally over for Christ's sake." He moved his Heineken to one side, put his forehead on the table and let out a sigh. Stein, as usual, spoke up for the group,

"We get the joke Johnny, it's just that the idea is so off the wall and flaky, that we're all a little stunned that's all." Stein looked around the table and asked, "Which one of you insensitive, male, chauvinist, pigs is going to volunteer to ask a fat woman to come sing at the party so we can all laugh at her? How about a show of hands."

The meeting lost its momentum and began going down hill. Jack noticed everyone looking at their watches and saw his opportunity to excuse himself and left for home.

He came in the next morning to clean out his desk. He had gotten a Perma-File box from Antonio in the back office. The box was free, but there was the usual price he had to pay when Antonio put the Spanish conversational full Nelson on him.

"Yak, Yak we are goin' to meeesss ju. Por que ju are goin' to Washington and leavin' gus? Comong Yak, stay here amigo."

"My country calls Antonio, I gotta do this," Jack said with a faux-noble look on his face. "Look Antonio, if they got rid of that asshole, cigar smoking, fatigue wearing, bearded son-of-a-bitch Castro, and they called you to go back to Havana to help out, you'd do it, right?" Antonio stood there with a blank stare going over yet another of Jack's famous 'out of nowhere' comments—Jack saw his opening for escape and made his move back toward the bond department. He passed Leon who had just arrived and was in the coffee room getting his fix of caffeine and sugar.

"Jesus Leon, you look like shit! How long did that meeting last anyway? Hell, I left at around 3:00 PM. I guess you didn't go straight home."

"Well, we got a little nomadic after you left. Cannon and Stein were on a quest and I got sort of swept along you might say. We hit a lot of watering holes. Actually, I think we hit all the watering holes. I finally got a cab home."

"I'm glad to hear that Leon. That is the first sensible thing you've done in all your carousing. You need to know when to fold them . . . know what I mean? I'm proud of you making such a rational decision"

"Jack, spare me the lecture. The only reason I took the cab was that I couldn't find my car."

"Well where is the goddamn thing Leon? How can you loose you car for Christ's sake?"

"I'm trying not to loose my patients Jack, but let me explain something to a guy who is not known for his social skills, at least as they relate to drinking and carrying on with the boys—you know, the manly stuff. Lets say I just lost track of where my car was. Anyway, I already hired a gumshoe to find it."

"Gumshoe? You mean a detective? You've got to be shitting me Leon. That's ridiculous. I'm surprised you even know a detective agency."

"I remembered the name from the divorce. I had to write the check to the agency my ex-wife hired to see if I was running around on her, and I remembered the name . . . another fucking Irishman", Leon said this with obvious disgust "...typical of you people. Don't you guys know how to do anything else but be cops? '*We peep while you sleep*'. I'll never forget their catchy logo—an eyeball in a window frame. It's the only way I remembered the name. I looked in the Yellow Pages."

"Well, call them back and cancel Leon. We'll just drive around the parking lots and find it. No sweat."

"Jack, this city must have 300,000 fucking cars and they are all downtown at the moment. Hell, we couldn't find the thing at three AM, much less in the middle of a business day. I'm not canceling anything."

"Did they tell you how much it could cost? I mean it sounds

pretty expensive. Maybe you ought to just wait until you get the call from the pound. Surely someone will have it towed today. It's got to be in somebody's way, unless it's in some chop shop over in Pasadena." Jack thought for a second, "Naaaahhh, what self respecting hoodlum would steal a Mercury Monarch for parts?"

"I'm just going to expense it anyway. We're in a new deal for Texas A&M and Stonebreaker said to just put it in as 'research'. Nobody checks that shit anyway. Besides, if it's stolen I can get a new one with the insurance money."

"Leon, I hope you wouldn't buy another one of those things. What ever possessed you to buy a Mercury Monarch in the first place? You look like a funeral director driving around in the one you have…or should I say had. And maroon! God what an ugly car. No wonder you're always bumming rides."

Leon could say nothing in response because he was always ragging on Jack about his Nova. Now it was Jack's turn. He considered mentioning that maroon was the Aggie color but decided to pass realizing how weak that response was. It really was bad though, an awful design. Mercury's were cool when he was a kid, they became the hotrod of choice, but they sucked now. Jack had apparently forgotten that Leon's wife had insisted on their buying that car and then when she divorced him, she would have no part of it. So Leon was stuck with her car. He suspected it was her last little chicken shit dig.

Jack was pretty social but he did not look forward to walking through the whole office shaking hands and saying goodbye like he was running for the Texas House. He figured he'd be there the rest of the day if he did that. On the other hand he couldn't exactly slink out the back door to the bond department, Perma-File in hand, either. If he did go out into the boardroom, he was committed to do everyone; it would be, as they say in the business, 'all or none'. It was a problem.

"Leon what am I going to do about saying my goodbyes out

there in the boardroom?" Jack was putting personal odds and ends into his box, "I mean I honestly don't want to talk to 90 percent of those people and I can't just see the five or six I'd like to."

"Write them a letter and Elvira can hand it out with all the other shit they hand out around here. With any luck they'll loose it anyway. Besides you'll be long gone then."

"Now there is a man who is thinking. That's a great idea Leon. I'll do it in longhand so it looks more personal."

"Jack, you write like a doctor. Nobody will be able to read it. Just have Elvira type the damn thing. Hurry up and lets get out of here. We'll go to The Sewer so you can say goodbye to Lung."

CHAPTER 23

Jack's going away party was at the Hyatt Regency in a relatively small room. It was a quarter of the size they normally use for weddings and bar mitzvahs. Ceiling to floor accordion doors closed the room off from some big gig going on next door. As he entered the room he heard the music stop. It sounded to Jack as if they had hired a DJ. The music came back on pretty loud with a raspy, woman's voice in a burlesque or cabaret style Jack thought he remembered from a Gillette ad he'd once heard on TV;

> The minute you walked in the place,
> (BAAAARRRRROOOOOMMMMM!!!)
> I could tell you were a man of distinction,
> A real big spender.
> Good lookin'-yes indeed
> (da da—da da—da da—da da—da da da da da)

Everyone was clapping as Sammy Stein led Jack and his wife to one of the big round tables. Jack was glad there wasn't a dais and microphone. He was hoping this would be small with no fanfare. In fact, the whole thing made him uncomfortable—being the center of attraction.

He finally saw the DJ over on the side—a hippie looking guy with shoulder length hair in a polyester jacket with wide lapels. When they sat down Jack leaned over to Stein and whispered,

"Not exactly one of 'The Few' Sammy." His sarcasm about this guy looking inferior, and not USMC material, did not escape Stein.

"Well Jack me boy, looks can be deceiving. That's Tommy LaRue. He was in my platoon in Korea—one of my guys. He got the Silver Star. I'll admit he looks strange, but he is a very talented musician. He'll do a good job tonight. He did my daughter's wedding in fact. He and a couple of his friends. We reconnected five years ago at a reunion and found out we were both living here in Houston."

"The Silver Star? No shit Sammy? Jesus."

"Jack, Tommy marches to a different drummer for sure. Never has any money so I have him do stuff for me like this. I took him out for drinks a couple days ago and filled him in on the cast of characters here. You know, so he could bring all the right records." Jack smiled and re-membered the 'Big Spender' song. Just then Tommy, the DJ, came over the sound system he borrowed from a friend and said in a theatrical tone,

"Good evening ladies and gentlemen, I have the first request of the evening from Leon, going out to Dominick Mortabella. It's by Patsy Klein. The song is Crazy.*"*

There was a bar set up in one corner of the room with one overworked bartender named Hey Zeus. Cannon and Stonebreaker alone took up half his time. Stonebreaker got special treatment beginning immediately after he handed this guy two twenties for his tip jar. After that, all Charlie had to do was to wave from the other side of the room and his next gin and tonic would be waiting for him at the edge of the temporary bar. Stonebreaker always prepared for the essential things in life, defining the word essential a bit differently than normal people. One time he told Leon that he had no life insurance because it was defeatist.

Danny McKay and Leon were in charge of selling the Fun Shares. That decision was the finding of the very same committee that rejected, by way of a unanimous voice vote, Johnny Cannon's idea to have a fat lady sing. Both of them agreed to have the Fun Shares elimination go on right through the dinner. Fun Shares, grossly simplified, is sort bingo for muni bond traders. Numbered tickets were sold and certain single digits of those numbers were eliminated until there were just a few remaining shares which competed for the pot.

That is where any similarity between Fun Shares and bingo ended. Leon's date, the racehorse he lusted after at the Christmas party at Searls, asked Cannon to explain how it worked since she was buying a few tickets. He intentionally made the explanation tortuous. When he had finished telling her every nuance of Fun Shares, she said,

"My God that's so complicated!" Johnny replied,

"Hey, if you want bingo for Christ's sake, they play it every Friday night along with their dance over at Saint Vitus—you know on Chimneyrock?" She had a puzzled look on her face the rest of the night.

"Here is another oldie but goodie, folks, going out to Johnny Cannon from Mr. Stein over here. It's Frank. Don't you love that guy?" The tune started,

"It's quarter to three. There's no one in the place except you and me." Cannon was drunk enough to feel honored at the dedication.

Leon Walla, Charlie Stonebreaker and Frankie 'Retro' Rizzo formed a syndicate, as did most everyone else, pooling their tickets thus spreading the risk. Of course, all of the ticket-syndication, short selling and the secondary trading of shares, were simply to complicate the game, making it far more fun. Sammy Stein and Charlie Stonebreaker were in charge of the operation side of Fun Shares. A thousand tickets at $5 each had been sold at the door, so the pot was to be divided among the winners with $3500 to the last remaining ticket, $1000 to the second to last, and $500 for third place. Stein got it started,

"O.K. folks, Leon's lovely date, aaaaahhhh TAMMY, Tammy, right, (he was tempted to say, but did not, 'I've had neckties that took more fabric than that mini skirt'), has agreed to pick the numbers out of the hat and her first number is four. So, anyone with the number four as the last number of their ticket, is dead. That number is killed." There were two or three loud, "SHIT"s, as tickets were thrown on the carpet in disgust. She drew the next number followed by other numbers, each accompanied by the same vulgar words, until only tickets with the last digit nine remained, leaving 10% (100) live numbers. Stonebreaker was over at the blackboard writing down the 'book value' of $50 per share. Stein then went to phase two,

"Lovely Tammy here," Stein looked over to his pal Tommy, the DJ, rolling his eyes, which did not escape Leon Walla who took it as some sort of Marine Corps secret handshake thing, "will pick a few more numbers to kill the *second* to last numbers, so we can reduce the outstanding live numbers to 20, and get this thing going." As she picked, and Stein 'killed' numbers, there was great gnashing of teeth of biblical intensity as worthless tickets became airborne, and the level of profanity rose. Jesus Christ's name was liberally employed.

This old Roy Orbison number is from Leon to his lovely date Tammy. It is Candy Man. *You gotta love a romantic like Leon folks.*

Tammy, who sort of considered this date with Leon as a charity thing, seemed a bit offended and leaned over to give Leon a little talk which was drowned out for everyone else by Roy's backup singers who sang,

Candy Man AAHH . . . Candy Man AAHH . . . Candy Man AAHH.

Charlie Stonebreaker now carefully printed out the remaining 20 live numbers on the blackboard, and updated the current 'book value' to $250 per Fun Share. He asked Jack's wife Mary to write each of the 20 numbers on the back of his business cards for the hat. He turned away from his work, choosing to take care of his personal needs first, by waving to his new friend, the bartender, for his next gin and tonic and announced,

"Fun Shares are now free to trade at a price of $240 bid, and $260 offered. For those of you non-muni people, unfamiliar with this, let me point out that the tickets are perforated and divisible into four parts. You can trade halves and quarters if you like."

Instantly the bar was mobbed so everyone could brace themselves for the trading. And the DJ took the opportunity to play another request,

"*This request is from Marc Rapport and the entire mishpacha, going out to Sammy Stein from the Grand Concourse. It's* Deuchland Uber Allis. *Oooopppsss! Folks can you believe it!?? I forgot to bring that old favorite by the Hamburg Hitler Youth Glee Club. So, we'll have to settle for the* Marine Corps Hymn *instead."*

All of a sudden the room was blasted with, *"From the Halls of Montezuma, to the shores of Tripoli…"*

Naturally, Jack Armstrong, Sammy Stein, the DJ, Tommy LaRue and one of the waiters serving the entrées, stood bolt upright until the song had ended. Leon leaned over to his date, trying not to look at her mini skirt riding up into dangerous territory, and said, "Jack and Sammy do all this John Wayne shit whenever they hear that song." Tammy looked at him, stood up also, and said out of the side of her mouth, "My dad was a Marine!" Leon saw his dream of a night in the arms of the love goddess slipping away, and decided to cut his losses by getting them more drinks. On the way to the bar Marc Rapoport asked,

"OK Mister big shot, are you a player, or are you satisfied going through your shallow existence as the cover bid?"

"So when did you change your name from Rapoport to Gutfreund? At least you kept within the same tribe. We've got some live numbers we'll offer at the market. You remember what 'at the market' is Rapoport? As opposed to those shitty bids you get me all the time? Hey, I got an idea. We'll swap you halves of every live number. That's subject to agreement from my partners."

"Meet me at the bar in two minutes Leon. Let me check." Leon saw Stonebreaker over at the bar and headed his way to get agreement on his offer to Rapoport. He heard someone say, "Hey, Leon." He kept walking to the bar saying over his shoulder, "Hold that thought."

"Charlie, let's swap halves of our live ones. I mean half of each ticket. We'll trade halves. Where is Rizzo?"

"Rizzo doesn't give a shit Leon, just do it." Charlie noticed Leon trying to get the bartender's attention with a five-dollar bill and said, out of the corner of his mouth,

"Leon, that five ain't makin' it. Know what I mean? I gave him a couple of twenties earlier. I'm afraid I've set the market and spoiled this guy. He'll probably tell you to stick that five up your ass. Here, I'll get you one." Charlie only had to raise his eyebrows to Hey Zeus and point, and Leon had his drink. As they walked away from the bar Charlie lectured Leon, "I'm surprised at you Leon. You need to step back sometimes and assess the situation. Number one; your firm is paying for the ticket to this gig, right? Number two; on the other hand, YOU are the one who will drink all this free stuff. So far, you are getting the better end of this deal. Number three; here is a situation where a hundred alcoholic muni guys, with fucked up livers, are asking only one bartender to take care of their collective thirsts, which he couldn't do with a goddamn fire hose. So, in order to distinguish yourself from all the other red noses, you need to make an investment, and early. I walk in, ask for my first gin and tonic, introduce myself, hand this Mexican $40 and say, 'Take good care of me tonight.' On top of that, I'll expense the $40 to the next syndicate I'm in and call it shoe shines and extra orange juice at breakfast. Am I making sense Leon? Actually, when he found out about the Fun Shares he wanted four tickets instead of one of the twenties so I sold him four of mine."

Stein sat down at an empty chair next to Rapoport and his Fun Shares partner Wide Load,

"I'm going to blow out my live tickets. If I do, I'll break even." He let out a sigh of resignation since he never won anything. "By the way Marc, I want you to know how very touched I was at the Nazi song idea."

"What are friends for? And you'll have to define 'breaking even'. We of the Jewish persuasion don't have that word in our vocabulary. You see when your distant ancestors were busy gathering and hunting and gathering and schlepping dead things back to the cave, mine were back in the warm cave trading all that shit and selling it to each other wholesale."

"Our next request is dedicated to Louie Napolitano, who incidentally, wins tonight's prize for coming the farthest...Brentwood, Long Island ladies and gentlemen. Let's give him a big round of applause! It is a longer drive to La Guardia than Stonebreaker's limo ride, so he's the lucky winner. The song is Mombo Italiano *by Rosemary Clooney."*

Everybody was laughing and when she got to the best part, Louie stood up and sang with her, "HEY GUMBA!!…"

Stonebreaker ambled over to the blackboard and got ready for the 'killing' of more tickets. Stein put down his drink and took the mike from the DJ Tommy LaRue,

"Tammy is all tired out from pulling those last few numbers, so I'm going to ask that heartbreaker Kitty McDonald to come up and pull ten numbers out of the hat." As Kitty approached the blackboard a chant broke out from Leon's table, "Kill. Kill. Kill. Kill." Kitty read off all ten ticket numbers to the howls and profanity of those who held those numbers, and the hoots of delight from those who had just before, sold or shorted them. Stonebreaker erased each number from the blackboard and then announced,

"Book value is now $500 per ticket Ladies and Gentlemen. Make your own markets. Do what you like. But in ten minutes we will kill seven more numbers. The remaining three numbers will all be in the money. Third place will pay $500, second place $1000 and the winner $3500." Stonebreaker looked toward the bar to give Hey Zeus the signal for another gin and tonic and was greeted by a thumb's-up, which either meant he got the secret drink signal or that Hey Zeus still had a live number.

By this time Jack, Rapoport, Stein and most everyone were out of live numbers. Jack's wife Mary had a live one and so did Leon. Leon decided he didn't feel lucky, so he stood up and yelled out,

"Offering one whole live one at $525!" Cannon was feeling a second wind all of a sudden and responded from two tables away,

"I pay $515 you little shit." Leon, who took offense, revised his offer side,

"It's now $540 for you Cannon—$525 for people with normal sized livers. When are you going to learn to trade you dope?"

"You're fuckin' done at $525 Leon!" It was Dowling who shouted that little gem out in spite of the women present. Jack leaned over to Sammy Stein and whispered, "Do me a favor Sammy and take that stupid son-of-a-bitch out by the dumpster and beat the shit out of him, will ya'. Can't we all just vote to kick him out of the business?"

Leon normally would have felt lousy at winning only $50 over an entire evening. He was usually a very aggressive gambler, but this night he had a premonition that he'd loose, so he bailed and felt good about it. He did not, however, feel good about his prospects for a successful date, which by his definition meant carnal knowledge of the lady. Tammy had all six of her tickets killed in the first round and had been surly ever since.

Stonebreaker returned from the bar where Hey Zeus let him know he still had a live number. Charlie grabbed the mike from the DJ and asked Mary Armstrong to come up to kill the last seven numbers. She read the first number and someone shouted "W H A T?" It was Dowling who not two minutes ago had paid $525 for the now worthless piece of paper. He sat there red faced while all the people who knew him laughed until their sides hurt. They all felt the same about the guy. Leon expressed it the best as he leaned over to Wide Load and said, "Danny, being stupid is sort of acceptable, but being an asshole too is just unforgivable."

Except for the accompanying vulgarities and groans by the holders of the final six tickets, things in the room were pretty quiet and orderly.

It was time for the finale and Charlie nodded toward the DJ who played the Olympic Fanfare while Stonebreaker erased the last seven killed numbers off the blackboard. The Fanfare over, Charlie himself picked the last three numbers pretty quickly,

"Ok, for the Bronze, it's," he pointed to the number on the blackboard and asked who that was. Leon shouted out that it was a little syndicate of sales assistants in his office none of whom were invited.

"Second place–the Silver–goes to." He pointed again but nobody said anything. Mortabella simply got up walked up to Stonebreaker with his hand out. Charlie handed him his $1000 and he just stuffed it all into his pocket leaving a big bulge. From behind the bar came Hey Zeus in a dead run, taking off his baroque gold and black vest and chucking it over his shoulder. He leaped on Charlie, who he considered his benefactor, his *patron*, his *jeffe*, knocking him to the carpet. It was a one-man, high school football game dog pile as Hey Zeus hugged and kissed Charlie who seemed defenseless. Finally, Hey Zeus got off Charlie, grabbed the microphone and yelled,

"Aaaaaiiiiiii Chihuahua!!" Charlie paid him his $3500 in small bills. The wad was two or three inches thick. Hey Zeus walked out of the room with both arms in the air like a bantamweight Mexican boxer and disappeared to the applause of the bond crowd. Stonebreaker thought there was something almost poetic about it. When he later expressed to Leon and Johnny Cannon, now making their own drinks, that it was like something out of a Damon Runyan story, neither had ever heard of Damon Runyan and both of them told him to go fuck himself.

Jack was over with the DJ when he saw Gator McCully and the Governor approaching. He was completely surprised and confused which the two visitors immediately recognized,

"Jack, the Governor was making a speech in the next room and I was about to fall asleep as usual," he said winking at Jack. "When I went to take a leak and heard the Marine Corps Hymn coming from this room I looked in and asked what was going on. Anyway, I told the Governor and he wanted to drop in. I hope you don't mind Jack."

"Not at all. Actually I'm honored. Can we offer you gentlemen a drink or anything?"

"Oh, there's Mary! I've got to say hello." As McCully moved off, the Governor asked Jack if he could say a few words, so Jack took the mike from the DJ and handed it to the Governor.

"Ladies and gentlemen, I don't mean to interrupt Jack Armstrong's going away party, but I was just next door giving a speech when my friend Gator McCully here, informed me that this party for Jack was going on. So, with the crust God reserves only for politicians and elected officials, I crashed your party. I wanted to say two things only. One is that I predict that your friend Jack will do a great job in Washington and make a real contribution up there— Lord knows we need good people in government. As I see it, one of the problems in our society is that good and able people too often avoid public office because of all the scrutiny. This vacuum sometimes is filled with the wrong people, or should I say, people with entirely misdirected motives. Too often they are more interested in their own fortunes and careers then they are in doing a good job for their states and districts. And I am not referring to someone who feels differently politically, it happens with Democrats and Republicans alike. At any rate, Jack will do well serving his country again just as he did with the Marine Corps. You will all be proud of him I am sure.

"The second point is that I personally admire the municipal bond community of which you all are a part in various capacities. I can't help but think that the vast majority of citizens, who drive on turnpikes, fly out of airports, attend colleges and send their kids to the local elementary school, seldom think where in the world the money to build these things came from. Schools, jails, bridges, airports, colleges, water and sewer systems—all vital to our society—are built with municipal bond proceeds. You men and women underwrite, distribute and make markets for these bonds and to me that is very important to how our society functions. And, as is often the case, few people understand this. The average guy out there doesn't know you and just what it is you do. The rich who buy the bonds know, naturally, but the average Joe six-pack, as the politicians call him, does not. You're roll and that of..." Just then Johnny Cannon seemed to stir, as if he had been asleep, stood and said,

"Roll? Roll?" Then he picked up his untouched dinner roll and threw it across two tables hitting Leon in the shoulder and knocking a cigarette out of his hand. The Governor and everyone else were speechless for a couple of seconds until Leon picked up his own untouched roll and, looking like Nolan Ryan, hummed one back at Cannon. Of course he missed by an entire table and hit Charlie Stonebreaker in his ever-present gin and tonic spilling it all over his prized E F Hutton tie. Jack yelled out, "Jesus Johnny, sit down! Somebody get control of Cannon!" Marc Rapoport reached up and yanked Cannon back into his chair, but not before Johnny, who had vastly more experience with judges than governors said, "I apologize Your Honor!" Jack simply glared and pointed at Leon and mouthed silently, "TEN YEARS OLD."

Jack turned to the Governor and the steely-eyed, plainclothes

State Trooper with the earpiece who, all of a sudden, was standing right next to his boss and said,

"My friend is a little drunk. He meant no disrespect Governor. I apologize. Please continue. I believe you left off somewhere around what great citizens we muni people are. The 'Joe six-pack' remark evidentially awakened something primal and deep within my associate Mr. Cannon." The room erupted in laughter. Both the Governor and Gator McCully had tears in their eyes. McCully, who was standing on the other side of the Governor from the trooper, leaned over and said, "See, I told you this guy was great!"

EPILOGUE

Jack Armstrong never came back to Texas except to visit. His wife Mary a.k.a. Radar, fell right into the Washington scene, made a lot of friends and ended up with a job on The Hill as soon as the kids reached high school. Gator McCully was right; Jack did make many contacts and ended up running the public affairs office of Vinson Elkins, DC office.

Glen Williams left the business to become what his friends called a professional hunter. His wife was a big lawyer in Houston and made plenty of money. He had always hated the bond business, so he ended up just screwed around looking after hunting leases for he and his buddies. Leon ran into him years later and Glen told him, "Leon, what always amazed me was that the bond business could hold that many shedskins."

Elvira Moore had been beyond retirement age at the time Jack left for Washington. His leaving prompted her to re-asses her situation and she resigned, moved to Port Aransas and got a part time job while her husband wade fished all day and got loaded at night. She managed all the Mexican housekeeping girls at a large condo complex on the beach, but got fed up with cleaning up vomit from the Aggies and UT students. She quit and started waiting tables at a place with seashells on the windowsills, right next to the ferry landing. Years later Rapoport told Jack that he ate there and hardly recognized her for the smile on her face! He said the only thing on the menu that wasn't deep-fried was the iceberg lettuce.

Bill Weekly managed to stay out of trouble, at least with the regulators, and along with three big producers, opened their own firm. One of their clients persuaded them to put up venture capitol in an outfit called Home Depot. They made an obscene amount of money and Weekly and his former secretary, now his devoted third wife, became regulars in the whiskey columns of Houston's newspapers. Sammy Stein visited Jack in Washington and had told him he had run into the Weeklys at a gala for The Alley Theater and described the third wife as being "all tits and diamonds".

Sammy David Stein, Johnny Cannon and Danny McKay eventually left the muni business to trade and sell the more esoteric and more lucrative investment instruments—principally government guaranteed SBA loans. They moved from one firm to another until they got disgusted and formed their own little boutique broker dealer made up of all the older bond guys. Nobody remembers the name on the door, but they do remember the name the rest of the business conferred on their firm—Jurassic Park. Johnny Cannon stopped drinking only to become equally obsessed with leading the noontime AA meetings near their offices. Danny McKay got on a health kick and lost a ton of weight and nearly all of his huge ass. His new clothes purchases at Norton Claymore were enough to make Aram Agajanian salesman of the year. Aram discreetly sent McKay's trousers to the winter headquarters of Ringling Brothers in Florida.

Leon Walla, on what appeared to be one of his more unsuccessful trips to Lake Tahoe, took his last gambling dollar and fed it into the huge, million dollar slot machine at about 2AM, on his way out the casino. He did not even bother to wait for the wheels to stop as he headed for the door. He began to hear bells as the cocktail waitress, he had tipped generously all night, grabbed him by the arm to drag him back to claim his fortune. To his delight, later that evening she was grabbing him somewhere else as they celebrated his jackpot. By the time he hit Houston, the million dollar wire from Harrah's had hit his checking account (with its usual two digit balance) at Texas Commerce Bank. The next afternoon he had a courier service deliver a single record of *"Take This Job And Shove It"* to the manager of his latest and last bond firm. Jack got a Christmas card from him, postmarked Manuel Antonio, Costa Rica.

Dominick Mortabella got rich, bored and left the business to become one of the "crew" of that huge geodesic dome thing in the Arizona desert, built and financed by that flaky Bass brother. Somehow or another he was sucked into that whole Orgo/Enviro thing. He had become convinced that turning one's pee-pee and turds into broccoli was the thing of the future. Many years later Leon could have sworn he saw Mortabella in his sneakers and blue jumpsuit on the evening news videos of that group who killed themselves out in California so they could meet up with the Hale-Bopp comet.

Charlie Stonebreaker remained at the same firm for his entire 30-year career in the muni business. His pal Rick, on the other hand, moved so frequently, that he actually ran out of muni bond firms. Charlie chided him once saying, "You know Rick, there is a $800 bid in the street for a complete set of your business cards." Charlie ended up with so much vacation time at what he called 'Preparation Bache', that they had to hang a picture of him outside his office so the employees would remember what he looked like when he came back from looking at Anasazi ruins.

Freddy Brister's midlife crisis came later in life than most of his colleagues. By the time he was 50 he realized he had a ton of money, since he never spent any of it, and he was irreconcilably bored with jamming bonds into his client's portfolios. He and his wife bought a building in San Miguel Allende, part of which long ago had been a ballroom. The local middle class residents once used it for parties their homes could not accommodate. The Bristers turned it into a bed and breakfast, which, based on their high school Spanish, they named "Las Cojonas Grande". The local Mexicanos found the name quite amusing and totally appropriate the better they became acquainted with Freddy.

Frankie 'Retro" Rizzo was so taken by Blanks White's Bar in Matamoras, Mexico, as a result of his trips to the bond outings, that he began taking vacations there. He eventually moved there and becoming an expatriate starting the first business he truly loved doing. He bought old 50s automobiles from Havana, restored them in Mexico and sold them in the US. He never felt uncomfortable with the Cuban embargo laws, since he convinced himself that what he bought in Havana was a completely different thing from what he exported into the States. He married a beautiful Mexican girl half his age that waited on him hand and foot. They ate nearly every lunch and dinner at Blanka White's. Leon Walla visited Frankie once a year. They'd sit at Blanka White's bar planning a reunion bond outing, which they both knew would never take place.